"Are you sorry you put yourself to so much trouble to find me a wife?"

When he asked the question, Jasper Chase cocked his head to one side, just like his son Matthew. His grin sparkled with impudence, yet there was an appealing warmth about it.

"Of course not." She tilted her chin and looked him in the eye. "I enjoy a challenge."

He nodded as if to say he did, too. "You have risen to it admirably. You must be very anxious to get away and start that school of yours."

"I am." Evangeline willed her voice to remain steady and positive, without the slightest quaver of doubt. If Mr. Chase heard it, she feared he might apply pressure to that weak spot to persuade her to stay.

But when she betrayed nothing he could exploit, Jasper Chase simply shook his head and repeated his earlier words with one minor but significant change. "How *will* we manage without you, Miss Fairfax?"

Books by Deborah Hale

Love Inspired Historical

The Wedding Season
  "Much Ado About Nuptials"
The Captain's Christmas Family
The Baron's Governess Bride
The Earl's Honorable Intentions
The Duke's Marriage Mission
The Gentleman's Bride Search

*Glass Slipper Brides

DEBORAH HALE

After a decade of tracing her ancestors to their roots in Georgian-era Britain, Golden Heart winner Deborah Hale turned to historical romance writing as a way to blend her love of the past with her desire to spin a good love story. Deborah lives in Nova Scotia, Canada, between the historic British garrison town of Halifax and the romantic Annapolis Valley of Longfellow's *Evangeline.* With four children (including twins), Deborah calls writing her "sanity retention mechanism." On good days, she likes to think it's working.

Deborah invites you to visit her personal website at www.deborahhale.com, or find out more about her at www.Harlequin.com.

The Gentleman's Bride Search

DEBOROH HALE

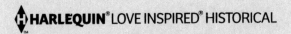

HARLEQUIN® LOVE INSPIRED® HISTORICAL

Recycling programs
for this product may
not exist in your area.

 LOVE INSPIRED BOOKS

ISBN-13: 978-0-373-28268-5

THE GENTLEMAN'S BRIDE SEARCH

Copyright © 2014 by Deborah M. Hale

www.Harlequin.com

Printed in U.S.A.

We have different gifts, according to the grace given to each of us. If your gift is prophesying, then prophesy in accordance with your faith; if it is serving, then serve; if it is teaching, then teach; if it is to encourage, then give encouragement; if it is giving, then give generously; if it is to lead, do it diligently.

—*Romans* 12:6–8

For Robyn and Deidre, my brave, brilliant girls, and for David, who fought a modern-day Goliath.

Chapter One

Vale of Eden, Northern England
July 1817

"He's home! Papa is home!" Ten-year-old Matthew Chase and his younger brother Alfie ran into the entry hall of Amberwood Hall shouting the news of their father's arrival to everyone within earshot.

A powerful wave of relief washed over Evangeline Fairfax, accompanied by a cold undercurrent of annoyance. Mr. Chase should have returned from Manchester several days ago for his summer holiday with his family. His guests were due to arrive soon, and she had been frantic with worry that he would not be there to welcome them.

The guests were not exactly *his,* Evangeline reminded herself. His mother-in-law had extended the invitations, at her prompting. It had taken weeks of planning and work to organize this house party, which could mean so much to her future. She did not want anything to spoil it—least of all her obstinate, work-obsessed employer.

She had to admit that description hardly fit Jasper

Chase when he strode through the door behind his elder sons. Her widowed employer seemed to have left the hard-headed cotton mill owner back in Manchester to become the genial, doting father of five. His youngest daughter, Rosie, rode on his shoulders, chattering away, while seven-year-old Owen clung to his hand. Emma, the oldest of the children, walked beside her father, staring up at him with an adoring gaze.

Seeing her dear pupils so happy brought a smile to Evangeline's lips and made her forget her simmering resentment of how much time Mr. Chase's business kept him away from them.

"Look, Papa! I lost a tooth!" Alfie grimaced to show the gap in his smile.

"How did you do that?" asked Mr. Chase, swinging Rosie down from his shoulders. "Take a tumble off the roof?"

"No!" Alfie laughed at his father's teasing suggestion. "It was only a tree. And the tooth was wiggly before that."

Evangeline recalled the boy's latest calamity, sustained while trying to rescue a nest full of baby birds that he feared had been abandoned by their parents.

While his son spoke, Mr. Chase cast a puzzled-looking glance around the entry hall. It was much tidier than usual and crowded not only with his children, but also with maids and footmen toting armloads of bedding and doing some last-minute cleaning.

"Welcome home, Jasper dear!" Mrs. Thorpe cast an anxious glance at Evangeline as she greeted her son-in-law. "You look well."

"Thank you, Mama." Mr. Chase stooped to kiss his mother-in-law on the cheek. "I hope all this fuss is not on my account. I would hate to think myself a guest in my own home."

Then perhaps he ought to *live* here and *visit* Manchester rather than the other way around. Evangeline bit her tongue to keep from saying what she had so often thought.

"It's not for you, Papa," cried Alfie before his grandmother could answer. "It's for the real guests. We're going to have a party!"

"A party?" A sharp note crept into Mr. Chase's deep North County voice. "What sort of party?"

"A house party, of course," Mrs. Thorpe replied in a cheerful tone as forced as her smile. Lately she'd grown worried that her son-in-law would not approve of their plans. "Only a very small one. A handful of friends who might enjoy spending a few weeks in this beautiful countryside."

Judging by the look on his face, Mrs. Thorpe had been right.

Mr. Chase spied Evangeline and fixed her with a glare that might have driven his mother-in-law to tears. "Did you know about this?"

Evangeline refused to be intimidated. During her miserable girlhood years at the Pendergast School for Orphaned Daughters of the Clergy, she had often stood up to harsh teachers and bullies who had picked on her friends. She'd learned not to betray any sign of weakness they might exploit. But the controlled fury in Jasper Chase's blue-gray eyes reminded her of the North Sea before a storm.

"Of course I knew." She tilted her chin defiantly. "The house party was *my* idea."

Beneath her intrepid facade, Evangeline tried to stifle an unexpected quiver of fear.

What had provoked that? She questioned her uncharacteristic response.

Mr. Chase was a tall man with broad shoulders and a powerful build. His dark hair and full dark brows could easily make him look severe. His features were handsome, but in a rugged way that did not seem entirely civilized.

But did she expect her employer to erupt in violence because she had vexed him? Hardly! In the six years since she had come to Amberwood to teach his children, Evangeline had never once seen him lose his temper. Not even with the older boys, who could be a handful at times. Perhaps it was seeing his control threaten to slip at last that shook her.

Or perhaps it was something even more unexpected she spied behind the anger in his eyes. He looked at her as if she had betrayed him.

"Reverend Mr. Brookes will be coming." Mrs. Thorpe's hands fluttered like a pair of small pale birds. "And Mr. Webster. You must remember him. I'm certain they will be delighted to see you again, Jasper dear."

Clearly his mother-in-law hoped it would ease Mr. Chase's annoyance to hear that his old friend and her late husband's business partner would be among the guests. Evangeline appreciated her efforts to smooth things over.

It seemed to work. At least it gave Mr. Chase a moment to recover his composure. Some of the blazing intensity faded from his eyes.

"Of course I remember Piers Webster, Mama. I used to see him quite often in Manchester. Miss Fairfax, might I have a word with you in private?"

Others might have quailed at the threat of a private interview with their displeased employer, but Evangeline relaxed a little. Mr. Chase was welcome to rail at her all he liked as long as his children were not around to hear and become upset. The girls and Owen already looked a little anxious.

"Certainly, sir," she replied in an unruffled tone that she hoped would reassure them. Then she signaled to the nursemaid. "Children, go up to the nursery with Jane and get your hands and faces washed for tea. I shall be along as soon as I finish talking to your father."

Emma tugged Rosie toward the stairs. "Are you going to take tea with us, Papa?" she asked.

"Of course, my love." All trace of annoyance vanished from his face, replaced by a comforting smile, for which Evangeline was grateful. "I wouldn't miss it. I hope there will be plenty to eat. My long ride in the fresh air has given me an appetite."

Not for the first time, Evangeline asked herself why a man who so obviously doted on his children could spend so much time away from them. She was only their governess, yet the thought of leaving her young pupils was the one blight upon her plans for the future.

The children headed off, Matthew and Alfie at a headlong run while the other three followed at a more sedate pace.

The smile quickly faded from Mr. Chase's lips as he turned and stalked toward his study. Evangeline marched after him with her back straight and her head high. What was the worst her employer could do to her, after all—dismiss her? She had been *trying* to leave Amberwood Hall for nearly two years!

When she stepped into Mr. Chase's study, he had already taken a position behind his writing table with his hands clasped behind his back, glowering at her.

Evangeline closed the study door and began to talk

at once, before her employer had a chance. "I hope you wanted to speak to me about my replacement, sir. You promised faithfully at Easter that you would engage a new governess as soon as possible. That was more than three months ago."

"I know when Easter was, Miss Fairfax." Her words seemed to take a little of the steam out of his overheated engine. "But I do not recall making any such promises. I am a very busy man. British industry is still trying to recover after the war and between last year's poor harvest and those misbegotten Corn Laws…"

"All the more reason why a new charity school is so desperately needed." Evangeline had long since run out of sympathy with Mr. Chase's business difficulties. "The patrons of the school have been very patient with me, as I have tried to be with you. But we cannot delay indefinitely while there are children who need our help."

The moment she'd received the letter from her old friend Hannah Fletcher, Evangeline had known this new charity school she'd been invited to set up was the Lord's calling. Her late mother had often told her the Almighty had some great purpose in store for her. When she'd been sent away to the Pendergast School, with its deprivations and petty tyranny masquerading as charity, that belief had helped Evangeline look to the future. She had tried to think of every hunger pang, chill and punishment as a lesson, training her for the work she would undertake one day.

It had been more difficult to continue believing in her future purpose after she left school to work as a humble governess. Surely this could not be the great service her mother had foreseen for her—teaching spoiled daughters of wealthy families a few superficial accomplishments. Raising the Chase children after their mother's death had made Evangeline feel she might have found her vocation at last. But when she learned of her friends' plans to endow a new charity school, she knew that was what she had been preparing for her whole life. She could no longer postpone her destiny to suit Jasper Chase's convenience.

His gruff voice broke in upon her thoughts. "There are children in this house who need you, Miss Fairfax. Or does *their* welfare not matter?"

"Of course it matters!" A surge of affection and protectiveness rose in Evangeline's heart. "At least it does to me. That is why I gave you so much time to hire them a new governess. Your refusal to use that time makes me question your commitment to your children, as well as your respect for me."

"I do respect you!" Mr. Chase insisted. "I would not have entrusted you with the care of my children otherwise. It is *because* I respect and value you as their governess that I do not want my children to lose you."

Was that true? His reply took Evangeline aback. All this time, she had taken his delays as a sign that he did not consider her needs worthy of his attention. Yet he claimed the opposite.

"I shall be sorry to leave them, too." The words caught in her throat, like tiny, sharp fish bones. Though she looked forward to the important responsibility of founding a new school, she had tried not to dwell on the prospect of leaving her young pupils.

"That's settled, then. You will stay." The relief in Mr. Chase's tone made Evangeline almost wish it were true. "And I will raise your salary."

"I do not want more money!" She threw up her hands. "And I do not believe it will be difficult to find a replacement. Have you tried at all?"

Her employer's hesitation gave her the answer she'd suspected. "You have not. Not a single inquiry among the other mill owners or even a notice in the newspaper?"

"I kept hoping you would change your mind." His look of remorse reminded Evangeline so much of his son Alfie, she found it difficult to stay angry with him… until he promptly changed the subject. "But that is not what I asked you here to discuss, Miss Fairfax. Would you kindly explain what possessed you to invite a bevy of strangers to stay at my house when I am trying to enjoy a quiet holiday with my children?"

She had wondered how long it would take him to get back to that. Part of her regretted intruding on the children's scarce time with their father, but she reminded herself it was he who had driven her to such desperate measures. "They are not *all* strangers. You heard Mrs. Thorpe. At least two gentlemen of your acquaintance will be among the party."

"Do not split hairs, Miss Fairfax. You know what I mean. These people will not be family."

That was true, Evangeline acknowledged privately. But she desperately hoped one of the guests at this house party might *become* a member of the Chase family.

Jasper brought his arms from behind his back to cross in front of his chest. "I am disappointed in you, Miss Fairfax."

His comment made her start. A complicated mixture of emotions played over her vivid features. Her full red lips compressed into a stubborn frown, but a shadow of guilt darkened her warm brown eyes. "I beg your pardon?"

He ought to tread cautiously in case the lady decided

to pack her bags and storm away, leaving him stranded and the children bereft. But he resented the way she'd turned this discussion back upon him then evaded his question with a quibble about its wording. "Never in the six years of our acquaintance have I known you to be anything less than direct and truthful with me."

"Nor have I been, sir."

"Sometimes a little too direct, perhaps." Hard as he tried, Jasper could not keep one corner of his lips from arching slightly. "But I much prefer that to being deceived."

Her expressive dark brows flew up. "Deceived? I would never...! How can you accuse me of...?"

Her indignation did not sway Jasper, for he sensed the lady was protesting too much. "You forget, Miss Fairfax, I have spent many years in the world of commerce. I have learned to recognize when a person is keeping something from me. I suspect you have acquired the same skill in the schoolroom."

By the time he finished speaking she had grown calm again. Perhaps she recognized the futility of trying to conceal something he wanted to know. "I believe I have, sir."

Her gaze fell—a sure sign of an uneasy conscience.

"There is something you are not telling me about this house party." Jasper did not pose it as a question but stated it as a fact. "Now kindly save us both time by telling me what I want to know."

"Oh, very well." She inhaled a deep breath then raised her head to meet his gaze. "It is no great matter so you might as well hear."

Before she could say anything more, they were interrupted by an insistent rapping on the study door. Miss

Fairfax glanced toward the sound then back at Jasper with her brows raised in a silent question.

"Go ahead," he growled, impatient with the ill-timed intrusion. "Answer it."

She opened the door to admit a flustered-looking footman. "Begging pardon, Mr. Chase, but Mrs. Thorpe bid me fetch you straightaway. Your guests have begun to arrive."

They were not *his* guests. Jasper barely stifled a gruff observation to that effect. They might be going to spend the next three weeks under his roof, but he had not invited them and he was far from certain he wanted them there. "Tell Mrs. Thorpe I will be along as soon as I am finished speaking with Miss Fairfax."

That was clearly not the response the footman wanted. "Mrs. Thorpe was very insistent, sir."

His mother-in-law was a good-hearted creature, but Jasper knew how little it took to throw her into a flurry and the effort it required to soothe her nerves again afterward.

"Oh, very well," he muttered as he strode toward the door.

As he brushed past his children's governess, he added, "This matter is not settled, Miss Fairfax, only postponed."

On his march back to the entry hall, Jasper tried to arrange his features into a hearty smile of welcome, but they resisted. However well-meaning the motives of Miss Fairfax and his mother-in-law, he resented the prospect of sharing his family holiday with a pack of strangers.

Still, none of that was his guests' fault. They would come to Amberwood believing he'd invited them. They did not deserve to be made uncomfortable or unwelcome. With that conscious alteration of his outlook, his features relaxed.

When Jasper spied a lanky gentleman in conversation with his mother-in-law, his lips spread into an unforced smile. "Norton! Welcome to Amberwood. It has been far too long, old friend."

He and Norton Brookes had grown up together when Norton was a pupil of Jasper's adoptive father. Though he came from a family of superior class and education, he had never lorded over Jasper, like some of the other boys. Jasper wished he had kept in closer touch with his old friend since their school days.

That made him regret the harsh manner in which he had questioned Evangeline Fairfax's motives for arranging this house party. Perhaps she had simply decided he might need something more in his life than work and his children. If she had, he owed her thanks rather than suspicion.

He glanced back down the hallway and spied Miss Fairfax lingering at the foot of the servants' stairs, watching his reunion with his friend. Jasper caught her eye and gave a rueful nod that he hoped would signal his apology. As soon as he was able, he would seek her out and properly beg her pardon for mistrusting her. He should have known a woman who cared for his children so well could not mean him any harm.

She acknowledged his nod with a fleeting smile that conveyed relief. Then she headed up the stairs.

"Jasper." Norton Brookes seized his hand and shook it warmly. "How good to see you again. And how kind of your mother-in-law to invite us! You must remember my sister, Abigail?"

He turned toward a tall lady with dark curls and a long, but attractive face that resembled her brother's.

"I do remember." Jasper bowed over her hand. "Though I fear I never would have recognized you, Miss Brookes. The last time we met you were still in the nursery."

Abigail Brookes's green eyes sparkled with lively mischief. "I was out of it more often than in, as you may recall, roaming the countryside like a proper little savage. I have been civilized since then, however. You needn't worry that I will smuggle hedgehogs into your house in my apron pocket."

Jasper laughed heartily. "My children would not object if you did."

"In that case I should very much like to meet them," Abigail replied. "How many do you have and how old are they?"

"Five altogether. Emma is eleven years old, Matthew nine and Alfie eight. Owen is six and Rosie, my youngest, is five."

They were too young to do without the woman who had cared for them the past several years. Somehow he *must* persuade his children's devoted governess not to abandon them.

A flurry of activity at the door signaled the arrival of more guests.

Jasper's mother-in-law greeted a tiny woman of her own age with a fond embrace then beckoned him over for an introduction. "You must have heard me speak of my dear friend Mrs. Leveson. Martha, may I present my son-in-law, Jasper Chase."

He bowed. "Welcome to Amberwood, ma'am. I hope you will enjoy your visit."

"It is a pleasure to make your acquaintance at last, Mr. Chase, after everything I have read of you in Hilda's letters." As Mrs. Leveson spoke, Jasper had the uncomfortable feeling she was sizing him up. He could not be certain whether he'd been judged adequate.

Next, his mother-in-law brought forward a young woman not much taller than Mrs. Leveson. Her golden-brown hair was tied up in two bunches of sleek ringlets that looked absurdly like sausages. Though Jasper guessed her age to be above twenty, she blushed and giggled like a child when he bowed to her.

"This is dear Martha's daughter, Gemma."

Jasper greeted Miss Leveson then turned to introduce her and her mother to the Brookeses. Mrs. Leveson appeared to size up his friend, as well. Gemma Leveson simpered when Norton asked if they'd had a pleasant journey.

Meanwhile, Abigail's dancing eyes warned Jasper that she was in danger of laughing. He was hard pressed to stifle a grin.

"We must show you to your rooms so you can rest from your journey." Jasper struggled to recall the expected duties of a host, which he had not been obliged to perform for quite some time. "Further conversation can wait until dinner."

No sooner had their guests been ushered away than more arrived.

"Mr. Webster, welcome!" Jasper shook hands with his late father-in-law's partner, a big, burly man whose genial air concealed a shrewd head for commerce. "You must feel as much out of your element in the countryside as I sometimes do. I trust business is thriving at Red Gate Mills."

Piers Webster shook his head, though his smile did not falter. "Beastly, and getting worse. But I promised Margaret I would try to put it out of my mind during our visit. You remember my daughter, don't you?"

"Miss Webster, of course." Jasper greeted the fair-haired lady with a dapple of golden freckles on her pretty nose. "I hope you did not have too much difficulty getting your father away from his mill."

"None at all," she replied. "It was Papa who insisted we accept your invitation."

Jasper and his mother-in-law talked a little more with the Websters until the footman returned to show them their rooms.

"Perhaps this house party was not such a bad idea, after all, Mama," Jasper said when their guests were out of earshot. He was not certain about the Levesons, but Norton and Abigail Brookes would be good company, as would the Websters.

"I am pleased to hear you say so, my dear boy." Mrs. Thorpe regarded him with a look that seemed to mingle relief and…pity? "You cannot grieve forever. Life moves on and there are the dear children to think of."

What did she mean by that? Jasper had no opportunity to ask because just then *more* guests arrived. The first to enter was a tall, striking lady with an elaborate hat perched on her carefully coiffed dark hair. In contrast, the woman who followed her was small and mousy looking, clearly doomed to lifelong spinsterhood.

Something about that impression made Jasper uneasy.

The handsome lady kissed his mother-in-law on both cheeks, exclaiming over the charming house and beautiful countryside.

Mrs. Thorpe beckoned Jasper to introduce her. "No doubt you have heard me speak of my goddaughter, Penelope Anstruther."

The lady thrust out her hand for Jasper to bow over.

"It is a pleasure to meet you at last, Mr. Chase. It was vastly kind of you to invite me."

"The pleasure is mine, Miss Anstruther and Miss…?" Jasper bowed toward the other woman, who started at his greeting and bobbed a timid curtsy.

"Oh…" Miss Anstruther seemed surprised to be reminded there was anyone with her. "*Mrs.* Dawson, my companion. I am informed you own a cotton mill, Mr. Chase. It sounds fascinating. You must tell me all about it."

Her interest in his business surprised Jasper, for he could not imagine anyone who would look more out of place in a cotton mill.

Then Miss Anstruther fixed him with a gray gaze he could only describe as…predatory. Suddenly everything that had been troubling him about this house party collided in his mind with his mother-in-law's earlier remarks. Though he had little experience with such gatherings, he believed it was customary to invite an equal number of ladies and gentlemen. This one had only two male guests while four were marriageable women—five if he counted Mrs. Dawson, who must be a young widow.

Why, this party was nothing more than a thinly veiled matchmaking scheme to find him a new wife! And his children's governess was clearly the mastermind behind it.

He would soon make it clear to Evangeline Fairfax that he wanted nothing more to do with matrimony!

Chapter Two

Mr. Chase had figured out the reason behind this house party. Evangeline could tell by the way she caught him looking at her when he joined the children for their tea.

The Amberwood nursery was a large, well-lit chamber that served as schoolroom, dining hall and playroom for the children. At one end it led off to the boys' bedroom and at the other to the girls' and their governess's. Previously, whenever Mr. Chase had visited the nursery, he'd scarcely seemed aware of Evangeline's presence except to question her about his children's health or their studies. All his attention had been focused on Emma, Matthew, Alfie, Owen and Rosie, as if to make up for the time he'd missed with them.

In all fairness, Evangeline had to admit Mr. Chase probably spent as much time with his sons and daughters in the course of a year as many fathers who lived under the same roof. That did not mean it was enough, she reminded herself, seeing the way their faces turned continually toward him, like flowers to the sun. With their mother gone, the young Chases needed *more* of their father's time. Matthew and Alfie could use his fond but firm guidance to curb their boisterousness. Quiet Emma and Owen needed the assurance that they were noticed and loved. Rosie just needed more kisses and cuddles.

If their father was too occupied with his business to provide the attention they required, perhaps an affectionate stepmother could make up some of what they lacked. Better yet, the lady might persuade her husband to devote a little less time to his mill and more to his family.

Those justifications ran through Evangeline's mind whenever she met a reproachful glare from her employer. However, they did not entirely soothe her conscience. She had always been an open, forthright person. What would her late mother think of the underhanded methods she had used to maneuver Jasper Chase into remarriage?

He had left her no alternative. Evangeline returned his challenging gaze with one of her own. Besides, her matchmaking scheme would not hurt anyone. If it succeeded, the result would benefit her employer, his children and her...not to mention one fortunate lady.

When they had finished eating and the nursery maid cleared the table, Mr. Chase addressed Evangeline. "We need to have another little talk, Miss Fairfax."

"As you wish, sir. But first I must take the children out to play in the garden then get them ready for bed." By that time, their father would be expected to dine with his guests. She would be asleep long before the party broke up for the night.

"Then I will join you in the garden." Mr. Chase smiled down at Rosie, who clung to his leg. "Would you like that, my love?"

Rosie gave a vigorous nod, making her red-gold curls dance.

Did he mean to confront her in the presence of her pupils? Evangeline's spirits sank. Would he tell them what she'd done? How could the children understand, especially Emma, who cherished the memory of her late mother?

"I would like it too, Papa!" cried Alfie. "What shall we play?"

The children argued about the choice of game in a good-natured way as they headed out to the garden.

"Let's play hide-and-seek," Mr. Chase said, putting an end to the debate. "You hide then Miss Fairfax and I will look for you. Off you go now. We will stand over here with our backs to you so we can't see where you go."

"Don't peek, Papa," called Matthew as he ran off.

"Come with me, Rosie." Emma took her little sister by the hand. "Help me find a good hiding place."

Their father lowered his voice, for Evangeline's ears alone. "Matchmaking, Miss Fairfax? I never thought you would stoop to such nonsense."

"It *isn't* nonsense," she replied in an emphatic whisper, vexed with him for confronting her now, when she must watch every word for fear of being overheard. "Your children need a mother and it is high time you found them one. Since you have little opportunity for courting, I thought I would make it easy for you by bringing several eligible ladies together. You ought to thank me."

"*Thank you?*" Jasper Chase thundered, then remembered where they were and tried to cover his outburst in a tone of false heartiness. "I mean…thank you…Miss

Fairfax, for reminding me it is time to look for my hiding children."

As they made a show of searching the garden, he continued in a casual murmur that could not disguise his exasperation. "If you had bothered to consult me, I could have saved you the trouble of arranging all this. I am done with matrimony. I have no time for anything but my mill and my children."

Had she gone to all this effort for nothing? The possibility stung Evangeline, as did a bewildering pang of pity for Jasper Chase.

"Do you even have time for them?" she muttered as she brushed past him to call out Matthew. The boy never could stay still long enough to win at this kind of game.

Mr. Chase soon found the rest of his children, though it took a while to discover Owen tucked between a shrubbery and the garden wall. The quiet little fellow seemed very pleased to play a game at which he could excel.

"Now you must all hide." Owen motioned them away with a sweep of his arm. "You, too, Papa, and Miss Fairfax."

"Come along, Miss Fairfax. You heard my son. We must find a hiding place." Her employer took Evangeline by the hand in much the same way Emma did little Rosie. She knew his motive was much different than his daughter's...as was her reaction.

Her strong will resented his taking charge so forcefully, yet another part of her responded to the warmth and restrained strength of his grasp.

A moment later, she and Mr. Chase were crouched behind a small shed where the gardener kept some of his tools.

Her employer turned toward her and continued in a

forceful whisper. "I spend as much time with my children as I can, while still earning enough to provide a good life for them. Don't you think I would rather come home to them every night when my work is done? There are times I miss them so much it is like someone gouged a great bleeding hole in my heart. But this is the home they have always known and the Vale is a healthy place for them to grow up. So I do what I must and make the best of it."

Suddenly he seemed to recall that he was still holding her hand. He released it abruptly with a rueful scowl.

Though her fingers tingled from being gripped so hard, Evangeline was too stunned by his outburst to take much notice. The raw regret in his blue-gray gaze made it impossible for her to doubt his sincerity.

For the past six years, she had been acutely conscious of how much her young pupils yearned for their absent father. She had suffered those same feelings after the deaths of her parents, so her heart had been quick to sympathize with the Chase children. She'd never stopped to consider how their father might feel about being parted from *them*.

"I did not realize, sir." She wished he had not let go of her hand, for just then she would have liked to give it a comforting squeeze. "You always go back to Manchester without any sign of reluctance."

"My work is important to me." A defensive note crept into his deep North Country voice. "You of all people should understand that it is about more than earning a wage. But I assure you, I leave Amberwood with much greater reluctance than I show. The children do not need me to make them feel worse about my going."

His explanation dealt Evangeline's conscience a smarting blow. At the same time she fought a bewildering urge to console him as she would one of the children.

"I found you." Owen's voice broke in on Evangeline's confused thoughts. "It was easy because I heard you talking. You must keep quiet if you don't want to be caught."

"Excellent advice, son." Jasper Chase emerged from behind the little shed. "I will do my best to remember it after this."

Evangeline followed, still feeling off-balance from the drastic shift in her perception of her employer.

While Owen hunted for his brothers and sisters, she addressed Mr. Chase. "I beg your pardon, sir, for being so insensitive to your true feelings. But you cannot deny you used to come home a good deal more often before…"

She hesitated, reluctant to speak of his wife's death with the children nearby.

Mr. Chase seemed to understand. He gave a curt nod that warned her there was no need to continue. Then he heaved a sigh. "I cannot deny it. Much as I enjoy being with my children again, coming back to Amberwood always reminds me of our loss."

For an unguarded instant, the grief he kept so well concealed from her and the children flickered in his gaze.

Though it made her throat tighten in sympathy, Evangeline refused to let it silence her. Instead, she chose her words with care and spoke them as gently as she could. "Is that not all the more reason to consider remarrying—for the children's sake and for yours? The right sort of wife might ease your unhappy memories, and help fill the hollow in your life that you try to plug up with your work."

Mr. Chase inhaled a deep breath and paused before answering. "I believe you mean well, Miss Fairfax, but I suggest you consider how *you* would feel if our positions were reversed. What if I invited a houseful of eligible bachelors to Amberwood to court you?"

"I found everyone," called Owen. "Now it is Emma's turn to seek."

Her employer's question hit Evangeline with the force of a runaway mail coach. How would she react if someone pressured *her* to marry? She had experienced that in the past and vowed never to let it happen again.

The other children scattered while Rosie ran to her father and caught him by the hand. "Will you help me find a hiding place, Papa?"

Mr. Chase did not wait for an answer from Evangeline but responded to his little daughter. "Of course, my love. Come along."

"Miss Fairfax?"

Evangeline roused from her preoccupation to find Emma staring up at her. "Aren't you going to hide?"

"Yes, of course." She wandered off, scarcely aware of where she was going.

She owed Mr. Chase an answer to his question. Evangeline now wondered if she did not owe him more than that.

How would Miss Fairfax react if he tried to make a match for her? When the question first crossed Jasper's mind, it had been charged with indignation. But the longer he dwelled on it, the more sincerely curious he grew to know the answer. It made him question why such an attractive, intelligent, accomplished woman had not secured a husband long ago.

He had no opportunity to ask her, even if he'd dared,

for the children's games required more of his attention. Later, while their governess got the children ready for bed, Jasper had to hurry off and dress for dinner. He returned to the nursery long enough to hear the children's bedtime prayers and kiss them good-night.

"Oh, Papa," cried Emma when she caught sight of him dressed up to dine with his guests. "You look so handsome! Doesn't he, Miss Fairfax?"

His daughter's question seemed to fluster her governess in a way Jasper had never seen before. Bright pink roses blossomed in her cheeks, making her look far younger than her years. The sight made him wonder once again how she could have remained unwed. Obviously she had no fortune or she would not be spending her life raising other people's children. But surely her looks, character and accomplishments should have attracted the interest of men wise enough to care for more than money.

"Very handsome, indeed," Miss Fairfax replied, though she had only glanced at him for an instant. "Now we must let your father get away to dine with his guests."

For some reason, Miss Fairfax's brusque compliment made Jasper self-conscious. He was used to thinking of himself as a practical man of business, a widower with five children, not an ardent young beau who made ladies weak in the knees. To hear himself called handsome was…unsettling.

Once the children were tucked in for the night, Jasper sensed their governess wanted to speak with him.

"What is it, Miss Fairfax?" He affected a severe look. If not for her meddling, he could have retired to his study for a quiet evening or gone off for a solitary walk. Now he would have to entertain a party of guests, several of whom might hope to become the next Mrs. Chase.

She opened her mouth to speak just as the nursery clock chimed.

"It can wait, sir." She looked relieved by the delay. "You mustn't keep your guests waiting."

"That would never do." His voice rasped with sarcasm as he stalked off.

By the time he reached the drawing room, Jasper was practically choking on his resentment of the situation in which Evangeline Fairfax had trapped him. The sight of his friend Norton Brookes eased his wrought-up feelings slightly. But the way Miss Anstruther tried to lure him into conversation at every turn set his teeth on edge almost as much as Miss Leveson's incessant giggles. He wondered if the ladies were aware of the purpose behind this house party. If they were, Abigail Brookes and Margaret Webster gave no sign of it, for they seemed more interested in talking to each other than to him.

The moment dinner was announced, Miss Anstruther seized his arm. "Since I will be seated beside you, Mr. Chase, we ought to go in together."

Jasper barely managed to bite back an exasperated sigh. He had almost forgotten the ridiculous rules of precedence that governed such gatherings. As host and hostess, he and his mother-in-law would sit at opposite ends of the dining table with the lady of superior rank seated on his right and the corresponding gentleman on Mrs. Thorpe's right. The rest of the guests would range on either side, with the most humble occupying the middle.

That would put Norton Brookes farthest from Jasper, while placing him between Miss Anstruther and Mrs. Leveson.

Adding that to his list of grievances against his children's governess, Jasper forced himself to smile at Miss Anstruther. "It will be…an honor to escort you."

He glanced toward his mother-in-law and received a subtle nod of approval as she accepted Norton Brookes's arm.

When Mr. Webster bowed to Mrs. Leveson and requested the honor of escorting her to dinner, Jasper held his breath, awaiting her reply. This party was a precarious mixture of minor gentry and prosperous business folk. Some people with claims to gentility went out of their way to avoid anyone in trade, no matter how great their fortune. Though Miss Anstruther appeared willing to unbend in that regard, Jasper was not certain Mrs. Leveson would be quite so broad-minded.

To his relief, she accepted Mr. Webster's invitation without the slightest qualm.

Abigail Brookes approached Miss Webster. "In the absence of any more gentlemen, shall we go in together?"

Margaret Webster did not appear troubled by the dearth of male guests. "I believe we can make do."

Gemma Leveson gave a tinkling giggle. "I reckon that leaves you and me, Mrs. Dawson."

Miss Anstruther's companion looked around anxiously at the other guests as if intimidated by having the slightest attention paid her.

"Come along, Verity," Miss Anstruther bid her in an impatient tone. "Do not delay us with your timidity."

Mrs. Dawson blushed and scurried to join Miss Leveson.

They proceeded in to dinner, which Jasper was

pleased to discover well planned and well prepared. Was this all his mother-in-law's doing, or had Miss Fairfax worked behind the scenes to make certain the house party would be a success? Jasper could not imagine where she'd found the time. Any family with five children was bound to keep their governess busy, especially when she must often act as both mother and father to them. Then again, Miss Fairfax had proved herself a woman of singular resourcefulness.

Had he shown his children's governess how much he appreciated her uncommon devotion? The question troubled Jasper. Could that be part of the reason Miss Fairfax wanted to leave his employ—because he had taken her for granted?

Just then he realized the table conversation had fallen silent.

"I...beg your pardon?" he asked Miss Anstruther, who was staring at him expectantly.

"I asked about your children," the lady repeated with a look of avid interest. "How do you manage all on your own with so many and your business to operate besides?"

Some of the other guests resumed their separate conversations, voices hushed as if to keep one ear out for their host's reply.

"I am hardly on my own." He nodded toward Mrs. Thorpe. "Their grandmother has been of invaluable assistance to me. And their governess is a treasure. I do not know how we would have managed the past few years without her."

Miss Anstruther nodded. "What a blessing it is to have reliable servants."

Her condescending remark irked Jasper. He was still annoyed with Evangeline Fairfax for arranging this matchmaking party without so much as a by-your-leave. But hearing her referred to as a mere servant vexed him even more. Clearly Miss Anstruther had no conception of the scope of Miss Fairfax's duties or how much she meant to his children.

Before he could say anything he might have regretted, Miss Anstruther added, "I do hope we shall have an opportunity to see the little darlings while we are here. I have always been vastly fond of children, haven't I, Verity?"

"Vastly fond," her companion parroted like a dull scholar giving a rote response.

"My Gemma dotes on children." Mrs. Leveson glared across the table at Penelope Anstruther as if this were a contest in which the lady had claimed an unfair advantage.

Jasper could imagine what his eldest sons would think of being called *little darlings,* but he suspected Rosie would love the attention. "I assure you, everyone will be seeing a great deal of my children, and hearing them, too."

"I heard them before dinner, playing in the garden," said Abigail Brookes. "They sounded as if they were having a jolly time. If I hadn't been dressed already, I might have stolen out to join in their games."

"That would have been amusing, wouldn't it?" Gemma Leveson cast a mischievous grin at Abigail. "Perhaps we shall have another chance while we are here."

Miss Webster had been very quiet but now she looked down the table at Jasper. "Your children are fortunate to have such an excellent governess, Mr. Chase. I was devoted to mine. It broke my heart when I outgrew lessons and she went off to a new position. Do tell us more about your children. How old are they? What mix of boys and girls?"

Miss Anstruther gave an offended sniff. "I was just about to ask that. Do tell us, Mr. Chase."

Jasper had never thought he would grow tired of talking about his children, but by the end of the meal he had been so thoroughly quizzed on the subject, he was eager to explore a new topic of conversation. With a sense of relief, he watched the ladies retire to the drawing room.

"We shall have to stick together, gentlemen." He rose from his chair and strode to the opposite end of the table, taking his mother-in-law's seat. "I fear we are badly outnumbered."

The two men chuckled—Piers Webster in a rumbling bass and Norton Brookes in a ringing tenor.

"I don't object to being surrounded by ladies." Mr. Webster leaned back in his chair. "Provided I am not their quarry."

Norton gave a rueful grin. "A poor vicar is not likely to be an object of interest to any lady. I reckon you can have your pick, Jasper. The only difficulty will be in choosing."

"I don't want to choose." Jasper hoped they would not be offended on behalf of their womenfolk. "This house party was not my idea."

Mr. Webster nodded. "Getting a push from your mother-in-law, then?"

"Something like that," Jasper muttered.

"Well, I won't pretend I wouldn't welcome you into my family." Mr. Webster folded his large hands over an ample expanse of waistcoat. "I'm not getting any younger and it would be a relief to leave my mill in capable hands, until a grandson were old enough to take it over."

Jasper appreciated the older man's frankness.

"Margaret is a fine lass, if I do say so," Mr. Webster continued. "She's got her mother's good looks, thankfully, and a sensible head on her shoulders."

"Which she gets from you?" Jasper asked.

The older man shrugged. "I like to think so."

"Any man would be fortunate to win a woman like your daughter." Jasper hoped he had not offended Mr. Webster by seeming to spurn her. "But I have my hands full with my children and my mill. Besides, I'm not certain I am ready to remarry."

"I wasn't anxious to think about marrying again for a great while after my wife passed on." Mr. Webster shook his head. "Now I wish I hadn't left it too late. Don't you make that mistake, lad."

Jasper glimpsed a shadow of profound regret in Piers Webster's eyes that made him wonder if he might be wise to take the older man's advice.

Evangeline rubbed her eyes and gave a deep, weary yawn. From her perch a few steps up the servants' stairs, she could hear voices coming from the drawing room, punctuated now and then by waves of laughter.

She wished she could hear who was speaking and what they were saying—who was provoking the laughter. Then perhaps she could gauge whether her matchmaking plans had any hope of success. Was Mr. Chase joining in the laughter or was he sitting in stony silence, too annoyed with her meddling to make any effort to enjoy himself?

After all she had done to arrange this party, it galled her to hang back and let events take their course. From her earliest years she had been accustomed to making things happen and her industrious mother had encouraged her.

"There are some people who claim Providence helps those who help themselves." Evangeline fancied she could hear her mother's words of encouragement. "But I believe the Lord helps those who help *others*. We cannot wait for Him to heal all the ills of the world. Or, worse yet, assume He does not care about the plight of those who need help. We who believe must act as His hands, feet and voice to work His will on Earth."

"I will, Mama," she whispered fervently.

Orphan girls, like her friends from school, needed her to provide the kind of safe, loving, stimulating sanctuary the Lord wanted for them. The Chase children needed her to find them a new mother who would make Amberwood the kind of home to which their father would want to return more often.

Yet as much as those goals compelled her, Evangeline could not stop thinking about what Jasper Chase had said to her in the garden. How would she feel if he tried to push her into marriage by arranging a party like this with several eligible gentlemen as guests? She knew the answer to that question all too well. She would feel manipulated. She would feel as if her wishes were of no consequence and her plans for the future did not matter.

Despite the fact that she had been up since early morning and put in a full day with the children, Evangeline knew she could not sleep until she had apologized to Mr. Chase. Even if it meant lurking on the servants' stairs waiting for the party to disband for the night.

As if on cue, she heard the drawing-room door open and Reverend Brookes apologize for being the first to retire. His sister claimed she was tired, too, but perhaps she only felt obliged to leave when her brother did.

Evangeline heard the door close, followed by foot-steps that paused a little ways away.

"Perhaps it was a mistake for us to come." Reverend Brookes sounded as tired as Evangeline felt.

"What makes you say that?" His sister gave a wry chuckle. "Just because Miss Anstruther is better bred than me, Miss Leveson is younger and Miss Webster prettier *and* richer, do you suppose I stand no chance at all of snaring your handsome friend?"

Somehow it irked Evangeline to hear Miss Brookes call Jasper Chase handsome. She told herself not to be ridiculous. She wanted all the eligible ladies to admire her employer and be eager to marry him if asked.

"Tosh," replied the vicar. "You have plenty of fine qualities to recommend you and Jasper is just the sort of man to appreciate them. There is more to him than a handsome face and a good income. You know that cotton mill of his in Manchester...?"

"What about it?"

Miss Brookes and her brother must be climbing the main staircase. Their voices were growing fainter. But the vicar's remark had piqued Evangeline's curiosity. Though her conscience chided her that it was ill-bred to eavesdrop, she stole up the servants' stairs and strained to catch the rest of the conversation.

"How admirable," she heard Miss Brookes say as they reached the upper floor. "I had no idea."

"Not many people do," her brother replied. "My friend heeds the Scriptures about doing good works in secret. Mr. Webster told me about it. I believe he considers the whole scheme a harmless eccentricity of Jasper's."

What scheme were they talking about? The curios-

ity Evangeline had hoped to slake only intensified. No
doubt this was her just punishment for eavesdropping.

It was clearly something to do with Mr. Chase's mill.
But what could be admirable about that? Often during
the past six years she had thought quite the opposite
about her employer's business, which kept him away
from his children so much. Whatever it was, why had
he never told her?

Curiosity battled conscience again, only this time
the latter won. Evangeline forced herself to descend the
stairs with as much stealth as she could manage. Five
steps from the bottom she sat down and resumed her
vigil. The brief snatches of conversation she had heard
ran through her mind as she tried to figure out the cru-
cial part she had missed.

A while later she jolted awake to find herself slumped
against the wall. Thank goodness she had not pitched
forward and tumbled down the last few stairs!

Hearing voices, louder and more distinct, she realized what had woken her. The party seemed to be breaking up for the night.

"It has been a most enjoyable evening," said Mr.
Webster. "In spite of the drubbing I took at whist from
the ladies. I hope we may play again, Mrs. Leveson."

"I expect we will have plenty of opportunities," the
lady replied. "Sleep well. I'm certain I shall after such
a fine dinner."

The others wished Mr. Webster and his daughter
good-night then the Leveson ladies lingered with Mr.
Chase, Miss Anstruther and her companion. The two
pairs of ladies did not address a word to each other
but made stilted conversation with their host. Evangeline sensed that neither wanted to be the first away to

bed, leaving the others to prolong their conversation with him.

Mr. Chase must have realized it, too, and decided he would have to be the one to end the impasse. "I regret I must bid you good-night, ladies. There is a small task awaiting me in my study which I must finish tonight. I look forward to seeing you tomorrow."

A subtle change in his voice made Evangeline doubt his sincerity, but she did not believe the ladies knew him well enough to catch it.

Did she know him at all after six years in his employ? Evangeline rubbed her eyes and rose to her feet as quietly as she could manage.

Now that there would be no advantage in outlasting one another, the ladies bid their host good-night and headed up the front staircase.

Mr. Chase strode away in the direction of his study. But instead of marching briskly past the servants' stairs as Evangeline expected, he turned onto them and started up the steps.

Coming unexpectedly face-to-face, they both sprang back, letting out stifled cries of alarm.

"Miss Fairfax!" Her employer clutched his broad chest. "What in blazes are you doing here at this hour?"

What could she tell him? Evangeline's heart pounded painfully against her ribs.

It was a natural reaction to such a fright, she told herself. Surely there could be no other reason for her heart to behave that way.

Chapter Three

The last person Jasper expected to meet on the back stairs was his children's governess. In all the time Evangeline Fairfax had been employed at Amberwood, he had never once seen her around the house after the children were tucked in for the night.

In fact, he hadn't thought he would meet *anyone* on the stairs. He'd hoped to slip up to his bedchamber quickly and quietly before the ladies reached the second floor. His sudden encounter with Miss Fairfax sent a jolt of alarm through him, magnified by embarrassment over his furtive behavior. He struggled to catch his breath.

Clearly he had given Miss Fairfax as much of a fright as she'd given him. She jumped back, a strangled squeak erupting from her lips.

"Miss Fairfax!" Jasper clapped a hand to his chest in an effort to settle it. "What in blazes are you doing here at this hour?"

She seemed to shrink from his question, but before she could answer, an alarming possibility occurred to him. "Is something wrong with one of the children? Alfie? Has he hurt himself again?"

His agitation seemed to steady her. "No, sir, nothing like that. The children are all sleeping soundly after their play in the garden. I am here to apologize for arranging this house party without your permission and for pushing you to remarry."

"You are?" Her admission surprised Jasper almost as much as her presence. Miss Fairfax was a strong-minded woman, not inclined to back down. What had made her change her mind?

She gave a convulsive nod. "I thought about what you said—how I would feel if our situations were reversed and you were trying to make a match for me. Of course, I would object to it in the strongest possible terms. I still believe it would benefit you and your children if you remarried, but it was wrong of me to force your hand this way. For that, I beg your pardon."

"You would not want to be married?" Jasper had never given the matter much thought until now. Never given *her* much thought, come to that. For all he'd noticed her, Miss Fairfax might have been a handsome, useful article of furniture in his home. He had never considered how she might feel or what she might want.

The lady shook her head vigorously. "Not every woman is desperate to snare a husband. For many, the role of wife is one to which they are well suited, but I have always wanted to do something more with my life. Something important in the Lord's service that will improve the lives of others. Perhaps that sounds foolish to you."

"Not at all." In fact, her fervent declaration echoed a deep conviction in his soul.

Perhaps Miss Fairfax sensed that and realized she might use it to her advantage. "Establishing a charity school is my calling in life, sir. I am certain of it. And that calling is not compatible with marriage. A man might be able to pursue his life's work with a wife to support him, but I do not believe the opposite is true."

Jasper wanted to contradict her but found he could not. What man could abide having his wife devote all her time and energy to a cause, however noble, if it meant neglecting their family?

That thought troubled him. Why should a woman be obliged to give up the comfort and love of a family in order to serve a higher calling while a man could have both? That was as unfair, in its way, as one class of people having too much while another had far too little. It also made him question whether he had neglected his family in the service of his cause.

"My children need you just as much." He was accustomed to giving orders, not pleading. But if he could keep Miss Fairfax at Amberwood, he would not feel he had failed his children. "They may not want for material things but they are motherless."

"No." Evangeline Fairfax pointed an accusing forefinger at him. "I will not let you hold me here with guilt. I am giving you a month's notice to find your children a new governess. After that, I intend to leave and responsibility for their care will be on your shoulders, not mine."

One month? If he looked for a year, Jasper doubted he could find anyone capable of truly replacing Miss Fairfax. "But...but...how can I search for a new governess and spend time with my children while entertaining a houseful of guests?"

Something told him she could manage such a feat if she had to. It galled him to admit he was less capable. But if he must for the sake of his children, he would.

"Your guests?" Her hand slowly fell, but not before

Jasper glimpsed a slight tremor in it. "I thought you would send them away or return to Manchester until they were gone."

He shook his head. "I may not be much of a gentleman but I have better manners than that. It wasn't my idea to invite these folk, but now that they're under my roof, they are my guests and I will extend them my hospitality."

"That is good of you, sir." Was she surprised to hear that he knew how to behave well? She did not sound it.

Jasper shrugged. "It still leaves me the problem of finding an opportunity to search for a new governess. I know it is my own fault for squandering the time you gave me. What would it take for you to stay two months, until the end of the summer? I give you my solemn word I will not ask for more time after that."

"What would it take?" she repeated. "I do not want more money, if that is what you mean. But if you promise to become acquainted with these ladies and keep an open mind about the possibility of remarriage, then I will extend my notice until the end of the summer. But not a day more."

Jasper did not answer right away, but mulled over her proposition as carefully as he would any business agreement. What she was asking could have a profound effect on his future and his children's. An extra month would give him more time to hire a new governess—or time during which he could try to persuade Miss Fairfax to stay. If he failed, then perhaps she was right and he should consider remarrying.

"Will you give me the night to sleep on my decision?" he asked. "It is not something I want to rush into."

"That sounds fair," she agreed. "You can tell me your decision tomorrow and we can go from there."

Jasper appreciated her directness. It was a refreshing change after an evening spent in the company of Miss Anstruther and Mrs. Leveson. Every time they spoke, their words seemed laden with hidden meaning he could not fathom. True, Miss Fairfax had gone behind his back to arrange this house party, but when he'd confronted her, she truly seemed to repent her actions. And he could not deny that his delaying tactics had forced her to take desperate measures.

"Tomorrow." Jasper could not suppress a yawn. "Now I think we had both better get some sleep. It has been a long day."

That was an understatement. He had risen at first light and set out from the inn in Kendal, where he'd spent the night after riding all day yesterday. Since reaching home, he had dined and played with his children, entertained a party of guests and spent more time in private conversation with Miss Fairfax than he had in the past several months put together.

"Indeed, sir." She struggled to stifle a yawn, too, with no more success than he'd had. "Good night, then. Rest well."

She started up the stairs, only to turn and fix Jasper with a questioning look when he followed her.

"The ladies may be lingering in the hallway bidding one another good-night," he explained. "I need you to go ahead and check whether the coast is clear."

She exhaled a sharp breath of exasperated amusement. "Come along, then. I will scout the terrain for you."

"Thank you, Miss Fairfax." Jasper gave a weary grin,

which he doubted she could see in the shadows of the unlit stairwell. "I know I can always rely on you."

A pang of regret pierced him as he spoke those words. He only wished he'd realized how very much he and his children had come to rely upon Evangeline Fairfax before they were faced with losing her.

A babble of voices from the nursery woke Evangeline the next morning. Forcing her heavy eyelids open, she glanced toward her clock to discover she had overslept by nearly an hour!

Dragging herself out of bed, she dressed with fumbling fingers, all the while chiding herself for her sluggishness. Usually she was up and about an hour before any of the children, ready to begin their day. If only she had not stayed up so late last night to speak with Mr. Chase. Surely her apology and ultimatum could have waited until morning.

"No, they could not," she muttered at her reflection as she pinned up her hair for the day. "Between the children and his guests, when else would I have found a private moment to speak with him?"

A splash of cold water on her face banished the worst of her sleepiness. She looked forward to her breakfast coffee with longing.

"What is all this hubbub?" she demanded as she entered the nursery to find Rosie chasing around in her nightgown, while Matthew and Alfie pelted one another with rolled-up stockings.

"I'm sorry, miss." The nursemaid pushed back a lock of hair that had escaped her cap. "I tried to keep them quiet, but they are so excited to have their father home."

"Don't fret, Jane." Evangeline stopped the boys' stocking fight with a firm look they had long ago learned to heed. "Go fetch us breakfast. I will restore order here."

"Thank you, miss." The girl heaved a sigh of relief. "I'll be as quick as I can."

While Jane hurried away, Evangeline turned toward her pupils. "Boys, get washed and dressed at once and no more horseplay or there will be consequences. Is that understood?"

"He started it." Matthew pointed at his brother.

"I don't doubt that." Evangeline caught Rosie's eye and nodded toward the bedroom she shared with Emma. "But you are older. You should know better than to egg him on. Off with you now."

Hearing the nursery door open behind her, she wondered at the speed with which Jane had fetched breakfast. But before she could turn to look, Rosie darted across the nursery floor on bare tiptoes, crying, "Papa!"

"Good morning, my love." Mr. Chase scooped his small daughter into his arms for a warm embrace. Then he stooped to hug Owen and Emma, who had been dressed and quietly reading books during the earlier tumult. "How did you all sleep? I've come to eat breakfast with you and help Miss Fairfax out if she needs me."

He looked up at Evangeline with a smile that made her forget her drowsiness and the upset in the nursery routine.

Her first instinct was to insist everything was under control, but Mr. Chase could see for himself that was not true. Besides, it would be good for him to experience some of what was involved in running an orderly nursery for five children. It might help him choose a new governess…and perhaps a new wife, wisely.

"Thank you, sir." She beckoned Rosie to her. "If you

would see that the older boys get dressed with a minimum of fuss, I shall look after this young lady."

Once the children were dressed, they gathered around the nursery table. With their heads bowed for grace, the young Chases looked like paragons of good behavior.

"Amen!" Matthew and Alfie chorused with gusto after Owen finished asking the blessing for their morning meal.

As the children tucked into their porridge and cream with hearty appetites and Evangeline savored her coffee, Jasper Chase asked, "What do you all think of this house party your grandmother arranged…with the help of Miss Fairfax?"

Though they had aired the matter thoroughly yesterday, Evangeline still squirmed a little at his mention of her underhanded behavior.

As always, Matthew was the first to get a word in. "It sounds like jolly fun, Papa."

Alfie's mouth was too full to permit him to speak, but he signified his agreement with a vigorous nod.

"I like parties," said Rosie. "Will there be cake?"

"Perhaps." Her father tried to suppress a grin. "Though it isn't quite that sort of party. What do you say, Owen? Emma?"

Owen shrugged. "It will be all right, I suppose."

Emma slowly stirred her porridge. "Will you have any time to visit with us or will you have to spend it all with the guests?"

Mr. Chase flinched and his grin faltered. But he came back with a reply that seemed to please his daughter. "I promise I will not neglect you in favor of our guests. They are welcome to join in our fun and games, but if they choose not to, that is their own lookout."

"I hope they do," said Alfie, who had finally cleaned his bowl. "The more the merrier!"

The boy's words seemed to restore his father's good humor. He winked at Alfie. "That's the spirit, son."

"Does that mean we can go fishing today?" asked Owen.

Mr. Chase nodded. "That sounds like a fine idea. I shall inform our guests at breakfast and ask who would like to come with us."

"Are you going to eat two breakfasts every day, Papa?" Matthew's eyes twinkled with merriment. "You will have to be careful you don't grow stout."

All the other children laughed. Mr. Chase joined in, as did Evangeline. She found it hard to imagine her tall, muscular employer ever putting on extra weight. He always seemed to be on the move like Matthew and Alfie.

"If we are to go fishing," she said when their merriment had settled down, "we will need bait. Why don't we go dig up some worms while your father and the guests are at their breakfast."

The boys all agreed eagerly, while Emma and Rosie wrinkled their noses.

"Good thinking as always, Miss Fairfax." Their father raised his coffee cup as if in a toast to her then drained it. "I shall ask Mrs. Gilman if she can pack us a picnic lunch of tea and cakes."

The children heartily approved his suggestion. Once they finished their breakfast, Evangeline sent them off to wash up and collect their caps and bonnets.

On his way out of the nursery, Mr. Chase paused near her and spoke in a soft voice. "I have decided to go along with this matchmaking scheme of yours. But only on condition that my children must be involved as much as possible in all my guests' activities. The last thing I want is for this house party to take away from my time with them."

"Of course, sir." Evangeline resented the idea that she would suggest anything that might limit her pupils' opportunity to spend time with him. "It will give you an opportunity to observe how each of the ladies gets on with the children. That way, you will be able to select the best possible mother for them."

A look of sorrow shadowed Jasper Chase's eyes, but he gave a resigned nod. He might not wish to remarry, but he seemed to realize the necessity, for which Evangeline was grateful.

A while later, Jasper glanced around the dining table at his guests as they ate breakfast. The gentlemen and Miss Brookes tucked into theirs with hearty appetites, while the other ladies picked away more daintily.

Having given Miss Fairfax his word that he would keep an open mind about remarrying, he considered each of the eligible ladies as a possible future wife.

Miss Anstruther was one of the best-looking, without a doubt, which made him question why she was still unwed when she must be every day of thirty. He did not consider her maturity an impediment—quite the contrary. In fact, he preferred it to the giddy, girlish air of Miss Leveson. She had been under his roof less than twenty-four hours yet already her incessant giggling had begun to grate on his nerves.

Abigail Brookes had a much more appealing laugh— robust and infectious. She was the least pretty of the younger ladies, yet still quite attractive in her way. Since she was the sister of a vicar, Jasper hoped she might approve of his work.

Margaret Webster had been quiet so far—preferring

to let those around her do all the talking. Jasper held that as much in her favor as her golden good looks. There was also the matter of her fortune, since she would one day inherit her father's prosperous cotton mill and other business interests. Jasper did not give a fig about that on his own account. But for the sake of the families who depended on him, it might make a vast difference. If he could persuade Piers Webster to reform his mill, other owners might give his radical ideas a try.

Miss Webster glanced up then and caught Jasper watching her. She blushed and ducked her head.

This was not lost on Miss Anstruther, who had been chatting away while Jasper pretended to listen. "My dear Miss Webster, I do believe you have made a conquest! Our host has been gazing upon your beauty for the longest time. You are blessed with excellent taste, Mr. Chase."

Though she spoke in a jesting tone, Jasper sensed something more behind it.

He had only ever courted one woman in his life, and it would be truer to say she had pursued him. Not that he'd minded—quite the opposite. But it meant he had little experience in the ways of women apart from his late wife and her mother. If he did take advantage of Miss Fairfax's matchmaking scheme to find a bride, would he be capable of securing the lady of his choice?

"Nonsense," he growled, casting his gaze down at his breakfast. "I would not be so disrespectful."

"Indeed he would not!" Mrs. Leveson huffed. "Mr. Chase could just as easily have been looking at Gemma. You should not make mischief, Miss Anstruther."

"Oh, Mama, she was only teasing," Gemma Leveson giggled and on this occasion Jasper did not mind it. "I'm sure Mr. Chase knows that."

"Of course." For the sake of peace, Jasper feigned a smile. "Very amusing, Miss Anstruther."

That did not entirely appease Mrs. Leveson, who seemed to have taken a dislike to Penelope Anstruther. "Young ladies were not so forward in my day as to rally their hosts."

From the far end of the table, Jasper's mother-in-law caught his eye. He sensed she wanted him to change the subject before the thinly veiled hostilities escalated.

"Speaking of amusing things—" Jasper raised his voice to include all his guests "—my children are eager for me to take them fishing this afternoon. If any of you would care to join us, you would be most welcome. Otherwise, my house, gardens and stables are at your disposal."

At his first mention of fishing, Miss Anstruther turned up her nose, the way Emma and Rosie had done at the prospect of digging worms. But when Abigail Brookes and Gemma Leveson said it sounded like a jolly outing, she agreed.

"Count me among your party, too," said Norton Brookes. "I can scarcely remember the last time I went fishing. Back during our boyhood, I reckon."

"I shall leave fishing to the young folk." Piers Webster mopped up the last of his eggs with a piece of bread. "But if Mrs. Thorpe and Mrs. Leveson would care to join me in a drive around this pretty countryside, I should be honored."

Both ladies readily accepted his invitation.

"What about you, Miss Webster?" asked Jasper's mother-in-law. "Would you prefer fishing or a carriage drive?"

"She'll go fishing, of course," said Piers Webster before his daughter could answer.

"And you, Mrs. Dawson?" Jasper asked when he realized Miss Anstruther's companion had once again been overlooked.

"Verity will come wherever I go," Miss Anstruther announced. "After all, what is the good of employing a companion if one does not have her company?"

Miss Leveson giggled, but her mother scowled, as did Norton Brookes.

Abigail turned toward Mrs. Dawson with an encouraging smile. "I'm sure it will be great fun!"

The timid young widow brightened visibly at the friendly overture. "Thank you, Miss Brookes. I believe it will."

While Jasper appreciated Abigail's show of kindness, he was not certain he could agree with what she had said. A simple fishing expedition with his children had turned into a sort of audition for a new wife.

An hour after Mr. Chase's children and guests trooped down to the stream with their fishing rods and creels, Evangeline finally had a moment to catch her breath.

Miss Brookes and Miss Webster were larking about with Matthew and Alfie, channeling the boys' high spirits while keeping them out of actual mischief. Miss Leveson had taken a great fancy to little Rosie, fussing over the child and addressing her in baby talk. The two sat in the grass by the riverbank chaining wildflower wreaths for their hair.

Mr. Chase and his friend Mr. Brookes were showing Owen how to cast his line into the water, while Miss Anstruther hovered nearby, frequently asking Mr. Chase for assistance as she fumbled with her fishing rod. Emma and Mrs. Dawson perched on the edge of the bank some distance away from the others. They talked quietly together as they held their rods and waited patiently for the fish to bite.

With the children all properly supervised, Evangeline took the opportunity to spread out the picnic rugs and unpack the vast hampers of food the cook had sent down.

She had not been at her task long when Miss Brookes approached and sank onto one of the rugs with a breathless chuckle. "May I trouble you for a drink, Miss Fairfax? Keeping up with those two young gentlemen is thirsty work."

"Gladly." Evangeline handed her a cup and pulled the stopper from a cider jug. "You and Miss Webster seem to be enjoying yourselves with the boys."

Miss Brookes nodded. "I haven't had such a jolly time since I used to tag along with my brother and his friends when we were young. Now that I am the sister of a vicar, everyone in Norton's parish thinks I ought to be prim and proper and never have a bit of fun. They forget what the Scriptures say about making a joyful noise."

Evangeline smiled as she poured the frothing brown cider into Miss Brooke's cup. The vicar's sister reminded her so much of her friend Leah Shaw. She wondered how rebellious, high-spirited Leah would adjust to the scrutiny of being Duchess of Northam. Miss Brookes might be the ideal woman to bring more joy back into Mr. Chase's life, the way Leah had with Lord Northam and his young son. While that thought brought Evangeline a sense of hope, it also inflicted a subtle sting, which puzzled her.

Miss Brookes took a deep drink from her cup then gazed around with a wistful smile. "I envy you your position here, Miss Fairfax. I've often thought what a fine thing it would be to earn an independent living."

"I am not certain most governesses would agree with you." Evangeline recalled the difficulties her friends had endured during their careers as governesses. "But I appreciate how fortunate I am to be employed at Amberwood. The children are all very good natured and Mr. Chase and Mrs. Thorpe never interfere with my management of the nursery."

"My brother will not hear of my finding work as a governess. Our mother was one before she married and it took a toll on her health. I hate to be a burden on poor Norton. His living is not large enough to support a sister and a wife…" Miss Brookes grimaced. "I beg your pardon for rattling on so. I am not accustomed to having another woman to talk to."

"There is no need to apologize," Evangeline assured her. "It is kind of you to confide in me as an equal rather than order me about as if I was a servant."

Abigail Brookes glanced toward Miss Anstruther and rolled her eyes. "I wonder if she would pursue Mr. Chase with such vigor if she knew what use he makes of his fortune."

The casual comment made the back of Evangeline's neck prickle. Could this be her opportunity to discover what the lady and her brother had been talking about last night? "One never knows. Miss Anstruther might consider it…admirable."

Miss Brookes gave an unladylike snort of laughter. "I should be astonished if she did. Fancy a man squandering the profits of his business on his workers rather than wringing every last penny from their labor? I suspect she would insist he put a stop to that foolishness."

Evangeline tried not to let her astonishment show.

Yet part of her was not altogether surprised. She recalled her late-night conversation with Jasper Chase and how he had not scoffed at her dream to do something important in the Lord's service.

Miss Brookes took another drink of cider. "You must be proud to work for such a charitable man. I would like to see the housing he has built for his workers. My brother tells me Mr. Chase sponsors all sorts of recreational activities so his workers will be less apt to spend their wages at the public house. If only more men in his position were so progressive."

Evangeline tried to look as though none of this information came as a surprise. It must take a great deal of effort to do so much for his workers' welfare, in addition to running his mill profitably enough to support his family. Her insides tightened with shame to recall how she had chided him about the time he spent away from his children.

"Thank you for the cider." Miss Brookes handed back her cup. "Now I must see if the boys have frightened all the fish away with their noise."

She scampered off, leaving Evangeline to digest this revelation about Jasper Chase.

Why had he not told her that he was doing something more than amassing a fortune for his personal use? Did he think she would not understand or care? Or did he think so little of her that it never occurred to him to tell her anything of consequence?

Indignation swelled within her, fueled by a bewildering sense of injury. But her conscience was quick to deflate it. Had she given Jasper Chase any reason to believe she might be interested in his work? All this time she had lived under his roof and raised his children, yet in many ways they hardly knew one another.

Perhaps that was just as well, Evangeline decided as she watched her employer converse with Miss Anstruther. It would be hard enough to leave the children for whom she had come to care so much. She did not need any other ties to prevent her from undertaking the task the Lord had given her.

Yet she could not deny that becoming better acquainted with Mr. Chase might be an advantage in helping her decide which of the ladies would make the best wife for him.

Chapter Four

Perhaps this house party was not such a bad idea, Jasper reflected as he helped Owen cast his fishing line on that pleasant summer afternoon. When he managed to forget the ultimate objective of the party, he actually found himself enjoying it. How long had it been since he'd spent leisure time in the company of other adults? He provided his workers with plenty of opportunities for recreation, yet it was a luxury he seldom permitted himself.

There was an unexpected advantage to having so many other people around, he realized as his gaze ranged over the party on the riverbank. Each of his children had someone to pay him or her exclusive attention. The older boys were larking about with Miss Webster and Miss Brookes. Emma was having a quiet chat with Mrs. Dawson, while Rosie was being fussed over by Miss Leveson. That left Jasper free to fish with Owen, who sometimes seemed to get lost among his brothers and sisters.

It was something he should do more often. Jasper resolved to spend more individual time with each of his children rather than always with the whole group at once.

"Papa?" Owen's voice was charged with suppressed excitement. "I feel something tugging on my line."

Jasper noted the tension on the line and the way the tip of his son's fishing rod dipped toward the water. "I think you have a bite there, lad."

"What should I do?" The child gripped the rod so hard, his arms quivered. "I've gone fishing before, but I've never caught anything."

"I shouldn't wonder, with your brothers around." Jasper gave his son an encouraging pat on the shoulder. "The trout likely hear them coming a mile away and swim off downriver. This fellow of yours must be hard of hearing."

Owen chuckled and the tension in his shoulders relaxed.

"Don't pull too hard," Jasper advised him, "or your line might break. Try easing your fish toward the shore. If he swims the other way, let him go as far as you can then bring him back. Be patient and you will tire him out."

It took a while and more coaching, but in the end Owen brought a fine fat trout near enough to the shore for Jasper to scoop it into a net.

That brought Matthew and Alfie running. "You caught a real fish! How did you do it, Owen?"

With an air of bashful pride, the boy gave a detailed account of how he had landed his catch. His brothers listened with avid interest and did not interrupt as much as usual.

Miss Fairfax strolled over to admire Owen's catch, as well. She did not look quite so much like a governess today. Perhaps because there were guests present, she had forgone her usual severely plain dress for a white frock sprigged with tiny blue flowers. Her sash and the trimming on her bonnet were a matching shade of blue. It suited her complexion and brought out intriguing flickers of amber in her brown eyes. A stranger might have mistaken her for one of his guests.

Jasper found himself comparing her with the other ladies. She was as pretty as Miss Anstruther without being conscious of her looks. She had far more good sense than Miss Leveson would ever have. She possessed more spirit than poor Mrs. Dawson or even quiet Miss Webster. Yet she seemed more capable and self-contained than Miss Brookes. He had taken her for granted since his wife's death, trusting her to raise his five greatest treasures without fully appreciating her many excellent qualities. In spite of her insistence to the contrary, he was certain it would be no easy task finding someone to replace her. It would be a far better use of his energies to persuade her to remain at Amberwood.

Miss Fairfax listened with patient interest as Owen once again recounted how he had caught his first fish.

"Well done!" She beamed with pride in her young pupil's accomplishment. "When we get home, you must take your fish to Mrs. Gilman and ask her to fry it up for tea."

"Papa must have some," Owen insisted. "He helped me catch it."

"I only gave you a little advice." Jasper rested his hand on his son's shoulder. "You were the one who hooked and landed it."

He glanced up to find Owen's governess watching them with a tender glow in her brown eyes that surprised him a little. He had never doubted Miss Fairfax gave his children the best possible care and instruction, but now he realized that she actually *loved* them. Was she aware her feelings for her pupils ran so deep? If so, how could she think of leaving them?

Miss Anstruther strolled over and spoke to Jasper. "How clever of your little boy to catch a fish, Mr. Chase. I have had no luck at all. You must show me the secret of it."

Owen pursed his lips in a frown of annoyance, perhaps at being referred to as a *little boy.* Meanwhile, Miss Fairfax withdrew to admire Rosie's wildflower crown.

"There is no great secret." Jasper tried to stifle his impatience with the interruption. He knew he ought to take advantage of this opportunity to become better acquainted with the lady, as he had promised Miss Fairfax. "It all comes down to a little good fortune and a great deal of patience, which Owen has in abundance."

"Owen," Miss Anstruther repeated. "What an interesting name. Were your ancestors Welsh, by any chance, Mr. Chase?"

Jasper shook his head. "All Cumbrian folk, as far as I know. My son is named after a friend of mine. Robert Owen shares my ideas about the responsibility of employers to provide their workers with a decent life. We believe it makes good business as well as moral sense."

"Indeed?" Miss Anstruther feigned a look of interest, but Jasper could tell she was uncomfortable with his radical ideas. "I was named for my grandmother. She was a Hervey."

Jasper tried to appear impressed, for it was clear she took pride in the connection. But he had no idea who these Hervey people might be.

"Do you come from a large family?" he asked her as Owen took up his rod and cast again.

"Alas, no." The lady heaved a sigh. "I envy your little ones all their brothers and sisters. My parents began their family late in life. I was their only child and now I am quite alone in the world."

Jasper knew how that felt. It made him warm to Miss Anstruther in a way he had not expected to.

"Shall I show you how to cast a line?" he offered.

The lady's face lit up, making her look even more attractive. "Could you, please? I fear I am all thumbs when it comes to outdoor pursuits. But I am keen to learn."

"That's the most important thing." Jasper picked up her fishing rod and showed her where to place her hands to get the best control.

Miss Anstruther made an effort, but he had to admit she'd told the truth about being all thumbs. At least she was able to laugh at her mistakes, in which he joined. When she finally made a fair cast, he complimented her.

To his surprise, Jasper realized how much he missed female company. Perhaps becoming acquainted with the other ladies would not be such an ordeal, after all.

With that in mind, he glanced toward Evangeline Fairfax, who was summoning everyone to eat. When their eyes met briefly, he offered her a broad smile to let her know he no longer resented her matchmaking efforts. Regardless of what came out of this house party, he knew she'd had his and his children's best interests at heart.

He expected an answering smile or perhaps a nod of approval. Instead, Miss Fairfax looked vaguely annoyed, though he could not imagine why. Was there no pleasing the woman?

What had come over her? Evangeline asked herself as she got everyone seated and served their picnic luncheon with the help of the footman and one of the maids.

Mr. Chase was doing precisely what she'd asked—getting better acquainted with one of the ladies. She should feel pleased, hopeful or some other positive emotion. Instead, when she'd watched her employer talking and laughing with Miss Anstruther, an unfamiliar sensation flared within her, making her insides clench and her cheeks burn. No appeals to reason could banish this perverse feeling, much to Evangeline's dismay.

Fortunately, everyone else appeared to be enjoying their excursion. The children were clearly delighted with the special attention being paid them.

"Look what we made, Emma." Rosie showed off the circlet of wildflowers nestled in her red-gold curls.

"How pretty!" her sister cried. "It makes you look like a woodland princess."

"Or a bride," Verity Dawson suggested.

Perhaps she had not meant to voice the thought. When the others looked at her, she ducked her head and mumbled something about ladies wearing floral wreaths on their wedding day.

"Quite right," declared Miss Brookes. Was she deliberately trying to draw attention away from Mrs. Dawson? "Plenty of the brides who get married at my brother's church wear bridal wreaths over their veils. I am often called upon to stand as a witness."

The mention of weddings seemed to make all the ladies pensive. Were they imagining themselves standing at the altar with Jasper Chase at their side?

Rosie paid little heed to the conversation of her elders.

"We made one for you, too, Emma." She jumped up and placed a ring of flowers in her sister's golden-brown hair and received a hug of thanks.

Matthew and Alfie made faces at one another, expressing their disdain for all the talk of flowers and weddings.

"Oh, Papa," said Matthew, "Miss Brookes told us about the things you and the vicar used to do when you were our age."

Alfie paused in his consumption of a cold-chicken drumstick. "Fancy a vicar catching tadpoles and flying kites."

"Alfie!" Evangeline and Jasper Chase both spoke at once in the same warning tone. "Mind your manners."

But Reverend Brookes laughed. "I'll have you know, I was a champion kite flier back then, Master Alfred, and I had no notion of becoming a vicar when I grew up. Perhaps you will be a vicar one day."

The children all burst out laughing at such an outrageous idea, but Evangeline did not discount it altogether. She knew what a loving heart Alfie had for all his boyish high spirits. He was the first to comfort his brothers and sisters if they were sad or hurt. Perhaps the ministry would be his calling in life.

"We should make kites and take them flying," Matthew suggested. "Up on Red Hill."

Abigail Brookes was quick to approve the idea. "That sounds jolly, doesn't it, Norton?"

The vicar nodded. "What do you say, Jasper? Shall we see if we still have our old knack?"

"It sounds like a capital idea." Mr. Chase took a little round meat pie from the platter. "Can you find us the necessary materials for kite-building, Miss Fairfax?"

"Of course, sir."

The strange feeling that had possessed her earlier seemed to have quieted. Now Evangeline savored the satisfaction of a plan well executed. Everyone appeared to be in fine spirits. Even Miss Anstruther seemed less haughty and Mrs. Dawson less timid. Best of all, Mr. Chase looked happier than she had seen him in years. Surely he deserved that after all the time he had spent tending to his mill and his children.

After eating luncheon with hearty appetites, the party did a little more fishing until the wind began to pick up and a bank of threatening clouds blew in.

Evangeline helped clean up after the picnic then sent the dishes and leftovers back to the house with the servants. Once that was done, she approached Mr. Chase and suggested it might be wise for them to seek shelter.

He glanced up at the sky. "I was having too good a time to notice. We are fortunate you were paying attention, Miss Fairfax."

Her employer's remark brought Evangeline a flutter of satisfaction. It was gratifying to know that he valued even her smallest contributions to the smooth running of his household.

"Come along, everyone," he called. "Let's pack up our gear and get back to the house before we are caught in a deluge."

A flurry of activity followed and soon the party set off back to Amberwood. Matthew and Alfie scampered ahead, calling to Miss Brookes and Miss Webster to chase them. Owen trudged along beside the vicar, with whom he conversed in grave tones. Emma and Mrs. Dawson held hands and walked quietly together while Miss Anstruther stuck close to Mr. Chase, who carried Rosie on his shoulders.

That left Miss Leveson on her own. She soon fell in step with Evangeline, who brought up the rear of the party. "Mr. Chase thinks the world of you, Miss Fairfax. How long have you worked for him?"

"Six years." Evangeline welcomed the compliment.

"I was hired to teach Emma and Matthew, but after their mother passed away, I took over supervising the care of the younger children, as well."

"You have done a fine job. They are lovely children—well behaved without being backward."

"Thank you, Miss Leveson." If there was one thing Evangeline could not resist, it was praise for her pupils. "They are as clever and good-natured a group of children as I have ever known, though I cannot pretend to be impartial."

"Their father must place a great deal of trust in your judgment," Miss Leveson continued. "I suppose he seeks your counsel about a great many things."

"Some, perhaps, to do with the children."

The lady gave an emphatic nod. "I thought so. I am certain you give him excellent advice about anything that might affect their well-being."

"I try to." Evangeline wondered where this conversation might be leading. "Why do you ask?"

"I thought you might want to warn him." Miss Leveson nodded toward Jasper Chase, striding along some distance ahead of them with Rosie on his shoulders, while Penelope Anstruther hurried to keep up.

"Warn him?" Evangeline repeated.

Miss Leveson slowed her pace and lowered her voice. "Surely you must agree it would be most unfortunate for your pupils if that woman manages to sink her claws into their father. She claims to be vastly fond of children, yet she did not pay any of them the least attention today. She was too busy fawning over their father."

That was true, Evangeline realized. No doubt it accounted for her strange antagonism when she'd watched the two of them together.

Miss Leveson dropped her voice even further. "I happened to overhear her talking to Verity Dawson, whom she treats abominably, poor creature. Miss Anstruther said the girls and the little boy were tolerable, but the older boys were a pair of boisterous ruffians."

The vague antagonism Evangeline had felt toward Miss Anstruther flared into defensive outrage. How dare she say such things about Matthew and Alfie when she hadn't exchanged a word with either of them? True, Matthew was constantly on the move, always talking and asking questions, but those were signs of his quick intelligence and boundless curiosity. Alfie could be a little bull in a china shop at times, but he had the most open, affectionate heart. Ruffians, indeed!

Her indignation quite choked her, but Miss Leveson seemed to mistake her silence for doubt. "Miss Anstruther went on to say that the boys should have been sent away to school long ago. I don't doubt that is just what she will do if she gains any influence over their father."

She couldn't, could she? The glare Evangeline shot at the distant figure of Penelope Anstruther might have set the lady's hat on fire. It had been their father's decision to educate the boys at home for as long as possible. With their mother gone and him away so much, he'd wanted his children to have each other's company. He was also reluctant for them to mix with young aristocrats who might shun them for having a father in trade or encourage them in false values like pride and selfishness.

Evangeline supported his decision entirely. She knew that a good boys' school would not be subject to the deprivations of the charity institution where she'd been so miserable. But the reports she'd heard about such places from the brothers of her former pupils did not inspire her with confidence. She feared school might stifle Matthew's curiosity and break Alfie's spirit.

"I thought I would mention it to you," Miss Leveson concluded, "since you seem so devoted to Mr. Chase's children."

"Of course," Evangeline replied rather absently. Her thoughts were racing so, she was scarcely aware of the other woman. "Thank you for this information."

"I felt it was my duty." Miss Leveson sounded convinced of her virtue. "I have taken such a fancy to these dear little ones."

With that, she hurried to catch up with Emma and Mrs. Dawson, leaving Evangeline to trail after the rest of the party, lost in thought.

If what she'd been told was true, it would be a calamity for the Chase children if their father wed Miss Anstruther. On the other hand, Miss Leveson's devious tattling did not paint her in a flattering light, either.

For the first time since she'd come up with the idea for a matchmaking house party, Evangeline questioned whether it was such a clever plan, after all. What would happen if Mr. Chase chose the wrong lady to be his second wife? Could she bear to be responsible for that?

"I believe I owe you an apology, Miss Fairfax," said Jasper as his children washed up for their tea.

"Do you, sir?" She had seemed distracted ever since they returned from their fishing expedition.

Jasper wondered if there was something troubling her. "I know I have difficulty admitting I am wrong. But in this case, I must make an exception. I am beginning to think this house-party idea of yours was not such a bad one, after all."

A rather pained look came over her vivid features.

He tried again. "In fact, it may have been a very good one. I was concerned it would take away attention from the children, but instead it has provided them with more. I enjoyed myself today as I have not for a very long time. For that I owe you my thanks."

Her expression lightened and warmed in response to his words, though he fancied a shadow remained in her brown velvet eyes. "I am pleased you had a pleasant time, sir. You deserve it after all you do for others."

Jasper sensed an unspoken "but" and wondered what it might be. Or was he only imagining things? "You did an excellent job today, making everything run smoothly for our outing, so we could all relax and enjoy ourselves."

"Thank you, sir." She looked gratified by his praise, yet her gaze seemed to avoid his, as if she'd done something wrong rather than doing everything right. "It was the least I could do after all my meddling in your life. I meant well, but now I wonder…"

"Don't fret," Jasper tried to reassure her. "Sometimes a person is right to interfere when they see a friend in need of help. Especially if that friend does not realize they need assistance."

Miss Fairfax still did not seem persuaded. Perhaps the situation called for more than words. He reached out, clasped her hands and gave them a gentle squeeze. "It has worked out for the best. Thank you for caring enough about my family to arrange all this."

His gesture of gratitude seemed to fluster his children's strong-willed governess in a way he had never seen before. Had he been so remiss about expressing his appreciation that she did not know how to accept praise?

Before he could think what else to say, Rose came running in from the bedroom she shared with Emma.

"I'm ready for tea, Papa. Are we going to eat Owen's fish?"

Jasper let go of the governess's hands and turned to pick up his youngest daughter. "Not today, little one. Mrs. Gilman needs to clean and fillet it. She promised Owen to have it ready for tomorrow. If I'd thought, we should have taken along a pan to fry our catch over a fire and eat with our luncheon. Fish always tastes best that way."

"We would only have gotten a bite each, among so many of us," said Matthew, suddenly appearing at his father's side. "It wasn't a very big fish."

"A good deal bigger than you caught," Jasper said, winking at his son to show he was only teasing. "Besides, you ought to recollect the story of the loaves and the fishes. Sometimes, when we are willing to share what we have, the Lord multiplies it further than we would ever imagine."

He knew that from experience. Mill profits, which might have evaporated to pay for luxuries, could make a good life for many more working families whose labor kept his business running. In turn, he believed his employees worked harder and more efficiently than the wretched starvelings hired by his competitors. One day he hoped to persuade the other owners that true Christian principles and good business could go hand in hand.

The other children soon joined them and they all sat down to a jolly tea. Each of the youngsters was eager to tell what they had done or discussed with Jasper's guests that afternoon...even Emma.

"I like Mrs. Dawson best," she replied when her father made a point of drawing her out. "She doesn't make a fuss or treat me like a baby."

Jasper glanced at Miss Fairfax to discover she was

biting on her lip to keep from grinning. He knew they were both thinking of how Miss Leveson had cooed and babbled over Rosie. Jasper pressed his lips tight together and looked away from the governess for fear they might offend his daughter with a burst of laughter.

"She is all alone in the world, you know," Emma continued in a tone of gentle pity. "She got married to a soldier but he was killed at Waterloo. I think she still misses him."

The way Emma still missed her mother? The thought gave Jasper a pang. He recalled how his late wife had doted on their first child, such a quiet, contented infant.

"I'm sure she does," Miss Fairfax spoke up when Jasper's memories rendered him silent. "But I believe she enjoyed herself today and was happy to make a new friend."

Her words seemed to comfort the child and encourage her to focus on how she could help Mrs. Dawson rather than dwell on the sadness of their bereavement.

Owen looked toward the nursery window where fat drops of rain spattered against the glass. "It's too bad we won't be able to play hide-and-seek in the garden after tea."

The other children murmured their disappointment, but their governess was quick to offer a suggestion. "What if we play downstairs before the guests come down to dinner?"

Jasper's children immediately cheered up, greeting the idea with enthusiasm.

"We will need your father's permission, of course." Miss Fairfax cast him a pleading look. "And we must promise to be very careful and not break anything."

"We promise!"

"Can we, Papa? Please!"

Jasper gave a cheerful shrug. "I don't see why not."

The children cheered and their governess flashed him a grateful smile.

"Perhaps we should ask Miss Brookes to join our games," he suggested. "She told me she wished she could have played with us last night."

Alfie nodded. "I think we should. I like her."

"So do I," said Matthew. "Miss Webster, too. Can we ask *her* to play, Papa?"

"If you like." Jasper wondered if the other children would want to invite their particular friends.

Before any of them should suggest it, Miss Fairfax rose from her place. "Let's get tidied up first. Rosie, how on earth did you manage to get jam on your nose?"

Jasper turned to the nursery maid, who had begun to clear away the dishes. "Jane, will you kindly inform Miss Brookes and Miss Webster that the children will be playing downstairs for the next hour, if they would like to join us?"

"Yes, Mr. Chase." The girl bobbed a curtsy. "Right away, sir."

Perhaps this would be an opportunity to become better acquainted with one of the other ladies. Jasper mulled over the idea as Jane bustled off to relay his invitation. Without Miss Anstruther around to claim his attention, it might be easier to engage Abigail Brookes or Margaret Webster in conversation.

Yet somehow, he could not dismiss the ridiculous impression that the ladies would be intruding on his family time with the children and Miss Fairfax.

Chapter Five

On the fourth day of the house party, Evangeline woke even earlier than usual. After checking that yesterday's rain had stopped, she dressed and arranged her hair with more than usual care. Mixing with Mr. Chase's guests had made her conscious of her appearance. She did not want to be an embarrassment to her employer, after all.

Once she was ready, she crept out to the nursery, where Jane had already lit a small fire and left a pot of coffee. Evangeline had just poured herself a cup when the nursery door eased open and Jasper Chase peered inside. She was not surprised to see him. The day before, he had asked if there was a time he might speak to her without the children present. She'd told him there was only this early morning hour or the evening after her pupils were tucked in for the night. Mr. Chase insisted he did not want to make her wait up.

Now he entered the nursery with quiet footsteps, closing the door softly behind him. Evangeline poured him a cup of coffee as he slipped into the chair beside her at the round nursery table. Of course, it would be easier to speak in hushed tones if they sat close, she told herself.

"Good morning," he whispered. "I hope you slept well."

She nodded. "Very well, thank you. I hope you are not tired from having to rise at such an early hour."

Mr. Chase shook his head as he took a sip of his coffee. "When I'm in Manchester I am accustomed to being up and about early. It is the late evenings sitting up with company that feel peculiar to me."

"I believe it will be a fine day." Evangeline wondered when Mr. Chase would explain the reason for his early morning call. "A bit windy, but that will not be a bad thing if you want to fly kites on Red Hill."

A slow smile spread across his face, beginning in one corner of his lips and rippling over to the other. "We had better, don't you think, after all the work we went to making them yesterday? It was a perfect activity to keep the children occupied on a rainy day."

Evangeline worked hard to suppress an answering grin. "Some of your guests seemed to enjoy kite-building as much as the children, Mr. Brookes and his sister, especially."

"Indeed," he agreed. "They both seem to appreciate this escape from the restrictions of vicarage life. I only wish I'd invited them to Amberwood sooner. I will not be so remiss in the future."

Reverend Brookes could visit much more frequently if his sister were the lady of the house. Evangeline was tempted to mention it, but something held her back.

Instead, she asked a question that had plagued her ever since Mr. Chase suggested this meeting. "I beg your pardon, sir, but the children will soon be stirring. What is it you wish to discuss with me?"

"Oh, that." He sounded as if he had forgotten his reason for being there. "You may have noticed the effort I have been making to get better acquainted with the ladies."

"I have, sir, and I appreciate it," Evangeline replied.

He already seemed to know Miss Brookes quite well. During yesterday's kite-making, the two had talked a great deal about a number of childhood visits he had made to her home. Though Evangeline was relieved to see his attention distracted from Miss Anstruther, she had not been as pleased as she should to witness his easy camaraderie with Abigail Brookes.

Mr. Chase looked rather self-conscious. "The fact is, I need to discuss the merits of each lady and seek advice about which might make the most suitable match. It would be awkward to broach the subject with my mother-in-law. I doubt Norton Brookes could be impartial since his sister is one of the ladies in question. That leaves you, Miss Fairfax. You know me, my children and my household. I trust your judgment as I do few others."

Evangeline ducked her head and bolted a mouthful of coffee to cover her intense satisfaction at hearing that.

"Besides," he continued, "this party was your idea to find me a wife. So I reckon you owe me your assistance."

"I suppose I do, sir." She acknowledged his claim with a rueful nod. "I shall be happy to help in any way I can, if you will tell me how."

"I would like your opinion of the ladies. Miss Anstruther to begin with. Do you think she would suit me and I her? Would she be a good mother for my children?"

Evangeline wanted to shout, "No, no, no!" at the top of her lungs, but she managed to restrain herself for fear of waking the children and perhaps offending their father. Had he taken a fancy to Miss Anstruther and wanted her to confirm the wisdom of his choice? Gemma Leveson's warning ran through her thoughts, yet she was reluctant to voice her opposition too forcefully. A strong-willed man like Jasper Chase might become more stubbornly attached to a lady of whom she disapproved.

Instead, she tried to be as diplomatic as possible. "Miss Anstruther is a very well-bred lady. She would get on well with your mother-in-law. But I am not certain she has much interest in your children. She has scarcely spoken to any of them since she arrived."

Mr. Chase gave a decisive nod. "I agree."

A powerful wave of relief swept over Evangeline. How could she have lived with herself if her actions ended up inflicting that unpleasant woman on her dear pupils?

"It is not her fault," he continued. "She grew up without brothers and sisters. I am not certain she has ever had contact with children before. Five must seem quite bewildering."

"That is no excuse." Evangeline's discretion deserted her. "I was my parents' only child, yet I became a governess."

That was no testament to a love of children, her conscience protested. She had been obliged to earn a living, and teaching was one of the only respectable ways a lady might support herself.

Fortunately, Mr. Chase did not take offense at her muted outburst. Instead, his blue-gray eyes twinkled. "But we cannot expect a mere mortal like Miss Anstruther to measure up to such a paragon as Miss Fairfax."

His teasing made Evangeline blush furiously. "I am not a paragon! How tiresome that would be."

"Compared to Penelope Anstruther, you are." He pulled a droll face that made Evangeline grin in spite of her embarrassment. "Besides, that is the paradox of paragons. If a lady believes she is one, she cannot possibly be. But if she denies it, chances are she is the genuine article."

She had heard Mr. Chase employ this kind of banter with his children, but he had never used it with her until this morning. She was not certain how she felt about it.

"Get away with you." She affected a mock scowl. "You are only flattering me to get me to stay at Amberwood."

"Perhaps a little," he admitted. "But that does not make it any less true. I am trying to make up for all the times I *should* have praised you in the past. If I thought flattery would persuade you to stay, I would lay it on with a trowel."

His eyes danced with mischief that reminded her of Alfie. She wondered if he had been like his son during his younger years. She could not help being amused by the image of him laying on thick gobs of praise the way a stonemason applied mortar.

"But back to my problem," Mr. Chase continued. "We are agreed that I can remove Miss Anstruther from my list of potential brides. Miss Leveson, too, I believe. Rosie likes her, but I am not sure about the other children. And I fear that giggle of hers would drive me mad inside a year."

Evangeline told herself she should be dismayed that Mr. Chase had casually rejected half the ladies she'd hoped he might wed. Instead, she felt elated. It must be relief that he could be trusted not to make an unsuitable match. She should have had more faith in his judgment.

"Even if the lady were more to my liking…" Jasper Chase grimaced. "I fear I could not tolerate having Mrs. Leveson for a mother-in-law."

Evangeline clapped a hand over her mouth to contain an unseemly burst of laughter that might rouse the children. They would be waking up on their own soon enough. For now she enjoyed this rare opportunity to talk privately with their father.

"Who does that leave?" He held up four fingers then lowered two. "Abigail Brookes. I believe she sincerely likes the children."

Evangeline could not dispute that.

"And I cannot deny I like her," Jasper Chase continued. "She was a wild little scapegrace as a child, but she seems to have matured into a very agreeable woman."

All that was true, Evangeline acknowledged. Abigail Brookes was not haughty and demanding like Miss Anstruther. Nor did she have Miss Leveson's flighty facade that masked a more calculating nature. Miss Brookes wanted to be a governess, which suggested an affinity for children. Her actions the past few days bore that out.

Then why did a sinking feeling come over Evangeline when Jasper Chase professed his fondness for the lady?

As he sat in the cozy, quiet nursery discussing prospective brides with Miss Fairfax, Jasper could not escape the feeling that he was a fraud.

In spite of the effort he had made to keep an open mind on the subject, he was still not convinced he wanted to remarry. Were the faults he had found with Miss Anstruther and Miss Leveson only excuses that might have been easily overlooked if he'd sincerely wanted to take a second wife?

Surely if he had been eager to wed, he would not have been so pleased when Miss Fairfax agreed that neither of the ladies was likely to suit him.

Now he raised the possibility of Abigail Brookes. He was certain her brother would approve of such a match. In turn, he would be delighted to have Norton for a brother-in-law. But could Abigail care anything for *him* or only his children? Jasper told himself perhaps the latter might be for the best. Then she might not feel neglected when he was obliged to be away so much on business.

Did Miss Fairfax guess the thoughts that were going through his mind? Perhaps, for her smile faded and an anxious look crept into her eyes. "Miss Brookes is, as you say, most agreeable. Matthew and Alfie are both quite taken with her. If they were twenty years older, you might have a pair of rivals for her hand."

It sounded as if Miss Fairfax might have her heart set on him wedding Abigail Brookes. Jasper was sorry to disappoint her, but something in him resisted her efforts to choose a wife for him. "I like Abigail, as if she were my sister or a friend, but I fear my feelings can never be more than that."

He expected Miss Fairfax to betray her frustration with him, but clearly she possessed even more self-control than he gave her credit for. The tension in her features eased and she released a soft, slow breath. "Do not be too sure. People's feelings can change, you know."

"Perhaps." Jasper could not conceal his doubts. "That leaves only Miss Webster. She seems pleasant enough, though we have had little opportunity to become acquainted. If I did not know better, I would say she was avoiding me."

The governess shook her head. "I am certain she is not."

Jasper shrugged. "At least it makes a refreshing change from being openly pursued."

"Or secretly stalked," Miss Fairfax muttered under her breath.

"Do you suppose it would be fair to Miss Webster if I tried to court her?" he asked. "Any romantic spark I ever possessed was snuffed out long ago by my responsibilities to my family and my business."

"Are you certain?" Miss Fairfax glanced up at him with a teasing half smile. "Perhaps it has only been hibernating and needs to be woken."

Her challenge seemed to stir something in him that had lain fallow for a very long time.

At that moment, Matthew popped his head out of the boys' room and Rosie out of the girls'. When she spied her father sitting at the nursery table, Rosie scampered across the room and scrambled onto his lap.

"Good morning, Papa!" She flung her dimpled arms around his neck and gave an affectionate squeeze. "What are you doing up so early?"

Jasper returned his little daughter's embrace with equal warmth. "I wanted a few minutes to talk to Miss Fairfax before she got busy with all of you."

Rosie contorted her face into an endearing look of puzzlement. "What did you want to talk to her about—us?"

Partly to avoid answering his daughter's question, Jasper opened one arm to Matthew. He was pleased when his son responded to the invitation by dashing over and exchanging hugs. He feared that all too soon the boy might consider himself too grown up for such gestures of affection.

"Will we be able to fly our kites today, Papa?" his son asked.

Jasper nodded. "I have consulted Miss Fairfax and she agrees that conditions appear ideal for kite flying."

"Can we bring a picnic again?" asked Rosie. She seemed to have forgotten her previous question.

"I believe that could be arranged." He gave her nose a playful tap with his forefinger. "After breakfast, why don't you go ask Mrs. Gilman. She cannot seem to deny you anything."

Their conversation soon roused the other children. Owen stumbled out, rubbing his eyes while Alfie yawned and stretched. Emma peeped out like a shy woodland creature from her den, but ventured out more boldly when Jasper smiled at her.

Miss Fairfax rose from her chair to begin her duties for the day. "Matthew, you should get dressed."

She approached Jasper with her arms open. "Come with me, Rosie, and pick out a dress for the day."

The child gave Jasper a parting kiss on the cheek then let her governess scoop her up and carry her away.

As the other children approached to receive some attention, Jasper realized that Miss Fairfax had subtly removed Matthew and Rosie to make room for them. Basking in the warmth of their affection, he reflected on the way his guests seemed to prefer one or the other of his children. Would he be able to find a wife capable of loving them *all,* different as they were?

Once Matthew and Rosie finished dressing, Miss Fairfax summoned the other children to get their clothes on. By the time they were all dressed and combed, the nursery maid had arrived with breakfast and they sat down to eat.

"Will you say the blessing this morning, Mr. Chase?" asked the governess.

Other nurseries might have a particular little prayer the children would say before meals, perhaps a short rhyme that became rote and slipped off the tongue with little thought. Jasper liked the way Miss Fairfax chose one of his children to ask the blessing in his or her own words. Sometimes he had to bite his lip hard to keep from grinning at the things Alfie and Rosie came out with, but it never failed to remind him to be thankful for the abundant blessings he had received.

"Very well." He watched the children fold their hands and close their eyes. "Heavenly Father, we thank You for this good breakfast. We thank You for the sunshine outside and the wind to fly our kites. We thank You for new friends, old friends and the love that fills this house. Help us to be mindful of our blessings and to share them with those who have less. Amen."

"Amen," murmured the children. Then they seized their spoons and tucked into their porridge.

"Not quite so much sugar, Rosie," Miss Fairfax cautioned Jasper's little daughter. "You are sweet enough, as it is."

Rosie broke into a broad grin and only sprinkled half the heaping spoonful of sugar onto her porridge.

Matthew began telling his brothers about plans for their excursion to Red Hill, while Rosie asked Emma to take her to the kitchen after breakfast to speak to the cook. Miss Fairfax followed their lively conversations, sometimes answering questions or slipping in a remark to praise or gently correct one of the children. As Jasper watched all this, he could not help feeling that she was as much a part of this family as he, if not more.

Would he ever be able to find a governess, or a wife, capable of filling her place? And why was this school she wanted to start more important to her than the welfare of his children?

The sun and wind had dried the grass by the time the Amberwood party set off for Red Hill, though the road was still muddy. Mr. Chase, Mr. Webster and Reverend Brookes rode on horseback, as did Miss Anstruther, in a stylish riding habit. The other ladies crowded into two carriages with the children. Evangeline shared one with Miss Brookes, Miss Webster and the three boys, while Mrs. Leveson and her daughter rode with Mrs. Thorpe, Verity Dawson and the girls.

Though Mr. Chase claimed he had no intention of courting Miss Anstruther, it vexed Evangeline to see how close the lady kept her horse to his, taking every opportunity to engage him in conversation. Miss Brookes and Miss Webster appeared to notice, too, but seemed to find her blatant pursuit of their host more amusing than annoying.

"I suppose she will need someone to help her down from her saddle when we reach our destination." Margaret Webster's bright blue eyes sparkled with merriment.

"Woe betide my poor brother if he offers to do the honors." Abigail Brookes gave an infectious chuckle. "He might get the toe of her riding boot in his ribs for his pains."

"You mean Miss Anstruther?" asked Owen in a tone of grave bewilderment. "Why would she kick the vicar if he tried to help her? That would not be very nice."

The two ladies glanced at each other, then toward

Evangeline, with apologetic grimaces. Matthew and Alfie were sitting up with the driver, not paying the other passengers a bit of mind. Clearly Miss Brookes and Miss Webster had thought Owen too young to take any notice of their banter.

Now Miss Webster wrapped her arm around the child's shoulders. "You are quite right, Owen. It would not be nice and I fear *we* were not nice to make a silly jest about such a thing. But that is all it was, a bit of thoughtless fun. I am certain you are too much of a gentleman to repeat any of it and risk hurting anyone's feelings."

Miss Webster's actions secured her Evangeline's good opinion on two counts. First, that she had frankly owned up to her mistake. Second, she'd taken notice of Owen in a way none of the other ladies had.

"Do you mean I should keep it a secret?" the boy asked.

It was clear from his tone that Owen found the prospect distasteful. As he should, in Evangeline's opinion. Her experiences at the Pendergast School had taught her that when grown-ups encouraged children to keep secrets, it often created a shadowy environment in which corruption thrived.

"Not...exactly." Miss Webster seemed to realize she was out of her depth. She cast Evangeline a look that pleaded for help.

"I believe what Miss Webster means, Owen, is that she is relying on your discretion. Do you remember what that is?"

The boy nodded. "It means knowing when to speak and when to keep silent. Like it says in the Book of Egg-lease...Eek-leasy..."

"Ecclesiastes." Evangeline pronounced the word

carefully, certain he would get it right the next time. "And you are correct. *'To everything there is a season.'"*

Miss Webster smiled her thanks to Evangeline then turned her attention back to Owen. "Something tells me you have an abundance of discretion, which is an essential quality in a gentleman."

Owen seemed pleased with the lady's praise and with being addressed as if he were much older than his years. Evangeline had noticed him giving Miss Leveson and her mother a wide berth after they chucked him under the chin and cooed what a pretty little fellow he was.

"You are a good judge of character, Miss Webster." Evangeline seized her chance to speak with the lady. "Owen is one of the most naturally discreet young men I know. You may rely on him never to embarrass anyone with an ill-considered word."

She was pleased this incident had given her an opening to become better acquainted with Miss Webster. If Mr. Chase could never feel anything warmer than sisterly regard for Miss Brookes, that left Margaret Webster as the only possible match remaining.

Just because she did not pursue him as blatantly as Miss Anstruther, did it mean she had no interest in Mr. Chase? Or was that like comparing Alfie and Owen in their reactions to people? Alfie's feelings were so emphatic and he never made any effort to conceal them, while Owen's were more difficult to guess from observation. That did not mean he felt them any less deeply— quite the contrary. Perhaps Miss Webster, like Owen, simply did not wear her heart on her sleeve. Evangeline hoped that by getting to know the lady better, she could decide whether Miss Webster might welcome an overture from Owen's father.

"You have taught your pupils well, Miss Fairfax," the

lady replied. "They are as delightful a family as I have ever met. You must be as proud of them as their father."

"I am very proud," Evangeline replied, warmly disposed to anyone who praised her young pupils. "I cannot begin to take credit for all their fine qualities. I only hope I have helped them make the most of their natural abilities. If I may say so, you have a natural way with children. Do you come from a large family?"

"Not anymore." Miss Webster shook her head with an air of regret. "I had two brothers, but the younger one was sickly and died of consumption. The older one joined the army and was killed in the war."

Evangeline was about to apologize for provoking such painful memories, when Owen piped up, "My mama died. Do you remember your brothers? I cannot remember my mama. Emma does and Matthew might, but it was very long ago, when I was only little. I wish I could remember her."

"I'm sure you do." Miss Webster clasped one of Owen's hands. "I never thought before what a blessing it is that I remember my brothers and my mother."

Evangeline tried to think of something to say that might comfort the child, but Miss Webster seemed to have managed quite well by acknowledging his sadness and letting him know that she understood. Perhaps she would be the right mother for the Chase children.

"My aunt had a large family," Miss Webster said, returning to Evangeline's question. "Perhaps that accounts for it. Most of her children were a good deal younger than I. Whenever I visited, I enjoyed looking after the little ones. I hope I shall be blessed with a family of my own one day—a big jolly one like Owen's."

Did she indeed? It sounded as if Miss Webster might not be as indifferent to Mr. Chase as he believed.

A few minutes later, they arrived at the foot of Red Hill, the tallest prominence in this part of the Vale of Eden between the lake-studded Cumbrian Mountains and the Pennines, which some called "the spine of England." While the riders dismounted and the rest of the party piled out of the carriages, Evangeline was kept busy watching that none of the children wandered off or strayed too close to the horses. Meanwhile, she parceled out the colorful kites they had built from bits of light strapping and scraps of silk found in an old trunk in the attic. Finally, she arranged for the picnic hampers and rugs to be carried up the hill.

As she watched the others pick their way up the winding path, Evangeline started when she heard her employer's deep voice close behind her. "How would we manage without you, Miss Fairfax? You arrange all our festivities and make certain everything runs smoothly. Is it as little effort as you make it appear?"

"Indeed it is not!" Her surprise and other unruly feelings found release in a burst of laughter as she spun about to face him. "There always seems to be a dozen things to do at once...besides keeping an eye on the children, which can be a handful on its own."

"Are you sorry you put yourself to so much trouble to find me a wife?" When he asked the question, Jasper Chase cocked his head to one side, just like Matthew. His grin sparkled with impudence, yet there was an appealing warmth about it.

"Of course not." She tilted her chin and looked him in the eye. "I enjoy a challenge."

He nodded as if to say he did, too. "You have risen to it admirably. You must be very anxious to get away and start that school of yours."

"I am." Evangeline willed her voice to remain steady

and positive, without the slightest quaver of doubt. If Mr. Chase heard it, she feared he might apply pressure to that weak spot to persuade her to stay.

But when she betrayed nothing he could exploit, Jasper Chase simply shook his head and repeated his earlier words, with one minor but significant change. "How *will* we manage without you, Miss Fairfax?"

Chapter Six

He must face the fact that Evangeline Fairfax was going to leave Amberwood in two months' time and there was nothing he could do to prevent her.

That afternoon, as flocks of woolly clouds chased one another across the summer sky over Red Hill, the Amberwood party enjoyed another lively outing. Meanwhile, Jasper grappled with the realization that there were some things even his strong will could not change and this was one of them.

"Why so solemn looking, old friend?" asked Norton Brookes, his voice breathless from running to get kites aloft for Emma, Mrs. Dawson and his sister. "Thanks to you, everyone is having a fine time. It would be unfair for you not to."

Jasper forced the corners of his mouth upward. "I am pleased to see that you and Abigail are enjoying your visit. I suppose you do not get to many house parties."

"I have attended a number in the past," his friend replied, "but they were not to my taste. Too much drinking, high play and late hours. Fishing, kite flying and the company of your charming children suit me much better. I am certain I shall return to my parish with my faith rejuvenated."

"I am glad to hear it." Jasper's smile grew more sincere. It seemed a number of good things might come out of this house party. Would they include a second marriage for him? "Now, shall we show my sons just what an expert kite flyer a vicar can be?"

Norton located an unused kite and held on to the roll of string while Jasper ran it up to the crest of the hill. There a stiff breeze caught it and tugged it out of his hand. His friend kept just enough tension on the string, unrolling it little by little until the kite soared high above the others. Matthew and Alfie cheered, as did Mrs. Dawson.

Out of the corner of his eye, Jasper could see Miss Fairfax and Miss Webster standing near Owen, watching the boy fly his kite. The two women seemed deep in conversation, which Jasper doubted had anything to do with kites. Now and then, one of the ladies would glance his way. He pretended not to notice, when, in fact, he was intensely aware of their scrutiny. He wished he knew what they were saying about him.

As he watched the flight of various kites, his thoughts returned to the prospect of Miss Fairfax's leaving. He had tried appealing to her affection for his children. He had tried to demonstrate his long-overdue appreciation for all she had done for his family. He was not proud of the fact that he had tried to make her feel guilty for leaving. Nothing had worked. If anything, she seemed more determined than ever to pursue what she clearly believed was her true calling in life.

He understood her determination more than she might realize. Anyone who tried to make him abandon his work at New Hope Mills would meet with similar resistance. He knew, because his late wife had tried. Her efforts had only succeeded in straining their marriage and making him question whether a man with his responsibilities could be a good husband.

"Papa!" Rosie's cry startled him out of his brooding. She scampered toward him, followed by Miss Leveson. "You'll never guess what I found."

Jasper noted the smear of bright red around his daughter's mouth. "It wouldn't by any chance be wild strawberries?"

"How did you know?" Rosie opened her dimpled fist to reveal a rather crushed handful of red berries, none bigger than an orange pip. "Would you like one?"

"Why, thank you." He plucked a berry from her hand and popped it into his mouth, savoring the wholesome sweetness. "I am very partial to strawberries."

"Your daughter is a darling little creature," Miss Leveson gushed. "We have such a lovely time together, don't we, Rosie?"

The child nodded as she crammed the rest of the berries into her mouth. When she had eaten them, she announced, "I like this party. We should have more."

Jasper gave the brim of her bonnet a playful tug. "Perhaps we shall. Now, I think you ought to go see Miss Fairfax and get your hands washed before you ruin your dress."

"Yes, Papa." Rosie skipped off toward her governess.

After hesitating for a moment, Miss Leveson followed his daughter, much to Jasper's relief. He watched as Rosie approached her governess and held out her berry-stained hand. Between the rush of the wind and the *whoops* of Matthew and Alfie, he could not make out what Miss Fairfax said. He could tell by her tone and gestures that she did not scold, but beckoned Rosie over to a small stand of trees that shaded the picnic rugs and proceeded to clean her up.

Miss Webster made some remark to the child that set her governess and Miss Leveson laughing, but she did not take her attention entirely off Owen.

It had been his wife's wish that their children grow up in the wholesome beauty of the Vale of Eden. Jasper had heartily agreed, though it meant long journeys back and forth from Manchester and a constant feeling of being pulled in two different directions. With the birth of each new baby, Susan had urged him more strenuously to leave the running of his mill to an overseer and spend more time with their growing family.

He had tried to explain how important his work was to him—not just the spinning and weaving, buying and selling for the sake of personal gain, but making the mill a success that would benefit his workers. Even for her and their children he could not abandon the work he believed the Lord meant him to do.

How could he expect Evangeline Fairfax to give up hers?

If the children must lose their beloved governess in two months' time, did he not owe it to them to fill part of the void she would leave with a new mother?

"There you go, Rosie." Evangeline examined the child's mouth and hands, which she had rubbed clean with a damp cloth. "If you want to pick more berries, I will give you a cup to put them in."

Miss Leveson took the child by one of her newly washed hands. "Come, Rosie-posey. What shall we do now?"

"Why don't you try kite flying?" Miss Webster suggested, thereby endearing herself further to Evangeline.

Though she was pleased to see Rosie getting special attention, she feared Miss Leveson's fussing and babying might spoil the child. If it did, she would have little time to correct the situation before she resigned her position.

"You can fly mine for a while," Owen said, holding out the string to his sister. "It's fun."

With further encouragement from her brother and Miss Webster, Rosie agreed to try. Miss Leveson hung about looking rather sulky. Perhaps she did not care to share the attention of her little pet.

Mr. Chase watched from a distance, though he seemed rather lost in thought.

Recalling what he had said about how his family would manage without her, Evangeline felt her resolve to leave Amberwood begin to weaken. Could that be why she had allowed Mr. Chase to dismiss three prospective matches without a word of argument? In the case of Miss Anstruther and Miss Leveson, she had positively encouraged him.

She must not let that happen with Miss Webster, to whom Owen had taken a fancy. The older boys liked her, too, and now she was taking an interest in Rosie. The other ladies all seemed to have their favorites among the children, except Miss Anstruther, who did not appear to care for any of them. The Chase children needed a mother who could love them all equally, as their father did.

If only Miss Webster would pay some attention to the children's father. He claimed the lady was avoiding him, but Evangeline could not imagine why. Perhaps she did not want to make a spectacle of herself by pursuing him the way certain others in the party did.

Evangeline glanced toward Miss Anstruther, who

kept edging closer to Mr. Chase while making a great
fuss about the difficulties of keeping her kite aloft. No
doubt she was trying to draw his attention and perhaps
get him to offer his assistance. Clearly she failed to realize he was not one of those men who found weakness
and ineptitude endearing qualities in a lady.

Suddenly Evangeline realized that Mr. Chase was
looking at her. Did he wonder why she'd been gaping
at him for the past several minutes?

To cover her embarrassment, she approached Miss
Webster, who was supervising the younger children as
they took turns with Owen's kite.

"He is so kind to his little sister." Miss Webster
regarded Owen fondly. "My young cousins bicker
amongst themselves all the time."

"There is a bit of that in our nursery, too," Evangeline admitted. "But for the most part, they get on well
together. I wish I could take credit for it, but I believe
the children have inherited their father's good nature."

"Mr. Chase seems a very amiable gentleman. Which
of the children is most like him?" Miss Webster sounded
sincerely interested, which encouraged Evangeline.

She thought for a moment. "None of them is exactly
like him, yet each has some of his traits. Emma has his
intense loyalty and sense of responsibility. You must
have noticed how she mothers the younger ones?"

"I have," Miss Webster replied. "Emma reminds me
of her dear mother. In character, I mean. Rosie looks
far more like her."

Evangeline nodded. "You are very observant. I believe Matthew and Owen get their cleverness from their
father and their enjoyment of a challenge. Alfie has Mr.
Chase's humor and his concern for others. Rosie inherited his sense of fairness."

The children shared some of their father's faults, too, but Evangeline saw no reason to mention those. After all, she was trying to make a good impression on Miss Webster. Besides, in both the children and their father, any small defects were more than outweighed by their good qualities.

"They are a fine family." Miss Webster cast a warm glance around at all the children. "No wonder Mr. Chase is so devoted to them."

"He does not show any partiality to one over the other," Evangeline added. "He has a special affection for each one."

Miss Webster looked toward Jasper Chase, who was trying to help Emma and Mrs. Dawson untangle their kites. "That is as it should be in families. I am certain Mrs. Chase would be pleased at how well her children have turned out. I knew her when our fathers were partners. Though I was younger, she was always kind to me."

This was the second time Miss Webster had mentioned the children's mother. Could that be what held her back from taking a romantic interest in Mr. Chase? Evangeline wondered. Did she think it would be disloyal to his late wife?

"I believe Mrs. Chase would have wanted her children to have a new mother to care for them as much as she did. Mr. Chase loved her a great deal. The past few years have been lonely for him, though he does his best to keep the children's spirits up."

"Poor man." Miss Webster's gaze softened. "It must have been very hard for him."

"I believe it has." The thought brought Evangeline a pang of conscience.

She had been so concerned about the children and

impatient with their father for not spending more time with them, she had not given much thought to *his* grief. When Mr. Chase came home for visits, he had been so determined to make his time with the children enjoyable that he'd seldom betrayed any hint of sorrow. His behavior gave Evangeline the impression that he had not been much affected by his wife's death. Only when she spoke to Miss Webster, trying to paint a flattering portrait of her employer, did she suspect how wrong she might have been.

"Mr. Chase seems to be enjoying this house party." Margaret Webster nodded toward him.

After much careful maneuvering, he had gotten his daughter's kite untangled from Mrs. Dawson's without bringing both hurtling to the ground. He received applause from the vicar and a hug from Emma.

"I believe it has done him good to mix with other people." Evangeline congratulated herself for having brought it about. "He needs to look to the future and begin living his life again."

"He is very fortunate," said Miss Webster, "to have someone who thinks so highly of him raising his children."

Evangeline was not certain what to make of the lady's remark. Her praise was not like Miss Leveson's transparent effort to ingratiate herself, but could there be some other motive behind it? "Everyone who works for Mr. Chase thinks well of him. He is a good, fair employer. I am certain his millworkers would say the same of him and better."

"Ah, yes. Mr. Chase's mill." Miss Webster shook her head as if puzzled. "The other owners say he is a fool to coddle his workers. They say it will give them dangerous ideas. But I do not see how it can be wrong to show people respect and treat them well."

Hearing Jasper Chase called a fool ignited a blaze of indignation in Evangeline. She was about to launch into a vigorous defense of him when a sharp tug on her hand made her look down.

Rosie stared up at her. "Is it time to eat yet? I'm hungry."

"So am I," said Miss Webster before Evangeline had a chance to respond. "All the fresh air and walking have given me an appetite."

She held out her hand to the child. "Shall we go ask the others if they are ready to eat?"

Rosie nodded and took her hand. As the two headed off together, Evangeline noticed Gemma Leveson and her mother shooting dark glares at Miss Webster, as if the lady had stolen her favorite plaything.

It soon became clear that most of the guests were as eager to eat as Rosie. They reeled in their kites then descended on the picnic hampers. For the next half hour, Evangeline was kept busy dispensing food and drink. Everyone ate with such hearty appetites that there was hardly a scrap left over.

"May we fly our kites a little longer?" Alfie begged his father when he had stuffed himself with cold meats, cheese, buns and pickled eggs.

"Go ahead," said Mr. Chase, "but only until everything is packed up to go home."

The guests dispersed and Evangeline began stowing the dishes, cutlery and linen back in the hampers. Mr. Chase lingered and set about helping her. "You and Miss Webster looked as thick as thieves a little while ago. Should my ears have been burning?"

"Perhaps." Evangeline could not resist teasing him

as she sometimes did the children. "Are a person's ears supposed to burn only when they are criticized behind their back, or will any sort of comment produce the effect?"

Mr. Chase feigned a severe look. "I have never studied that particular old wives' tale. Why do you ask?"

"Because—" Evangeline found herself enjoying their banter "—Miss Webster and I were only saying good things about you."

"What sort of things?" Mr. Chase looked doubtful.

Did he not realize how much good there was to say about him?

"I cannot tell you." Evangeline returned the last of the plates to the hamper, cushioning them with napkins. "It might make you vain."

He gave a self-deprecating chuckle. "That would never do, would it?"

"It certainly would not," she replied tartly. "I cannot abide vain men. I will tell you this much—Miss Webster thinks well of you, she likes your children a great deal and she approves of your enlightened approach to business."

"Enlightened?" Mr. Chase seemed to savor the word. "Did she say that?"

"No. I did." Much as Evangeline wanted to make a match between Mr. Chase and Miss Webster, she could not lie. "She said something similar but I cannot recall her exact words. The point is, I am certain she would welcome your attentions, if you could evade Miss Anstruther long enough to speak to her."

"Whose fault is it that Miss Anstruther is sticking to me like a plaster?" He parried her playful jab.

"Yours, of course," she retorted, "for being so handsome and charming."

Jasper Chase laughed so hard he rocked back on his heels. "Touché, Miss Fairfax! How is it I never realized how amusing you can be?"

Evangeline accepted the compliment, though she had not been jesting.

Two days after their excursion to Red Hill, Jasper slipped into his children's nursery in the early hours of the morning and waited impatiently for their governess to rise.

This matchmaking party of hers was not going at all the way it should and he felt a pressing need to discuss it with the one person capable of setting matters right. After all, Miss Fairfax had done a remarkable job raising his children. Helping him secure a suitable wife should be easy compared to that.

After several minutes that felt much longer, Evangeline Fairfax emerged for the day. Preoccupied with inserting one last pin into her chestnut hair, she did not notice Jasper at first.

When she suddenly spotted him, the governess gave a violent start. "Mr. Chase, do you mean to make a habit of visiting the nursery at all hours?"

Jasper shrugged as if to ask why he should not. "This is the only time I can be tolerably certain of a private word with you. Given the present situation, I find it necessary. And since you are responsible for the situation, I think you ought to oblige me."

"I suppose I should." Once again, she took a seat beside him so they could speak softly, yet still hear one another. "What is it you wish to discuss?"

The frustration that had been building within him for the past two days eased in anticipation of unburdening himself to her. "This is not working...with Miss

Webster, I mean. Her father keeps dropping broad hints about what a good idea it would be for me to marry her, but I cannot manage more than a nodding acquaintance with the lady. Whenever I come near her, I sense an impenetrable barrier between us. I cannot talk to her with the ease I talk to…you."

Miss Fairfax seemed surprised, but she was quick to offer an explanation. "That must be because you have begun to care for Miss Webster and it makes you awkward when you try to converse with her. With me you can relax because we have known each other so long and I am not an object of your affections."

"Perhaps." Jasper dismissed a nagging whisper of doubt. "Though I do not believe all the difficulty is on my side. Are you certain Miss Webster does not dislike me?"

"Quite the contrary," the governess insisted. "She had nothing but good to say when we spoke of you the other day. Perhaps you are only imagining this hostility."

"She is not *hostile*." Jasper tried to explain what he sensed from Margaret Webster. "And not exactly frightened. Wary might be the best way to describe it, as if she thought I might pose a danger to her."

The governess's dark brows lowered over her large brown eyes. "Perhaps she is afraid of appearing ridiculous if she shows too much interest in you, the way a certain lady does. Or perhaps she is reluctant to endanger her heart by becoming attached to you when there is so much competition for your favors."

"No serious competition," Jasper scoffed, once again dismissing a qualm of doubt. He found it difficult to think of himself as a prize for which ladies would vie.

"You and I know that," Miss Fairfax replied, "but

how can Miss Webster? Perhaps you are not approaching her in the proper way."

"What way is that?" Frustration made his question come out louder than he meant it to. "It has been a long time since I courted a lady and even then…"

"Even then…?" she prompted him to continue, an amber glint of curiosity in her eyes. "Surely you must recall what you did to engage the affections of your wife."

"That's what I am trying to say," Jasper admitted. "I did not have to do anything in particular to win Susan."

It was clear Miss Fairfax had no idea what he meant. How could she advise him properly if she did not understand?

"Before I met my wife, I was too occupied with my work to give any thought to romantic attachments. By industry and application, I had risen to become the overseer of Mr. Thorpe's mill. One day his wife and daughter paid a visit. I was smitten on the spot, but I never thought of being so bold as to pursue the master's daughter."

The memory of his first sight of Susan Thorpe glowed softly in his mind. "I could scarcely believe it when her parents invited me to dine with them. When I discovered she fancied me as much as I did her, I thought I must be dreaming."

Those days seemed so long ago. Where had they gone? Had Susan ever regretted marrying that driven young man? Did she ever wish she'd settled for one of the suitors her parents wanted for her—a man who might have devoted himself to her entirely and not cared about anything else?

"So it was 'love at first sight'?" Miss Fairfax spoke

the way she might have to one of his children who had fallen ill or woken from a bad dream.

He nodded. "Since I was reluctant to anger her father and risk losing my position, she had to take the lead if anything was to come of our feelings for one another."

Jasper reminded himself that he was not telling Miss Fairfax all this simply to confide in her. There was a point to it. "So you see, I've never had to court a lady. That is why I have no idea how to begin with Miss Webster. I need your help."

Evangeline Fairfax squirmed in her seat. "What more can I do? I already talked to her about you. I praised you to the skies."

Jasper had an answer ready for her. "You're an excellent teacher. You have taught my children everything from music to natural history. I want you to teach me the proper way to court Miss Webster."

Chapter Seven

Teach Mr. Chase how to court his future wife? Evangeline's mouth fell open as all the muscles of her face went slack from shock.

"Will you do it?" he demanded as she sat mute. "You are the one who is so anxious for me to remarry. I would say you owe me all the assistance you can provide."

His words pierced her bemusement and provoked a response. "Have you gone mad? That is the most preposterous idea I have ever heard!"

"Keep your voice down!" he demanded in a fierce whisper, glancing from his sons' bedroom door to his daughters' door. "I assure you, I have all my wits about me. What is so preposterous about my suggestion, may I ask?"

Did he truly not understand? Evangeline found it hard to believe. "Where do I begin? I suppose I should be flattered by your confidence in my abilities, but the reason I am able to instruct your children in certain subjects is because I have studied them myself. I know far less about romantic attachments than you do. How could I possibly teach you anything?"

Part of her wished the children would wake up and

put an end to this absurd conversation. It flustered her to think of tutoring her employer in the art of wooing. She wanted him to remarry, but there were limits on what she was prepared to do to bring it about. Unfortunately, the Chase children must have been thoroughly tired out from all their recent excursions. Not a sound from either bedchamber suggested they might wake anytime soon.

After a moment, their father came up with an answer to her challenge. "You have never been paid romantic attention by a gentleman? I find it hard to believe that such an attractive lady cannot have had a great many admirers."

The haste of his words suggested they were sincere, which made them all the more gratifying. Evangeline struggled to suppress a delightful little thrill. She reminded herself that susceptibility to flattery was as great a weakness as fear of failure or ridicule.

She rolled her eyes and pretended to dismiss his remark. "What lessons could I possibly teach such a skilled flatterer? As for my lack of suitors, I could make the same claim you did—that I have been too devoted to my work to seek romantic attachments. I told you, I have no wish to wed."

"First of all, I was not trying to flatter you." He sounded offended that she would accuse him of such a thing. "Second, even if you were not interested in marriage, I do not see why that should prevent determined gentlemen from trying to change your mind."

"There was one who made the attempt," Evangeline confessed with reluctance. She did not care to dwell on the one time she had been the object of romantic pursuit. "But I finally put a stop to his nonsense. He refused to heed my efforts to discourage him. He tried to persuade me that I should devote myself to a woman's proper role of wife and mother."

His efforts to mold her into the kind of biddable wife he wanted had soon destroyed her budding affection for him. He had made her realize that her teachers were right in claiming she was not cut out for marriage. "The only lesson I could draw from his efforts would be what actions to *avoid* if you wish to find favor with a lady."

Jasper Chase did not seem any more daunted by her objections than Mr. Preston had been. "That would be a start at least. Besides, you are a woman. Surely you can imagine some ways a gentleman might secure your regard."

She could tell her employer had his mind made up. If he had decided he needed her to teach him how to win Margaret Webster's affections, he would keep insisting until she agreed. She might as well consent at once and save herself the argument. He would soon discover how little she knew about anything romantic. Then he would stop pestering her and work out for himself how best to approach Miss Webster.

"Very well." She blew out a forceful breath to make it clear she was agreeing under protest. "When am I supposed to conduct these courting lessons? I presume you do not wish to take time away from the children any more than I do. After they go to bed for the night, you are busy with your guests."

"What is wrong with this time?" he asked. "We are both early risers and have no other calls upon us until the children wake."

As she considered his suggestion, Evangeline found herself torn. On one hand, she enjoyed this quiet solitude at the beginning of the day and was reluctant to give it up. Then again, she found these private conversations with Mr. Chase enjoyable in a different way.

"Agreed." She gave a brisk nod. "Now, how do you expect me to present these lessons? Will you require a lecture? Should I assign practice exercises?"

Mr. Chase ignored her ironic tone. "Not lectures. I thought you could suggest some action I should take then we could discuss why it is important and how to do it properly. But practice exercises are a splendid idea! After we practice together, you can suggest ways I might improve. Later in the day, I can try out my new skill on Miss Webster. The next morning, I can report my progress and you can offer further suggestions."

"It might work." Evangeline could not conceal her doubts, though Mr. Chase had a way of making such an absurd proposition sound almost reasonable.

"Let us begin, then." He sat straighter in his chair and fixed her with an expectant gaze.

"I beg your pardon?"

"We might as well start now, don't you think?" Jasper Chase made a sweeping gesture to indicate the empty nursery. "There is little more than a fortnight left until the guests leave. I must begin to make some headway with Margaret Webster soon if I am to have any hope of winning her."

Evangeline could not disagree with that. But must they start this very minute? She had hoped to have time to come up with a suggestion that might not sound altogether ridiculous. Then again, an ill-prepared lesson might make Mr. Chase realize his folly in applying to her for romantic advice.

"If you insist." She tried to recall anything her school friends had written her about their early acquaintance with their husbands.

Perhaps Mr. Chase could invite the lady to use his library, as Captain Radcliffe had done with Marian Murray. Of course, that would only work if Miss Webster was as devoted a book lover as Marian. Sustaining an injury so Miss Webster would have to supervise his convalescence would not be practical, even if it had brought Hannah Fletcher and Lord Hawkehurst together.

After Evangeline had spent several minutes in thought, Mr. Chase began to drum his fingers on the table. "Come, Miss Fairfax, surely you can think of something."

"I can think of a great many things," she snapped. "That does not mean they will be of any value."

"Let me be the judge of that." He made a beckoning motion with his hand. "Out with it—the first thing that comes to mind."

"Ask her about herself." The words tumbled out before Evangeline had a chance to give them any thought. "But that must be obvious."

He employer gave a discouraged nod. "It is and I have tried it already to no avail. I have asked about her home, her family, her opinion on a number of subjects. She always gives the briefest answer that provides no opening for further conversation. Then she slips away before I can think of another question to ask."

Evangeline could picture the fruitless, frustrating exchange. "I do not mean asking for superficial information about her. Try to discover something she cares about deeply. If you give her an opportunity to converse on the subject, I am certain she will take it."

Mr. Chase continued to look doubtful. "How am I to find out this great interest of hers if she will not talk to me long enough to tell me?"

"Why not ask her father?" Evangeline suggested.

"You said he seems anxious for a match between you. He might be happy to help."

"You may be onto something, Miss Fairfax." Jasper Chase nodded, slowly at first, then with increased vigor. "I knew my faith in you would not be misplaced."

His praise of her abilities pleased Evangeline more than his earlier compliment on her appearance. She told herself the satisfaction she felt must come from moving a step closer to finding her employer a wife.

"Now to practice my lesson." Mr. Chase turned the full force of his gaze upon her. "Tell me all about this school you are so eager to set up. Why is it so important to you?"

Eagerness to talk about her school made Evangeline open her mouth, but deeply ingrained reluctance to discuss her past seemed to paralyze her vocal cords. Could a wealthy, successful man like Jasper Chase possibly understand what she and her friends had endured at the Pendergast School and the zeal it had fired in her to provide other girls with a more compassionate alternative?

What had he done wrong? Jasper wondered as he awaited some response from Miss Fairfax. He'd assumed she would be keen to talk about the project that was more important to her than his children. Instead, the lady looked as if he had threatened her with a loaded weapon!

"Is there some difficulty?" he asked. "I thought your school was a subject you cared a great deal about."

"It is!" Even as the words burst out of her, Jasper sensed her resistance. "But I doubt you would find it of interest."

"I would," he insisted.

It was more than simply the chance to practice a skill

he would need for courting Miss Webster. It was an opportunity to become better acquainted with the most important person in his children's life. Jasper regretted not having done it sooner.

"Please." He fixed her with a beseeching look that she seemed reluctant to meet.

His appeal worked. After a moment's hesitation, Miss Fairfax replied, "It will be a place to educate and care for the orphan daughters of clergymen. I attended such a school when I was a girl, but it was the bleakest, harshest, most repressive place—quite the opposite of what was needed. I want to do it properly."

Jasper had to seek far back in his memory to recall a bleak, harsh, repressive place. But when he did, the images sprang to life, provoking powerful emotions. It had never occurred to him that strong-willed, managing Miss Fairfax might harbour similar memories and perhaps bear similar scars upon her heart.

"Tell me more about your old school," he urged her. "Where was it? When were you sent there?"

Again she hesitated, which he could now understand. But at last she began to speak. "The Pendergast School is in Lancashire. I went there at the age of nine after my father died. The trustees enriched themselves off the endowment, leaving only a pittance to operate the school. We were always short of coal for the fires. Food was scant and of the poorest quality. The teachers were ill-paid and overworked, so many of them took out their frustration on the girls."

Her words lit a blaze of outrage within Jasper, as injustice and abuse always did. He might have vented those feelings with some pithy remarks, but Evangeline Fairfax gave him no opportunity. Now that she had begun to speak, more words poured out.

Perhaps sensing Jasper's sympathy, she told him about the dampness and overcrowding that had bred disease. She told him about the bullying that was a deplorable consequence of any group having too little of life's necessities.

"That is monstrous!" Jasper growled when he could no longer contain his indignation. "If ever there was a situation calculated to crush young spirits, that vile place sounds like it. How did you manage to turn out so well?"

His words seemed to release Miss Fairfax from the grip of her dark memories. But before she could reply, a small voice piped up from the direction of his sons' bedroom.

"What monsters, Papa?" asked Owen as he rubbed the sleep from his eyes. "Was Miss Fairfax telling you a fairy tale?"

"Something like that." Jasper beckoned his youngest son toward him. "Fortunately, like most fairy tales, it all works out in the end, thanks to the bravery and goodness of the heroine."

As he spoke, it occurred to him how many fairy tales were stories of girls, often orphaned, who had to overcome great hardship to secure the happy ending they so richly deserved. Evangeline Fairfax had all the makings of a fairy-tale heroine come to life. And he had only heard the beginning of her story. Now Jasper longed to learn more, but he would have to wait.

Owen padded over to the table and crawled up into his father's lap. "Miss Fairfax tells good stories. They make me see pictures in my head. She says that is called 'magination."

No doubt his governess could evoke dramatic images of the characters' suffering, drawing on her own experience.

The boy snuggled into Jasper's arms and asked his governess, "Will you begin the story again, please, so I can hear?"

"I'm afraid that will have to wait until bedtime." Miss Fairfax reached out and bestowed a fond caress on the child's golden-brown hair. "Now I must wake your brothers and sisters. You have all slept in late this morning."

She rose and headed for the girls' room with her accustomed brisk composure restored. But Jasper had glimpsed the downtrodden charity pupil Miss Fairfax kept as well hidden as he did the overworked bobbin boy. There were some who might look down on the lady for her early misfortunes, but the knowledge of what she had overcome only raised her in Jasper's estimation.

As she roused the other children for the day and took refuge in familiar nursery routine, Evangeline sought to push her recollections of the Pendergast School back into the deepest recesses of her memory. Though those experiences had helped to make her the person she was and spurred her to establish a better school in its place, she seldom permitted herself to dwell on her darker memories from those blighted years.

As she helped Emma and Rosie dress for the day, she recalled the drab, ill-made dresses the Pendergast pupils had been obliged to wear, all identical. Which had been worse—the flimsy fabric that afforded little protection from the pervasive damp chill or the way the strict uniformity sought to stifle any flicker of distinctiveness.

Watching the children eat their breakfast of porridge studded with plump raisins, followed by buttered eggs and muffins, Evangeline sickened with the memory of watery gruel that had no taste at all unless the cook let some of it burn to the bottom of the pot. Unappetizing as it had been, she'd wolfed it down to dull the gnawing ache that seldom left her belly.

While the children larked about with their father, Evangeline was more than usually indulgent with them, recalling the frequent punishments that had been a way of life at the Pendergast School. The slightest infraction of numerous, often conflicting, rules had earned penalties that ranged from whippings to standing on a chair for hours or being deprived of meals that were already inadequate.

Jasper Chase was right. It had been a situation calculated to break young spirits.

As she watched him exchange a fond smile with Emma while patiently answering a series of questions from Matthew, it dawned on Evangeline that Mr. Chase truly seemed to understand what she had endured. His indignation had been so tangible she could almost feel its sharp edge. Somehow, his outrage on her behalf soothed the feelings her memories provoked.

She told herself it would be worth her distress if the things she'd told her employer made him understand why it was so vital for her to establish a new school. At the same time, her memories reproached her for allowing him to delay her mission for as long as she had. There were girls, perhaps no older than Rosie, suffering the same hardships she and her friends had endured, when she might have spared them. That was not Mr. Chase's fault, but hers.

Evangeline roused abruptly from her troubled thoughts to find her pupils staring at her.

"Did you hear me?" asked Matthew. "Are we going on another outing today?"

"I—I have no idea," she replied. "You will have to ask your father about that."

Alfie turned at once toward Mr. Chase. "Can we, Papa? Please! It was jolly fun to go fishing and kite flying."

"So it was," Mr. Chase agreed. "But I am not certain poor Mrs. Gilman is up to preparing a picnic luncheon *every* day. Why don't we stay at home today and find ways to amuse ourselves here?"

The children could not hide their disappointment, especially Rosie and the older boys. But when their father suggested they play pall-mall and some other outdoor games, they grew more enthusiastic.

"Can we go for a walk," Owen asked Evangeline, "while Papa and Granny and the others are having their breakfast?"

She nodded. "That sounds like a fine idea. You may bring your butterfly net in case we see any interesting specimens."

A brisk walk with the children would do her good. Fresh morning air and movement might be just what she needed to lift her thoughts out of the dark place into which they had fallen.

As the children hurried off to get ready for their walk, Mr. Chase leaned toward her and spoke softly. "I am sorry to have brought up all that business about your younger years. I had no idea how deeply personal an undertaking it would be for you to set up this new school. If I had known, I would have tried to assist you rather than dragging my heels and throwing obstacles in your path."

He reached across the table and covered her folded

hands with one of his. It felt protective yet sympathetic and encouraging. "I hope you can forgive me."

"Of course." She had to force the words out—not because of any reluctance to do what he asked, but because her throat had grown tight. "I should have told you long ago."

Perhaps she should. But it had never crossed her mind that he might care about the circumstances of her girlhood. Besides, she had never before trusted anyone sufficiently to reveal this vulnerable facet of her character—least of all her dynamic, successful employer.

"I wish you had." Jasper Chase patted her hands then drew his back. "But now that I know part of your story, I am anxious to hear the rest. I will be waiting for you tomorrow morning."

The thought of that encounter made Evangeline want to run away as fast and as far as she could get in twenty-four hours. Yet another part of her could scarcely wait for tomorrow morning to come.

Early the next morning, Jasper sat in the nursery again, sipping a cup of good strong coffee as he waited for Evangeline Fairfax to join him.

After yesterday, he would not blame her if she refused to come out until she heard his children stirring. Agreeing to give him courting lessons had been one thing, but she could not have expected to relive the worst experiences of her life. In her place, he would have wanted to bury those memories even deeper. Yet here he sat, waiting for her to tell him more about the wretched past that had shaped the woman she'd become.

His anticipation was whetted to a sharp pitch by the time he heard Miss Fairfax begin to move about quietly in her room. At last she emerged, with an air of mingled eagerness and reluctance.

"Good morning." He held a chair for her. "I was not certain you would join me this morning."

"Neither was I." She sank onto the chair. "But I could not resist the smell of coffee."

Jasper gave a low, rumbling chuckle as he resumed his seat and poured her a cup of the bitter but invigorating brew. "You are a woman after my own heart, Miss Fairfax. I hope you slept well."

"Well enough." She pulled the cup toward her and inhaled the aroma rising from it. Then she took a sip, closing her eyes as if to savor the taste. "The children had a fine time yesterday. I noticed you managed a longer conversation with Miss Webster. Perhaps you do not require lessons from me, after all."

Jasper shook his head. "Quite the contrary. The only reason Miss Webster spoke with me was because I took your advice. I asked her father about her interests and he said she is very partial to music. So I asked her if she might favor us with a recital some evening."

"What did she say to that?" Evangeline Fairfax seemed less self-conscious now that they were discussing Miss Webster.

"She claimed she would feel uncomfortable being the center of attention for all that time. But she suggested we might get up a little concert with everyone having an opportunity to perform. What do you think?"

Miss Fairfax seemed surprised to be consulted, but she did not hesitate to give her opinion. "It sounds like a fine idea. The more I hear of your Miss Webster, the better I like her. I believe she will make you a very good wife."

He nodded absently. Margaret Webster was not *his*.

Besides, it was not Miss Webster he wanted to talk about now. "I wonder if the children might take part. I know you have been teaching them music and I thought they might enjoy entertaining our guests."

"Indeed they might," she replied. "Let me know when you decide to have this concert and I will do all I can to assist Miss Webster."

"Did they teach music at your old school?" Jasper seized the opportunity to return to that subject.

"I wondered when you would get around to asking about that." Miss Fairfax looked at him the way she sometimes looked at Alfie when he misbehaved—as if she knew she ought to scold him but found his antics too amusing.

Jasper tried to mimic his son's winsome grin. "You didn't think I would forget, did you?"

She pursed her lips into a tight frown that he sensed she found hard to maintain. "I thought after your conversation with Miss Webster, you would have more profitable things to think about."

"There is more to life than profit." The words popped out by reflex because he spoke them so often to the other mill owners of Manchester, who seemed to regard the sentiment as blasphemous. "Tell me more about how you managed to escape from that wretched school with your spirit intact."

"I do not wish to dwell on the hardships of my youth," Evangeline Fairfax insisted in a firm tone. "I put them behind me long ago and that is where I mean them to stay. I refuse to give them the power to distress me further."

He of all people ought to understand that, yet Jasper could not conceal his disappointment.

Perhaps seeing it so plain on his face made her relent a little. "But I will tell you what made those conditions bearable and helped me rise above them. It was my faith in the Lord and the support of my friends. Six of us banded together, as close as sisters. Each of us brought some special quality or ability to the group that enriched us all and made us stronger together than we could ever have been on our own."

Her eyes took on a fervent glow as she spoke of her friends. Her account fascinated Jasper, who had never experienced that strong a bond, even with Norton Brookes.

He leaned forward, his chin cupped in the palm of his hand. "What sort of qualities did each of you bring to the group?"

The lady's tense frown softened. It was clear she needed less urging to speak about that part of her past. "Marian Murray had the courage of a lion when it came to defending others. Leah Shaw could always make us laugh, no matter how bleak things looked."

Jasper gave an approving nod. Those were excellent traits for comrades to possess, especially in such circumstances. He was glad that young Evangeline Fairfax had been blessed with such friends.

"Rebecca Beaton was unshakably loyal." Her tone warmed as she spoke of her friends. "We could count on her to encourage us when our spirits were low. Hannah Fletcher was conscientious and capable. She would gladly turn her hand to anything to help one of us. Grace Ellerby was kindhearted and understanding. We could always confide in her and know we would get a sympathetic hearing."

"What about Evangeline Fairfax?" he asked when she paused. "What did she contribute to this group of friends? Something equally valuable, I'm certain."

Miss Fairfax cast him a doubtful look. "The other girls called me their 'intrepid leader,' which I suspect was a kind way of saying I was insufferably overbearing."

A week ago, he might have agreed with her. But at the moment Jasper could not bear to hear her criticized—even by herself. "There is more to leadership than that. I reckon it is as admirable a quality as those others you mentioned."

As she took another sip of her coffee, Miss Fairfax glanced up at him with an air of gratitude that moved him to add, "Proper leadership inspires a group with purpose. It brings out the individual skills of each member and welds them into a powerful force for the good of all."

"You do make the quality sound admirable."

"Because it is. I am only saying what I believe your friends would say about you. I believe you have done the same thing for my children. You have cultivated their special qualities and made them a true family—loving and loyal to one another. For that, we all owe you a great debt."

Miss Fairfax lowered her gaze. "That is very kind of you to say, especially since you have experienced the other side of my leadership—deciding what is best for others and imposing my will on them even when they disagree."

Jasper gave a rueful shrug. "It is not always easy for people to recognize what is best for them. My children, for example. Given the choice, they would eat nothing but sweets and stay awake all night. Insisting they take proper nourishment, keep regular hours and learn their lessons is not tyranny but kindness, even if they cannot always recognize it."

"It sounds much nicer when you put it that way." Miss Fairfax picked up the coffeepot and poured what was left into their two cups. "I suppose being a governess does provide scope for exercising leadership."

Jasper nodded. "That ability will make you an excellent headmistress of your school."

"Speaking of which," she replied, "we must not forget your reason for coming here this morning. I have given some thought to what other lessons might be helpful in winning Miss Webster. I believe the next topic we should concentrate on is telling her more about yourself and the things that interest you. After all, she will want to gain a sense of whether you are the kind of man with whom she would like to spend the rest of her life."

"I suppose that stands to reason." Jasper could guess where such a lesson might lead and it was a direction he would have preferred to avoid.

But how could he resist, when Miss Fairfax had given him a glimpse of her painful past?

"Does that mean you would be willing to tell me about your extraordinary cotton mill," she asked, "and why it is so important for you to operate it the way you do?"

"*Willing* might be a bit strong a word for it." He bolted the last of his coffee. "But I reckon what's sauce for the goose is sauce for the gander."

"Are we going to have goose?" Rosie ran across the nursery and jumped into her father's lap. "But Christmas is a long time away."

"So it is." Jasper embraced the child with a rumbling chuckle born as much of relief as amusement. "Then I suppose the goose will just have to wait."

As he bent forward and rubbed noses with his small daughter, he realized how fast she and the others were growing up. He knew Miss Fairfax wanted him to spend more time with his children so their younger years would not seem to disappear so quickly.

Surely he owed it to her to explain why he could not.

Chapter Eight

Why was Mr. Chase reluctant to tell her about his mill?

Evangeline considered the possibilities that Sunday morning while she prepared her pupils for church.

Surely he did not think she would disapprove of his innovations as haughty Miss Anstruther might. Perhaps it was modesty that made him hesitate to proclaim his admirable work, though somehow she did not think so.

"Remember," she warned the children as she gave their appearance a final inspection before they set out for church, "you must be on your very best behavior this morning so you will be a credit to your father and grandmother."

"I will try." Matthew sighed. "But it is a long while to sit still with nothing to do."

Alfie nodded in agreement.

"You could try listening to what the vicar says." Evangeline decided to take the precaution of not letting the brothers sit together, where they might egg each other on into mischief. Instead, she would place one on either side of her, where she could keep a close eye on them. "Why don't we make a game of it. After church,

I shall ask three questions about the service. There will be a special treat for everyone who can answer one or more correctly."

"Can I play, too?" asked Emma. "Or is the game only for Matthew and Alfie?"

"You are all welcome to play." Evangeline plumped the bow on Emma's bonnet and reflected on how much the child had grown since she'd first arrived at Amberwood. "However, I believe some of you may find it less of a challenge than others."

Emma and Owen exchanged a significant look. They were always attentive and well-behaved during Sunday services, while the older boys chafed at the stillness and solemnity. Rosie stayed quiet enough, but only because she watched the other worshippers to see what they were doing and wearing.

After trying to smooth down a tuft of Alfie's hair that stubbornly insisted on sticking up, Evangeline said, "Let's go so we don't keep your father's guests waiting."

They marched off with Emma leading the way, holding Rosie's hand. The older boys followed, while Evangeline and Owen brought up the rear.

Mr. Chase beamed with pride when his children appeared in the entry hall. "A very handsome family, if I do say so."

"Indeed they are," Mrs. Thorpe agreed. "Good morning, my darlings."

The children greeted their grandmother with decorous affection, no doubt mindful of several guests present. Evangeline made certain to catch the eye of each of her pupils and give them a discreet smile or nod of approval.

"Now that we are all assembled," said Mr. Chase,

gesturing toward the door, "I believe our carriages are waiting."

Alfie looked about with a puzzled frown. "Not everyone is here, Papa. Were some of them allowed to miss church?"

His father gave an indulgent chuckle. "No one will miss anything. Mr. Brookes rode out some time ago because our vicar asked him to help out with the service. And since the morning is so pleasant, Mrs. Dawson, Miss Webster and Miss Brookes decided they would walk to church."

Alfie surveyed the remaining guests and seemed satisfied that everyone was accounted for. "That's all right, then. We can go."

He looked puzzled when the grown-ups laughed.

As the party headed out to the carriages, Jasper Chase cast Evangeline a glance over his son's head and grinned.

With the vicar and three of the ladies gone ahead, the others were able to crowd into two carriages for the short drive. The three elder members of the party shared one with Emma, Owen and Rosie. Evangeline had the dubious pleasure of squeezing into the other with Mr. Chase, his elder sons, Miss Anstruther and Miss Leveson.

On the drive to church, the ladies vied with one another to engage their host in conversation. When one succeeded, the other would make little secret of her vexation. Evangeline heartily envied the three who had insisted on walking, though she wished Miss Webster could have ridden with their party. Confined to the carriage, she would have been obliged to converse with Mr. Chase. Evangeline could have watched to see what he might be doing wrong. Then she could advise him how to correct his behavior during future lessons.

The carriages passed the trio of walkers just before they reached St. Oswald's. The children called out to the ladies, who waved and called back to them.

No sooner had they arrived than the church bells began to ring and everyone hurried inside. Evangeline was pleased to see Mr. Chase holding his two youngest children by the hand. She had the two older boys, while Emma accompanied her grandmother.

Miss Anstruther and Miss Leveson appeared most anxious to secure a place as close as possible to Mr. Chase, but Evangeline managed to foil them. She nudged her employer toward the pew in which Miss Webster had taken a seat. Then she, Alfie and Matthew squeezed in to fill the remaining space.

She could imagine the indignant glares being directed at her, but she ignored them. Instead, she concentrated on Mr. Chase and Miss Webster. To her satisfaction, they began a whispered conversation over the head of Rosie, who snuggled between them. Unfortunately they did not have long to talk, for the service soon commenced.

"Don't forget our game," Evangeline whispered to the boys.

Her diversion worked so well, she wished she'd thought of it sooner. Matthew and Alfie concentrated on every word of the service as if their young lives depended on it. Perhaps it also made a difference that one of the clergymen was a guest in their home, who had gone fishing with them and helped them build kites. It might have reminded them that the Lord was with them not only on Sundays, but throughout the week while they studied and played.

When the time came to pray, Evangeline silently beseeched the Lord to further her plans by opening Margaret Webster's eyes to all of Mr. Chase's fine qualities.

He was beginning to make a little progress with Miss Webster, Jasper reflected when he woke early Monday morning with an unaccountable sense of urgency. Part of his success was thanks to Evangeline Fairfax, who had contrived to get him seated next to the lady at church. Remembering his lessons, he had engaged Miss Webster in a brief conversation about her favorite hymns.

Rosie had done her part, too. Wedged between them, his little daughter had rested her head against Miss Webster's arm. Frequently during the service, she had exchanged smiles with the lady. By the end, they were holding hands and, afterward, Miss Webster talked to him at some length about Rosie and the other children. However she might feel about him as a suitor, Jasper sensed that Margaret Webster would not object to becoming a stepmother of five.

When he had turned to find Miss Fairfax watching them, she rewarded his success with a smile of approval that warmed him from head to toe. A wave of gratitude rose within him for the patience she had shown, bearing with his children in spite of his selfish delays. She could have given her notice at any time, leaving him to scramble for a replacement while she went off to set up the school that meant so much to her.

As he headed to the nursery the next morning, Jasper wished he had thought to ask much sooner why the school was so important to her. If he had, he would have discovered he could sympathize with her motives far more than most people. He understood her compelling need to purge the ills of the past and try to set them right for the future.

When he reached the nursery, he found Miss Fairfax waiting for him. Over sips of coffee, she commended his progress with Miss Webster then suggested they get on with his next lesson.

Jasper nodded toward the door. "If you have no objection, I thought we might take my studies outside where there will be no danger of the children overhearing."

Before she could protest, he added, "I asked Jane to supervise the nursery until we get back. I am certain a walk in the fresh air will do us both good."

"You seem to have it all arranged." Miss Fairfax did not sound pleased to have him take charge of the situation without consulting her. "I suppose there is nothing to do but go fetch my bonnet."

By the time she returned, Jane had come to keep watch in the nursery.

"We should not be long," Miss Fairfax told her. "But you may give the children their breakfast once they are all awake."

She and Jasper scarcely exchanged a word as they made their way outdoors. He wondered how many of the servants noticed their passing while quietly going about their early morning duties. He hoped this whim of his would not expose Miss Fairfax to gossip below stairs.

Such thoughts faded from his mind when they emerged into the green, dew-dappled countryside at sunrise. Jasper inhaled a refreshing breath of morning air then beckoned Miss Fairfax toward the path that led down to the brook. He did not want to linger too near the house where their voices might waken sleeping guests or someone might look out a window and see them together.

The path was narrower than he'd realized. Two adults could walk on it side by side, but at this hour they were obliged to keep close together to avoid getting skirts and boots drenched with dew.

"Are you going to tell me about your mill?" Miss Fairfax asked. "Or did you just bring me out here to enjoy the morning air?"

Jasper risked a glance at her only to find her gaze fixed on the path ahead. "I was trying to decide how to begin."

"I know your mill is more than a commercial enterprise." Her tone sounded almost accusing. "You provide housing and food for your workers?"

"I *sell* them food." Jasper was careful to make the distinction. "They may buy from me or from the shops if they prefer because I pay them in cash, not those miserable tokens. Most of them buy the food I make available because the quality is better and the price cheaper than they can find elsewhere."

"Tokens?" Evangeline Fairfax sounded mystified. "Are you saying some mills do not pay their workers in shillings and pence?"

Jasper gave a sharp nod. "Not some—most. Instead, they pay with tokens that have no value outside the company truck shop. The food and goods they sell there are poor quality and overpriced so the owners can make more money off their workers."

Contemplating such greed, at the expense of those who worked so hard for so little, ignited a blaze of righteous anger inside Jasper. "One thing I refuse to sell is spirits. I don't stop my workers from buying it elsewhere if they must, but I am proud to say few of them do. The life they have at New Hope Mills is agreeable enough that they are not inclined to seek escape in a gin bottle."

"I should think not." Miss Fairfax gave an indignant sniff. "Your workers must feel blessed to have an employer who cares about their welfare as much as you do. How did you come to own New Hope Mills? You said you were an overseer for Mr. Thorpe when you first met your wife."

"That's right." The keen interest in her voice intensified Jasper's natural inclination to talk about the work that was so important to him. "I'd worked my way up to overseer. Mr. Thorpe was a good employer. He ran his mill better than most and he rewarded hard work and initiative. After I married Susan, I persuaded him to make some changes in the way we did business. He died a few years later and I took over the mill. That was when I built housing for our workers and expanded my efforts to encourage temperance among them. In the meantime, I did everything in my power to keep the operation profitable so other owners would see it is possible to make money without treating our workers unfairly."

"Well done," said Miss Fairfax. "Very well done, indeed."

When Jasper glanced over, he caught her gazing at him with shining eyes. He was so accustomed to being ridiculed for his radical ideas that her obvious admiration made him feel a foot taller. Yet it troubled him to think that what he was doing should be considered extraordinary.

"It is no more than any employer should do if he would be a true servant of our Heavenly Master. No one seeing the working conditions in most Manchester mills can possibly believe that is God's will."

"I wish you had told me all this long ago." The governess's footsteps slowed. "I would not have been so critical of the time you spent away from home if I had known it was for a higher purpose than simply making your fortune."

It eased his conscience, knowing she grasped the importance of what he was trying to do and understood the sacrifices he was obliged to make in his family life. "I assumed you must have been told already by my wife or her mother. You and I have never had much time to talk about anything but the children."

"That is true."

They walked on in silence for a few moments then Miss Fairfax spoke again. "What made you care so much about bettering the lives of your workers?"

There was the question he'd known she would ask. The question he had not wanted his children to hear him answer. If Evangeline Fairfax had not confided in him about her wretched experiences at the Pendergast School, Jasper was not certain he could have answered her now. But she *had* confided in him and he owed it to her to return the favor.

"My family all worked in a cotton mill when I was a boy. It was a hard life but it was all we knew. We were fortunate not to have more mouths to feed and that my father wasn't a drunkard. He wanted a better life for me, so he sent me to a Sabbath school run by Parson Ward."

By now the path had reached the brook. The gentle babble of the water put Jasper more at ease, allowing him to speak about the worst day of his life. "When I was the age of our Emma, there was a fire at the mill. With all the fluff floating about, the air itself seemed to go up in flames. Ma ran to find my sister, Rose, and Pa grabbed me. It was bedlam—everyone trampling each other in a blind panic to get out. The doors were soon jammed with bodies. Pa picked me up and threw me over the heads of the crowd. I knew if I lost my footing I'd be run down and crushed. By the grace of God, I managed to make it out alive..."

His voice trailed off, his throat as tightly choked as the doors of that burning mill. Instead of fresh country air, he smelled a sulfurous inferno. His eyes stung and began to water as if from the thick smoke and shimmering waves of heat consuming everything in their path.

"Your parents?" Evangeline Fairfax murmured as her footsteps slowed. "Your sister?"

Jasper could only shake his head and fight to maintain his composure.

Miss Fairfax helped by continuing to talk. "Now I see why you did not want your children to overhear us. I am sorry to have brought it all back to you. I should not have pried into your past."

"No!" The denial burst out of Jasper. "You deserve to know after what you told me about yours. I cannot pretend I enjoyed reliving those memories, but it is a relief in a way—like opening an engine valve to reduce the pressure building up inside it."

"I shall have to take your word for that." Miss Fairfax attempted to lighten the mood, for which Jasper was grateful. "I am woefully ignorant about anything to do with machinery. But I understand what you mean about a sense of relief. I have felt it, too, since I spoke to you. Perhaps putting the very worst things into words gives us a little power over them. It reminds us that we have survived and been strengthened in the process."

"Perhaps." Her explanation sounded as reasonable as anything.

By unspoken agreement they turned and headed back

to the house. The children were likely awake and curious about the absence of their governess and their father.

"What became of you after the fire?" The concern in Miss Fairfax's voice was unmistakable. She knew what could befall an orphan child. No doubt she also realized that her experience, as difficult as it had been, was not the worst that could happen. Did she picture Matthew or Alfie in that situation?

Jasper wanted to put her mind at rest. "I was fortunate. Parson Ward took me in temporarily. When he discovered I had no other family, he adopted me and educated me with Norton Brookes and several other boys our age. Some might say the deaths of my parents brought me a better life and a brighter future than they could have given me if they'd lived. But I would give anything to have been able to prevent that fire."

"Of course you would." Evangeline Fairfax seemed to understand in a way few others could.

Jasper wished he had talked all this over with her long ago. "When I finished my schooling, I went to work for Mr. Thorpe. I joined the philosophical and literary society and a committee on the board of health. That is where I met Robert Owen and others who were eager to promote improvements in safety and working conditions in the cotton industry. I felt I owed it to my family to do my best to change things."

He marked the way Miss Fairfax nodded. It conveyed more than simple agreement. It assured him of her sympathy with his ideals. Not since his friend Robert Owen had gone away to Scotland had Jasper felt such kinship with another person regarding this important aspect of his life.

"You should tell your children," Evangeline Fairfax suggested. "Not about the fire, of course, but about New

Hope Mills—why you operate it the way you do and why it is such important work."

With anyone else Jasper would have disagreed strenuously. But with Evangeline Fairfax, he could not, for he knew she believed in his work and loved his children.

"Why do you say that?" he asked. "You and I learned at too young an age what a harsh place the world can be. I want to protect my children from that knowledge for as long as I can. That is the other goal I have worked hard to accomplish."

"I know." She sounded apologetic yet determined to persuade him. "It is not only the noise and crowding and smoke of Manchester you want to shield them from. It is the way so many people are obliged to live. But your children must learn someday. If they understand what you are trying to do and why, they may not mind so much that you must spend so much time away from home."

Jasper could not deny the truth in what Miss Fairfax had said and it troubled him. "Do my children think I do not care for them, that I want to be away from them so often?"

Their governess knew his children better than anyone. She had shown herself willing to speak her mind, especially where their welfare was concerned. Jasper trusted she would tell him the truth no matter how hard it might be for him to hear.

"They know you love them." Miss Fairfax soothed one of his greatest fears. "No one who sees you with them can doubt that. But there are times when I fear they blame themselves or each other for your long absences. They wonder if they were better behaved or more entertaining company you might be inclined to spend more time at home."

Though offered in a tone of gentle compassion, her words pierced Jasper's heart to a dangerous depth. This was worse than he had feared. He would rather his children think him a bad father, incapable of loving them as they deserved. He could not bear to have them doubt or blame themselves for his absences.

"It never occurred to me they might feel that way." His shoulders slumped. "You are right, Miss Fairfax. I must speak to the children at once and try to make them understand. Will you help me?"

"Me?" Her step lurched slightly, as if she had caught her foot on a bit of uneven ground. "What can *I* do?"

Jasper reached out to steady her, but she avoided his hand in her independent way. She might be willing to assist him, but it was clear she had difficulty accepting help from others. Could that be a consequence of her school years, when she'd been called upon to be a source of strength and leadership for her friends?

"I expect you will think of something," he replied. "You know my children so well. If we find a way to explain the importance of my work, perhaps it will help them understand why *you* feel obliged to leave them when the time comes."

He had thought she would grasp his reasoning and approve the idea. He did not expect Miss Fairfax to flinch and let out a half-stifled gasp, as if he had struck her.

Jasper Chase was not a cruel man—quite the opposite, in fact. Even when Evangeline had privately questioned his commitment to fatherhood, she had never doubted his basic good nature.

Now, as they returned to the house from their early morning walk, she knew he did not mean to distress her. But when he spoke of her leaving and how it might affect the children, his words seemed to knock the air out of her.

She tried to tell herself he was wrong. Of course his children would be sorry to see her go, but they would not feel *responsible* for her decision to leave. Would they?

"Are you quite well, Miss Fairfax?" This time, when Mr. Chase put his hand out to steady her, Evangeline was too preoccupied with thoughts of the children to avoid it. "That is the second time you have lost your footing. Perhaps I should not have dragged you out for a walk before breakfast. I hope you will pardon my thoughtlessness."

"Nonsense." She shook her head and tried to ignore the agreeable sensation of his hand on her arm. "In the past, I have done a great deal of work first thing in the morning and never been the worse for it. I am certain you must have, too."

She pictured him laboring on the floor of a cotton mill at the age when she had been doing chores in the damp, chilly rooms of the Pendergast School. She'd never suspected the two of them might have so much in common. For his sake, she wished they did not.

"That is true enough," he replied in a rueful murmur. "What made you falter, then, if not hunger?"

Part of her wanted to make up some other excuse— anything but the truth, which Jasper Chase might use to persuade her to stay at Amberwood. Having exchanged such painful confidences with him recently made it difficult to be less than candid now. "If you must know, it was what you said about telling the children I will be leaving. I never considered that they might blame themselves. It came as something of a shock but I have recovered. I am capable of walking the rest of the way without assistance."

"Of course." Mr. Chase released her arm one finger at a time, as if doing so required some effort.

Once his hand broke contact with her arm, he let it fall to his side and started back toward the house. Hurrying to catch up, Evangeline braced for him to take advantage of her reluctant confession. To her surprise, he did not.

"We needn't mention your plans until the time draws closer. But I would like to talk to the children about my situation as soon as possible. Once we finish breakfast, we should speak to them together. I will explain about my work at New Hope Mills as best I can. Stop me whenever you think necessary to help them better understand. Can you do that for me?"

Evangeline nodded. "I am certain Matthew will interrupt you with plenty of questions, but I will do my part."

"Thank you." Jasper Chase caught her eye, which she had been trying to avoid. "I know I can rely on you."

There was no more treasured compliment he could pay her. Evangeline looked away quickly but could not conceal her satisfaction.

As they approached the house, about to slip in the side entrance nearest the nursery, they met Mr. Brookes on his way out, accompanied by Verity Dawson. Both couples gave a start then pretended they had not.

"More early birds out enjoying the morning air—excellent!" The vicar's hearty tone rang hollow.

"Indeed it is," replied Mr. Chase as if there was nothing unusual about them meeting like this. "If you are heading toward the river, keep to the path for the grass is very wet just now."

"Then perhaps we should confine our stroll to the lane instead." The vicar's forced smile looked anything but happy. "If that is agreeable to you, Mrs. Dawson?"

"Perfectly." The lady's reply was barely audible. Her shifting glance made her look as guilty as if she and Mr. Brookes had been caught committing highway robbery.

"Enjoy your walk." Mr. Chase ushered Evangeline inside. Clearly he was as eager as his friend to end their awkward meeting. "I will see you at breakfast."

As the other two hurried away, Evangeline doubted any of them would mention their early morning encounter over breakfast. She and Mr. Chase spoke no more on their way to the nursery. But when they passed a looking glass in the hallway, she was dismayed to glimpse a furtive look on her face, identical to Verity Dawson's.

She had no reason to be ashamed, her conscience protested. She was only discussing her pupils with their father. No doubt Mrs. Dawson and Mr. Brookes had an equally innocent reason for taking an early stroll together. Yet their reaction suggested they might have something to hide.

Did the vicar and Verity Dawson suspect the same of her and Mr. Chase?

Chapter Nine

"Where have you been?" Matthew demanded when his father and governess returned to the nursery.

The children were clustered around the table eating breakfast. All five looked up with expressions that echoed Matthew's question.

"Jane wouldn't tell us where you went," said Alfie.

"I didn't know, myself," the nursery maid protested.

"We were worried." Emma's quiet reproach hit Jasper hard.

"There was no need for that." Miss Fairfax rested her hands on Emma's shoulders in a gesture of reassurance. "We couldn't get into any trouble around Amberwood... at least not without some assistance from Alfie."

The children laughed at that, Alfie loudest of all. The tension Jasper had sensed in the room eased.

"Your father and I had some matters to discuss," Miss Fairfax explained. "We did not want to be interrupted or wake you, so we went outside. I hope you haven't eaten all the porridge. Our walk has given me an appetite and I expect your father is hungry, too."

"Now that you mention it, I am rather." Jasper tried to infuse his voice with the gratitude he felt. Her calm, caring manner seemed to have relieved his children's fears.

He sank onto a chair between Alfie and Rosie while Miss Fairfax took a seat between Matthew and Owen. She ladled a generous helping of porridge into a bowl and passed it to him.

"What are we going to do today?" asked Matthew.

Jasper shook his head. "I hadn't thought. The weather looks fine, so something outdoors perhaps. Do you have any suggestions?"

The words were scarcely out of his mouth before his son replied, "Could we go for a boat ride down the river like we did last summer?"

Matthew's brothers and sisters were quick to approve the idea.

Jasper considered his son's suggestion. "That will take a bit of planning to accommodate all our guests. But as soon as I can arrange it, we will go."

The children seemed satisfied with that.

"The parish fair is on Saturday," said Emma. "Can we go?"

"Please, Papa!" Rosie turned her most appealing look upon him. "It's such fun."

Jasper smiled at his daughters. "That sounds like a fine idea."

The children cheered.

By now they had all finished their breakfast. Jasper hurried to clean his bowl. "Before we do anything else, there is something I would like to talk to you about."

"What is it, Papa?" For once Rosie beat Matthew to the question.

Jasper hesitated. Fatherly instinct urged him to shield his youngest daughter, like the delicate blossom for which she was named, from the blight of harsh reality.

He glanced at Evangeline Fairfax, whose vivid features radiated encouragement.

"Why don't you go to the chair, sir." She nodded toward a large upholstered armchair beside the nursery hearth where she often sat to read to her pupils. "The children can gather round you."

"That is an excellent idea." Jasper scooped Rosie into his arms and carried her to the chair. He sat down with his little daughter on his knee.

The others followed. Matthew and Emma stood on either side of the chair, while Alfie and Owen sat on a footstool in front of it. They all gazed at him expectantly.

"It's about my mill." He searched for the right words. "*Our* mill, I should say. Miss Fairfax thought you should know more about it. You see, it is run rather differently than other cotton mills in Manchester."

He repeated some of what he had told their governess about the dangers and hardships faced by textile workers, including many children their age.

As he spoke, they responded in different ways according to their temperaments. Matthew began to fidget. Alfie's eyes flashed. Emma and Owen stared at him in thoughtful silence. Rosie began to suck her thumb. She looked puzzled, as if Manchester was a very strange place she could not understand. Yet in other respects his children were in complete agreement—their sympathy for the workers and their outrage at the injustice. It echoed Jasper's feelings and stirred his heart. Never had he felt quite so close to his children. He sensed a bond linking them to the family he had lost so long ago.

"That's not right!" Alfie burst out at last, as if the indignation brewing in his warm little heart could no

longer be contained. "Those children ought to be playing and learning like we do, not working all the time."

As gently as he could, Jasper explained how many
families needed their children's small wages in order
to get by. He told them some attended Sabbath schools,
as he had done.

Miss Fairfax had helped Jane clear the breakfast
table, but now she rejoined the family. She sank onto
the floor beside the footstool and put her arm around
Alfie. "Tell them about New Hope Mills, sir, and all
you have done to improve the lives of the people who
work for you. I'm sure they will be very interested and
very proud."

The children nodded and murmured their agreement.
All fixed him with looks of admiration and affection.

Jasper told them how he had abolished payment with
shop tokens and built better housing for his workers.
The children seemed most interested in hearing about
the recreational activities he provided, from sporting
events to concerts to a small lending library.

Rosie removed her thumb from her mouth. "I'd like
to go to a concert. Will you take me to Manchester the
next time they have one, Papa?"

Before he could answer her question, the rest were
clamoring to go, as well.

Jasper shot their governess a look that appealed for
her assistance.

She did not fail him. "You will not need to go all the
way to Manchester to see a concert, Rosie. Miss Webster is very fond of music and your father has asked her
to organize a concert here at Amberwood. I hope you
will all take part in it."

"I will!" Rosie bounced excitedly on Jasper's knee.
"I want to sing that song about the little bird."

The boys were quick to suggest pieces they could perform and soon they were all talking about the concert. The notion of visiting Manchester seemed to have been forgotten, for which Jasper was deeply grateful.

When the children let her get a word in, Miss Fairfax suggested they go down to the music room and practice while their father joined his guests for their breakfast.

"Before you go," said Jasper, remembering the purpose of this talk, "there is one more thing I would like to say."

They quieted and gave him their full attention once again.

Jasper looked into each beloved young face, trying to impress his point upon them. "It is not an easy task running New Hope Mills the way I do while still making money from it. But I believe it is important work that needs doing."

Alfie gave an emphatic nod while the others murmured their agreement.

"That is why I must spend so much time in Manchester," Jasper continued, "when it would be a great deal more enjoyable to be here with you."

The children seemed to accept his explanation, disappointed by what it meant for them but understanding the necessity. Jasper congratulated himself.

Then Owen spoke up. "I think we should go live with you in Manchester, Papa. Then you will be able to see us as much as you like and we can help you with your work."

Matthew and Alfie were quick to agree, as was Rosie. Emma looked torn by the choice between leaving her beloved home and seeing more of her father.

"That is a very kind offer, son." Once again, Jasper silently appealed to Miss Fairfax to rescue him. "But

Manchester is not nearly as pleasant a place as the Vale of Eden. And besides…what would your grandmother do without you?"

"She could come and visit us," said Alfie.

"And we could all come to Amberwood for Christmas and the summer," Matthew added.

"I suppose…but…" Desperation seized Jasper by the throat. "Perhaps when you are older. Miss Fairfax, tell the children why it is better for them to stay here at Amberwood."

He waited confidently for her to assist him.

Instead, she patted his youngest son on the shoulder. "I think it is a wonderful idea. Well done, Owen!"

Her response struck Jasper like a knife between the shoulder blades. After years of respectful tolerance, he thought the two of them had finally become allies. How could Evangeline Fairfax have picked this critical moment to betray him?

"What possessed you to encourage that mad idea of my children moving to Manchester?" Jasper Chase glared at Evangeline from behind his writing table a few hours later.

She had sensed her employer was not happy with her after their talk with his children, but they'd had no opportunity to discuss the encounter until he summoned her from the music room to his study. His face had a livid cast and every feature was clenched so tight, it looked as though something might snap.

"I do not think it is a mad idea at all." Evangeline strove to calm Mr. Chase by speaking in an even tone. "Owen is an uncommonly sensible boy for his age. I believe it would do you and the children good to live as a family rather than occasional visitors. Since you have important work that requires your presence in Manchester, it makes sense that *they* ought to join you."

It puzzled her why he could not understand that and why the very idea seemed to enrage him.

He took a deep breath and made an obvious effort to maintain his composure. "After our talk this morning, I thought you understood. A large industrial city is not a proper place to raise a young family. My children are better off here in the country."

"Are they?" Though she tried to remain calm, Evangeline felt her temper rising.

She felt something else, too, which dismayed her. Since coming to Amberwood, her attitude toward Jasper Chase had been one of wary neutrality at best, though she'd worked hard to conceal it from the children. As a consequence, she'd felt free to say whatever she liked to him, regardless of whether he wanted to hear it. Yet in a perilously short time, her attitude had undergone a drastic change. She had come to admire Jasper Chase and sympathize with him. As a consequence, she *did* care that he was vexed with her. But why should he be? She only wanted what was best for him and his children…and his new wife. Surely the lady would expect to see her husband more often than the distance between Amberwood and Manchester would allow.

Somehow the image of the Chase family with Margaret Webster at its center no longer appealed to Evangeline as much as it had before.

Such confused, heightened emotions threw her off balance and made her defensive. "Are your children better off separated from their father? You heard them this morning. They care about your workers and they want to help. If you truly wish to see your work continue and spread, I believe you have far more to hope from your children than from the other mill owners. But you must act soon to get the children involved before they begin to resent your work as a rival for your attention."

Her arguments did not sway Jasper Chase except perhaps in the opposite direction. His full, dark brows clashed together over flashing eyes. One powerful hand slashed the air, demanding her silence. "That is quite enough, Miss Fairfax! Since you are determined to abandon my children, you have forfeited the right to have a say in how I choose to raise them. From now on, I will thank you not to encourage them in thinking they should live with me in Manchester."

His words bit into Evangeline's heart the way her teachers' switches had once bitten into her hands. She found herself vulnerable to Jasper Chase's criticism in a way she had not been before. It puzzled her why that should be. One thing she did know was that she could not abide it.

She tilted her chin and stiffened her spine, wishing she was capable of making herself physically taller. "You are a fine one to talk about me abandoning your children! I have been with them night and day for the past six years, caring for them when they were ill, comforting them when they were sad or frightened. You only came home long enough to take them on outings and play games. Your work in Manchester is important, but your children need to know you will be with them through bad times as well as good."

"I want to spare them from bad times!" His hand crashed down upon the writing table with thunderous force. "Can you not see that? I want to protect them from squalor and ugliness and misery the way my father protected me from the smoke and flames at the cost of his own life."

The pain of that memory seemed to drain the power from his anger, the way a fire sucked all the air from an enclosed chamber. His shoulders slumped and his eyes dimmed with a lifetime of unshed tears. "It costs me more than you know to be away from my family, Miss Fairfax. That may be why I want the time we do spend together to be as happy as possible."

Jasper Chase's sorrow and regret affected Evangeline in a way his hostility never could. It flowed beneath her defenses, weakening the foundations until they threatened to crumble. Might she have better success reaching him if she changed her approach?

Making a conscious effort to soften her voice, she asked, "Could it be that you are driven to protect the family you have now because you could not protect the one you lost?"

She did not mean it as an accusation but rather a possible insight into his actions.

Jasper Chase did not take her question in the spirit she had intended. His head snapped back as if he'd been dealt a powerful blow. He stared at her with a deeply aggrieved look. "I will thank you not to speculate on my motives, Miss Fairfax. I have tried to do the best I can for my family while endeavoring to make a positive difference in the lives of people few others pay any regard."

Evangeline tried to summon the words to assure him that she did not question his feelings for his children or the vital importance of his philanthropy. But the look of misery etched on his bold, handsome features paralyzed her tongue. Her words had sown the pain in his eyes and in his heart. She feared she would only make matters worse if she said anything more.

Mr. Chase heaved a deep sigh. "Perhaps you are right

to believe it is impossible to do important work and raise a family properly. I have no choice but to try. If you have any respect for me or love for my children, please do as I ask. Whether they or you realize it, my family is better off here."

Of course she loved his children! Evangeline bristled at the mere suggestion that her feelings might be otherwise. As for their father, her respect for him had increased so much during the past ten days that she might almost mistake it for a different feeling altogether.

"Please, sir..." Could she make him understand when she was not certain she understood, herself? For far too long, she had questioned his feelings for his family. But she had been wrong. Now that she knew about his work and his past, she had begun to value Jasper Chase as he deserved. That did not mean she was mistaken about the importance of him spending more time with his children.

"I think you have said enough, Miss Fairfax." He backed away from his writing table to stand before the window. There he angled himself to look outside. "And I have probably said too much. If it will not be possible for you to oblige me, perhaps you ought to consider leaving Amberwood sooner than we discussed."

Was he politely threatening to dismiss her if she refused to obey him? Evangeline could not decide if she was more aggrieved or outraged. Her head felt too tight suddenly to contain her raging thoughts, as did her chest to hold her stormy heart.

"Indeed, sir." She spoke with clipped precision, desperate to maintain her composure. "I believe you *have* said altogether too much."

With that, she marched out of his study without asking his leave to go. She did not trust herself to stay another minute without risking a humiliating outburst of tears.

What had he done? Jasper chided himself that evening when his temper had cooled. The last thing he wanted was to have Evangeline Fairfax leave Amberwood after having managed its nursery so capably for the past six years. He wished she did not have to go two months from now to open her charity school and he could not abide the prospect of her leaving immediately.

Throughout the afternoon, as his children and guests had amused themselves in the garden, he had done his best to stay away from Miss Fairfax. Part of him feared he might say something that would provoke her to pack her bags that very night. Another part worried that he might back down and grovel in an effort to persuade her to stay.

He could not avoid her when he'd gone to the nursery to hear his children's prayers and tuck them in for the night. Yet somehow she'd managed to maintain a safe distance between them without betraying any hint of their discord to her young pupils. He'd rather expected the children to besiege him with more pleas to go to Manchester, but no one had said a word about it. Jasper wondered if Miss Fairfax had spoken to them on the subject and what she had said. But he would rather have jumped off the roof than ask her. He'd left the nursery and headed to dinner in a fog of bewilderment.

He was grateful not to have to talk much during the meal that evening. He allowed Miss Anstruther to drone on, with occasional caustic interjections from Mrs. Leveson, while he nodded at appropriate intervals.

Meanwhile, his thoughts returned to his unsettling interview with Evangeline Fairfax.

He had been unduly severe with her, which he regretted. A month ago, it would not have surprised or troubled him to disagree with her. They might have argued over their difference of opinion, but he would not have felt the sting of personal betrayal. Nor would he have lashed out at her so fiercely.

Back then, Miss Fairfax would not have presumed to comment on the most painful experience of his life because she would have known nothing about it. Had he been foolish to trust her with such a sensitive confidence, giving her ammunition to use against him if she chose? Jasper's caution and sense of privacy agreed it had been a mistake, but part of him was still not convinced. Confiding about his past, with someone capable of understanding its effect on his present character and choices, seemed to lighten a burden he had not realized he was carrying.

But if Evangeline Fairfax understood him so well, his conscience challenged, did that mean she was right about his reasons for wanting to keep his children away from Manchester? And were those reasons good enough to justify it?

While his guests ate and conversed around him, his thoughts continued to spin, always coming up with more questions than answers. He went through the motions of dining, scarcely noticing what he put in his mouth. It came as a surprise when his mother-in-law rose and led the other ladies away. If Jasper expected to be left to reflect in peace, Piers Webster soon disabused him of that notion.

Looking from Jasper to Norton Brookes, the older man shook his head. "What's gotten into the pair of you?

You hardly said two words between you during dinner. You looked as if your minds were a hundred miles away. Not bad news from Manchester, I hope. Ever since the war, it's been nothing but labor agitations."

So Norton had been distracted during dinner, as well? Jasper wondered if it had anything to do with Mrs. Dawson.

Though he did not want to argue with Piers Webster, Jasper was anxious to steer the conversation away from the question of what had preoccupied him and his friend. "If the workers were treated better there would be no need for agitation. Unless something is done to improve conditions, it will only lead to more violence."

That was another reason he wanted to keep his children as far as possible from the industrial heartland. With workers increasingly desperate, there had been riots and killings, machinery destroyed, mills burned. The government's response had been to increase repression, banning large gatherings and making it a hanging offense to wreck machinery. In Jasper's opinion, that was like adding fuel to a boiler then jamming the pressure valve. An explosion was inevitable.

"You may be right," Mr. Webster conceded with obvious reluctance. "None of your lot were mixed up with that Blanketeers March in the spring, yet you haven't gone bankrupt."

This hint of respect for his work made Jasper forget Evangeline Fairfax…at least temporarily. "I do not make as great a profit as some, but I am able to provide a good life for my family. What more can a man ask?"

He appealed to his friend. "We cannot take our money with us when we leave this life, can we, Norton?"

"Indeed not." Norton Brookes roused from his abstraction enough to quote Scripture. "'Lay up for your-selves treasures in Heaven, where neither moth nor rust doth corrupt, and where thieves do not break through nor steal. For where your treasure is, there will your heart be also.'"

Jasper thought his friend's words ended on a wist-ful note.

"It is hard to argue with the Good Book." Piers Web-ster leaned back in his chair and laced his fingers over his waistcoat. "Tell me more about your mill, Chase. What changes should I make first if I wanted to try your system?"

"Do away with tokens and reform your truck shop." Jasper rattled off his answer, eager to take advantage of Webster's unexpected receptiveness.

A lively conversation followed, with the older man challenging a number of his ideas, while Jasper ques-tioned the old way of doing business. He thought he was making some headway toward persuading his late father-in-law's partner that his radical ideas had some merit, after all.

"This is fascinating," Norton Brookes remarked at last in a tone that contradicted his words. "But is it not time we joined the ladies?"

Jasper would have preferred to continue discussing his ideas, but Mr. Webster sprang to his feet. "Quite right, Vicar. We should not keep the fair ones waiting."

The three men exchanged a few more words about business as they headed to the drawing room.

"You must tell Margaret about this system of yours." Mr. Webster glanced around the room where some of the ladies were chatting.

There was no sign of Miss Webster among them. Her father asked Mrs. Thorpe her whereabouts and was directed to a screened alcove. Gesturing for Jasper to accompany him, Mr. Webster strode toward it and found his daughter tracing a shade of Verity Dawson.

Margaret Webster cast her father and Jasper a teasing grin. "So you gentlemen have decided to grace us with your presence at last." She held up her work for their inspection—a tracing of Mrs. Dawson's profile. It had been cast on a sheet of paper by a special lamp. "It is a fine likeness, don't you think? Verity has such a lovely, delicate profile. Now I only need to transfer it to black paper and cut it out."

"You made a fine job of it." Her father thrust Jasper forward. "Now you must trace one of our host. His profile may not be delicate, but I reckon it is handsome enough."

Mrs. Dawson wasted no time taking his hint. She offered Miss Webster a few breathless words of thanks then fled the alcove.

"Papa," Margaret Webster protested, "you should not order everyone around to suit yourself. Mr. Chase might find it tiresome to sit still so long. He might rather enjoy more of Miss Anstruther's conversation. He seemed quite engrossed by it at dinner."

The lady was amusing herself at his expense. Jasper wondered if that might be a sign of romantic interest.

He chuckled to let her know her irony had not escaped him. "I have held a monopoly on Miss Anstruther's conversation long enough for one evening. As I am sure your father can tell you, a little healthy competition is better for business."

Miss Webster laughed. "Then this party must be thriving, for there is plenty of competition for your attention, sir."

Her father looked pleased with them both. "You

young people seem to be getting on well. Sit down, my boy, and let Margaret trace your shade. She is a dab hand at anything artistic."

Jasper did as he was bid. "I'd be grateful if you would, Miss Webster. My children might like a profile of me to hang in their nursery. Would you be kind enough to oblige me for their sakes?"

"Certainly." She hung a fresh sheet of paper on the easel and picked up her sketching pencil. "Now look that way and try to keep as still as you can. I will try not to take too long."

"Don't rush," her father advised. "Make a good job of it. Now I must excuse myself. Mrs. Thorpe wants me to make up a foursome at the card table."

After he hurried away, his daughter set to work. "Don't mind Papa, Mr. Chase. He is the best of men, but no more subtle than a brickbat."

Was that why Miss Webster had seemed uncomfortable around him, Jasper wondered, because she was embarrassed by her father's blatant efforts to push them together? He could hardly blame her for not wanting to appear ridiculous.

"Subtlety is not necessarily a virtue." He tried not to move his mouth too much as he spoke. "When people make themselves plain, you know where you stand."

Miss Webster's pencil scratched softly against the paper. "It was plain to me that you had something on your mind at dinner and it was *not* Miss Anstruther's conversation."

It took a great deal of willpower for Jasper not to keep from turning to look at the lady. Though she had not asked in so many words what preoccupied him, there could be no mistaking her curiosity. While he shrank from telling her about his disagreement with his children's governess, he fancied he could hear Evangeline Fairfax urging him to talk about himself with Miss Webster.

"You are very perceptive," he said, continuing to stare straight ahead. "In fact, there was something troubling me. My children want to come and live in Manchester. What do you think of that?"

"Manchester?" Her tone crackled with scorn. "Why would they want to live there?"

Until that moment, Margaret Webster had been only the least objectionable of the ladies Miss Fairfax had selected as a possible match for him. Now he'd discovered something important they might have in common.

"You do not like the city?" He tried not to influence her by betraying his own opinion.

"Why would I?" Her pencil sounded louder as it moved over the paper. "So crowded and grimy and the smell! Your children are fortunate to have such a lovely home in the country. The only town I would care to live in is Bath. I visit there as often as I can."

The tightness in Jasper's shoulders eased. How pleasant it was to converse with someone who agreed with him. He knew he should take advantage of this time with Miss Webster while they were almost alone. What would his resident matchmaker advise him to do?

"I have not had the pleasure of visiting Bath." He darted a sidelong glance at her. "Can I prevail upon you to tell me about it? What makes it such a superior place?"

"I shall be glad to," she replied. "The only difficulty will be in deciding where to begin. I admire its history and its elegance…"

As the lady warmed to her subject, Jasper congratulated himself on making some real progress with her. In spite of his earlier quarrel with Miss Fairfax, he looked forward to giving her a full report.

Chapter Ten

The birds outside her window woke Evangeline the next morning with their joyful singing. She wished they would all fly away and let her sleep, for she had gotten little rest in the previous hours. Hard as she'd tried to put her argument with Jasper Chase out of her mind, bits of it had run through her thoughts over and over, making her head ache and her stomach churn.

Her employer had made no further mention of her leaving Amberwood. Then again, he'd had little opportunity with the children always present. He must know as well as she how they would react to such an announcement. She resented his attempt to intimidate her that way. It reminded her of how the Pendergast teachers had made Leah and her obey by threatening to punish their more sensitive friends.

The tactic had worked in both cases. In their later years at school, she and Leah had been less overtly rebellious. After her interview with Mr. Chase, Evangeline had warned his children not to mention going to Manchester until their father got used to the idea. Though, after the way he'd reacted, she doubted he would ever get used to it.

Perhaps it was just as well they'd had this falling-out, Evangeline reflected as she dragged herself out of bed to face the day. Lately she had become too close to him for her peace of mind. She'd begun to question whether someone else might do just as well at founding a new charity school, while the Chase family might find her impossible to replace.

It would not be the first time her liking for a strong-willed man had tempted her to abandon her plans for the future. Fortunately she had come to her senses when Mr. Preston tried to remake her into his ideal of the perfect submissive wife, as she was coming to them now. Her teachers had been wrong about a great many things, but they had been right to warn her that she would only get a husband by subduing her strong will. Men like Jasper Chase would always insist on having their way, even when their way was wrong and hers was right!

With that thought, Evangeline stabbed the last pin deep into her hair and marched out of the room as quietly as she could manage. Only consideration for her sleeping pupils kept her from slamming the door of her bedchamber behind her.

The sight of Jasper Chase sitting at the nursery table made her jump back with a barely stifled shriek stuck in her throat.

"What has you so nervous this morning?" he demanded in a gruff whisper. "Have you been reading Gothic novels before bed?"

Evangeline was inclined to view the question as a deliberate insult until she recalled that his late wife had enjoyed reading such books. Besides, he was pouring her coffee—a service for which she was willing to forgive a great deal.

"I did not expect to see you here this morning." She

marshaled her dignity as much as possible after her foolish fright.

Mr. Chase appeared puzzled for a moment and then surprised. "You mean because of our discussion? I thought the issue was resolved in a most satisfactory manner."

As she took a seat opposite him, Evangeline gave a derisive sniff. "Satisfactory for *you,* perhaps. I do not respond well to being bullied, especially when the harm is threatened to others."

She would have said more, but the rich aroma of the coffee was impossible to resist. She settled for fixing her employer with a fierce scowl as she lifted the cup to her lips.

"Bullied?" he sputtered, clearly hard-pressed to keep his voice down. "Threatened? I did no such thing."

Evangeline's brows flew up. "Then what did you mean by saying I must leave Amberwood at once if I did not discourage the children from asking to go live with you in Manchester? Was it a jest, perhaps, that I misunderstood?"

Though his unexpected presence had given her a turn and they were arguing again, Evangeline found herself strangely glad to have him there. They might not always agree, but at least Jasper Chase treated her like a person worthy of his confidence.

"It was not a jest," he muttered. At first, Evangeline assumed he was cross with her. But the more he spoke, the more she sensed he might be angry with himself. "But it was not altogether in earnest, either. It was certainly never meant as a threat. I only wanted to impress upon you the depth of my feelings in the matter."

"You certainly did that." She wanted to stay vexed with him but it was not easy. Perhaps she had been more forceful than necessary in her arguments. And perhaps she ought to have consulted him before encouraging Owen's idea of going to Manchester.

"I suppose you often received threats at that wretched school you attended." Jasper Chase bent forward to sip his coffee. Somehow it looked like a bow of contrition.

Evangeline nodded. "When the teachers discovered some of us could not be cowed by ridicule, deprivations or the switch, they resorted to punishing our innocent friends for our acts of defiance. That was most effective from their point of view, but I considered it wickedly unjust."

Her employer's bold, attractive features darkened and his fingers clenched around the handle of his cup. Evangeline thought she glimpsed a flicker of shame in his blue-gray eyes. "Do you intend to egg my children on about going to Manchester again now that you know I will not dismiss you for it?"

"No." Even if she had not cared about waking the children, Evangeline could scarcely coax her voice above a whisper. Her conscience chided her as a traitor to the welfare of her pupils. "I still believe I am right, but you are their father and I do not wish to cause strife between you. Especially not with the changes they will soon face."

"Thank you." He stretched his hand across the table and for a foolish instant Evangeline thought he meant to clasp hers.

Though caution and propriety warned her not to respond to the compelling invitation, she could not stop her hand from inching toward his.

Fortunately, before it reached him, Mr. Chase motioned toward her cup. "Can I get you more coffee?"

"Yes, please!" She nearly upset the cup in her haste to push it toward him.

If he had noticed her reaching for his hand, Mr. Chase was enough of a gentleman to pretend otherwise. "I know you believe the children should be near me, but I am not alone in my opinion that the city is no place for them. Miss Webster agrees with me."

Why did his casual remark sear through her in a white-hot flash? By contrast, Evangeline's reply was so cold she wondered that her breath did not frost the air. "Does she? You discussed the matter with her?"

Jasper Chase nodded. "Last night, after dinner. She noticed my preoccupation and asked the cause. That was kind of her, don't you think?"

"Very kind." Evangeline felt as if her face were paralyzed into a bland mask that bore no relation to the emotions churning within her.

Until now, she had viewed Margaret Webster as a good prospective stepmother for her pupils and a fine wife for their father. If Miss Webster agreed to marry her employer, Evangeline would feel free to leave Amberwood with a clear conscience, knowing the family was in capable hands. But Jasper Chase's account of his conversation with Miss Webster changed all that.

"We spoke at some length," he continued, "while she was tracing my shade. An excellent likeness she made of it, too."

Evangeline gave a nod of feigned interest. All the while, she could not help thinking that tracing the outline of a person's shadow might take skill and a steady hand but no particular talent. Her friend Rebecca could sketch a portrait that not only captured an accurate likeness of the sitter but a glimpse into their heart and soul, as well.

"I told her about the children hankering to go to Manchester," Jasper Chase went on, oblivious to Evangeline's reaction. "She said she could not understand why anyone would want to live there when they were fortunate enough to have a place in the country."

"I see." Evangeline forced her frozen mouth to work.

He nodded. "I will admit I was skeptical of this matchmaking scheme of yours at first, but I am beginning to see the wisdom of it. My children do need a mother. If they have one, I expect they will be happy to stay at Amberwood with her and give up any notion of living in Manchester."

Would they? Evangeline was not so sure. If Mr. Chase married Miss Webster, the lady would be little more than a congenial stranger to his children. Evangeline was as close to a mother as most of the young Chases had ever known. Yet they still hankered to spend more time with their father, like a true family. Did he believe the children would become so much more attached to Miss Webster than to her that they would no longer miss his regular presence in their lives?

That thought stung. So did the lady's disagreement with her about where the children should live. At least their father had unselfish reasons for his opinion. Did Miss Webster favor the children remaining in the country because she preferred to live there? Did she seek to curry favor with Mr. Chase by agreeing with him? Or was she one of those women who believed a man's ideas were always right?

None of those possibilities endeared her to Evangeline. She turned a deaf ear as her employer praised the superiority of Miss Webster's understanding, but her attention revived when he said, "I think you will be proud of me."

She was already proud of the life he had fashioned for himself from the humblest beginning and the commitment he had made to improve the lives of others. "Why is that?"

"Because," he replied, "I followed your advice. I told Miss Webster something about myself and encouraged her to talk about something of interest to her. We had a most satisfactory conversation."

"I am pleased to hear it." That falsehood weighed heavy on Evangeline's tongue.

"I thought you would be." Jasper Chase looked absurdly like his son Alfie when the boy received her praise. "That is why I came here this morning."

Evangeline gave a rueful grin. "To boast of your conquest?"

He chuckled as if he believed she had intended to amuse him. "I have not made a conquest of Miss Webster yet. But with more of your excellent lessons, I hope to."

He wanted her help to win the hand of a woman she was no longer certain would be the right sort of wife for him? Evangeline struggled to swallow that irony, which she found a good deal more bitter than her coffee.

Miss Fairfax did not seem nearly as enthusiastic about helping him as she had been at first. Jasper found her change in attitude rather annoying, considering this matchmaking business had been her idea.

He'd resisted it in the beginning but lately he had begun to change his mind. Would the same ever be true of Miss Fairfax's claim that the children belonged with him in Manchester? Jasper did not want to believe it, but he could not be entirely certain. That was why he'd been so grateful to Margaret Webster for agreeing with him.

There was a great deal more about the lady to recommend her as a prospective bride. She had a pleasant personality and got along with all his children. Her
background was similar to his late wife's and she preferred to live in the country. Besides, her father seemed
anxious for a match between them. If they were related
by marriage, Piers Webster might be willing to try some
of Jasper's reforms.

Was that enough on which to build a marriage? Jasper's heart demanded. Shouldn't he feel something more
for a woman he would consider making his bride?

Perhaps not, he tried to persuade himself. Marriage
based on romantic feelings was for the young. He had
responsibilities to his family and his work that must
come before sentiment. He did not want to care for any
woman so much that his feelings for her might distract
him from his work.

In response to his request for more courting lessons,
Miss Fairfax shifted in her chair as if it had suddenly
grown uncomfortable. "I am not certain I have anything
more I can teach you, Mr. Chase."

"Surely you must," he appealed her. "Two lessons
in any subject is hardly a proper course of study. Your
first two lessons proved most valuable."

Evangeline Fairfax avoided his gaze. "The extra
sleep would likely provide more benefit than coming
here so early every morning to consult with me."

She might be right, yet Jasper found himself reluctant to give up these early morning chats. Even when
Miss Fairfax urged him to talk about the past he would
rather forget, this time with her seemed to get his day
off to a proper start. It was like the coffee they shared.
The brew might be bitter or a trifle too hot, but it was
always stimulating and made him hanker for more.

"Why are you so reluctant to assist me all of a sudden?" he asked. "I thought you wanted me to marry Miss Webster as soon as possible so you could leave to set up your school."

Now that he understood her motives for wanting to take on that task, he no longer begrudged her need to leave Amberwood.

"Of course I do," she insisted. "It's just that..."

Jasper had been told enough falsehoods in his life that he had could recognize one when he heard it. "Do you no longer approve of Miss Webster because she agrees with me that the children are better off here than in Manchester?"

In response to his blunt question, the governess met his gaze head-on. "I cannot deny it has given me second thoughts."

"Why?" he demanded. "Because you want to leave a deputy behind who will act and believe just as you would, even if that puts her at odds with me? Is that any way to insure my children's happiness, by having their parents in constant disagreement?"

Miss Fairfax flinched at his questions, making Jasper suspect she had not considered the matter in that light. "I do not want any such thing. But neither do I want your children to have a mother who never questions their father's decisions and always believes he knows best about everything. Such an arrangement might make for a peaceful household but at what price? I know you want what is best for your children, but your judgment is no more infallible than that of any other man or woman."

Even when he thought he had her outwitted, Evangeline Fairfax had a knack for challenging him in a way he found difficult to refute. Jasper could not decide whether to be indignant or amused. Perhaps a little of both with a helping of grudging admiration thrown in for good measure.

"I never claimed to be infallible." He could not suppress a self-mocking grin. "I only want a wife who will understand the importance of my work and support me in it. Not one who will view it as a rival and constantly seek to distract me from it."

The moment the words left his mouth, Jasper knew he had said too much—especially in the nursery, where one of his children might wake and overhear. He cast a furtive glance toward the bedroom doors.

Relieved to see no sign of the children stirring, he resolved to change the subject. "Come now, will you give me another courting lesson or must I blunder along on my own? What more proof do you need that I do not consider myself infallible?"

"Not on this subject, perhaps." The lady's resistance seemed to be waning. "Very well, then. I have another suggestion or two that might help you."

"Excellent!" Winning her cooperation pleased him a great deal. "The days are slipping by and I need to make more progress with Miss Webster before she leaves."

Miss Fairfax gave a terse nod. Though she had agreed to assist him further, Jasper sensed he had not entirely overcome her reluctance.

"Do not laugh," she warned him, "for my next suggestion may seem tiresomely obvious. You should praise the lady. Not with shallow flattery of her looks, though the occasional compliment of that sort might not go amiss. Express your approval of her understanding, her conversation, her way with children…her artistic talent."

Was it his imagination or did that last suggestion sound rather ironic?

"Whatever quality or skill you praise," Miss Fairfax continued, "make certain you are sincere. She may be able to tell if you are not and that would be as bad as an insult."

Jasper nodded. "It is rather obvious but still important. I reckon I should make more effort to praise people—not only Miss Webster but my children and my workers. Now, to practice my lesson."

"That will not be necessary." In spite of her brusque reply, Miss Fairfax blushed a little. "I have no doubt you can do it, provided you remember to."

"Nonsense," Jasper said, waving her objection. "Any skill benefits from practice, though finding qualities to praise in you does not present much of a challenge."

"You see?" Miss Fairfax sounded almost severe, but the deepening color in her cheeks told a different story. "You are a skilled flatterer already. That is the sort of subtlety that should endear you to Miss Webster."

"I was not trying to flatter you." The thought offended Jasper somehow. "Only stating the truth. Surely you know how much there is to admire about you. Your strength of character to have survived that wretched school with your spirit unbroken. Your generosity in forging your circle of friends when it would have been easier to look out for yourself."

As he gathered breath to continue, Miss Fairfax cut him off. "Well done. You have obviously mastered the lesson. There is no need to continue."

Jasper could imagine her taking that tone as she examined one of his children's compositions.

"I am not finished," he replied as he might have if one of his workers interrupted him. "You have been patient with me during the past two years. Instead of appreciating your forbearance, I imposed upon it to an inexcusable degree. You were justified to issue your ultimatum. You have done everything in your power to insure my children continue to be properly cared for. If they are not, the responsibility will be mine, not yours."

It puzzled him that Evangeline Fairfax reacted to his words with increasing agitation rather than pleasure. When he finished speaking, she jumped from her seat as if it were strewn with hot coals. "Thank you, sir, but that is quite enough. I do not want any of the children to overhear you. I am certain I hear them stirring."

Jasper could not detect any sounds from the children's rooms that suggested they might be awake. Perhaps six years of caring for his children had made their governess's hearing more acute.

She rushed to the girls' door and pushed it open. "Just as I thought, Rosie is awake and anxious to see her papa."

She entered the bedroom and returned a moment later with the child in her arms. Rosie yawned and rubbed her eyes. Odd as it seemed, Jasper suspected her governess had woken his daughter to prevent him from praising her any further.

Had he truly mastered his latest lesson in courting, Jasper wondered, or failed to grasp it at all?

Why could she not bear to hear Jasper Chase say such kind things about her?

Evangeline continued to ponder that riddle later in the day, when the Amberwood party went on a boating excursion down the river Eden. Had all the criticism heaped upon her at the Pendergast School made it impossible for her to accept any kind of praise?

Somehow she did not think that was the answer. She and her friends had always tried to build up one another's confidence beyond the power of any teacher or bully to tear down. It had worked better for some of the girls than others, but she was reasonably certain she did not think any worse of herself than she deserved. If anything, her experiences at school might have made her too quick to shrug off criticism without taking time to consider whether there might be a grain of truth in it.

Then what had flustered her so much about the things Jasper Chase said that morning? Intuition warned her she might be better off not knowing.

As she helped get the children seated in the barge Mr. Chase had hired for their voyage, Evangeline found her gaze drawn toward her employer and Miss Webster as they engaged in conversation. An unaccountable stab of pain lanced her heart when she saw him look into the lady's eyes and murmur some words to her.

Whatever he said clearly pleased Miss Webster. She glanced up at him through her flirtatious fringe of lashes and made some reply that Evangeline did not catch. He responded with a chuckle, then suddenly glanced up and caught Evangeline staring at them.

A ridiculous spasm of shame urged her to look away and pretend she had not been watching. But Mr. Chase did not appear to resent her interest. Instead, he raised his bold, dark eyebrows in a way that suggested he was seeking her approval. He must have paid Miss Webster a compliment and been gratified by her simpering response.

Simpering? Evangeline chided herself for such a harsh thought. Miss Webster had reacted in the way any woman might when she received praise from an attractive man. It was precisely the way she *should* want Miss Webster to respond, just as he was behaving the way she should want him to. But instead of satisfaction and approval, Evangeline was gripped by darker emotions she did not understand.

Mr. Chase beckoned his daughters to join him and Miss Webster. He took Emma on his knee while Rosie climbed onto the lady's. So intently was Evangeline watching them that she did not notice the vicar's sister lean close to her.

"It looks as if our handsome host has made his choice." Miss Brookes's gleeful whisper caused Evangeline to start violently.

"F-forgive me!" she stammered. "My thoughts were elsewhere."

If Abigail Brookes guessed where that might have been, she gave no sign. "I cannot blame him. It is the best match of the lot. My poor brother will be disappointed, though. If he could get me off his hands, he might be able to afford a wife."

The rest of the party were all talking, so no one seemed to overhear Miss Brookes's confidential murmur. Neither did they notice her subtle nod toward the stern of the barge. There sat the vicar and Verity Dawson on either side of Owen. They spoke quietly to the boy, pointing out sights of interest along the riverbank. But when their gazes met over the child's head, Evangeline sensed another unspoken conversation taking place.

Her heart went out to them, though her sympathy was accompanied by an unwelcome pang of longing.

"I like boats!" Matthew announced to no one in particular. "They are always taking you to someplace new. I want to be a sea captain when I grow up."

Evangeline's gaze flew to the boy's father. At his son's words, Jasper Chase's features set in a rueful frown, which she was certain she could interpret. Clearly he hoped his children would carry on his work once they were grown. But how could he expect that unless they were brought up from an early age to understand his commitment to improving the lives of mill-workers and their families?

As the other children chimed in to tell what they would like to do in the future, Evangeline took the opportunity to respond to Abigail Brookes. "Are you not the least bit sorry on your own account?"

Should she have done more to encourage Mr. Chase to consider Abigail as a wife?

The vicar's sister shook her head. "I have concluded that some women are not suited for marriage. I believe you and I fall into that group, Miss Fairfax."

Was that true? Part of Evangeline agreed most emphatically. She had important work to do, which was not compatible with family life. Besides, she could never be happy subduing her strong will in order to conform to a husband's wishes.

And yet, as she watched Jasper Chase talking and laughing with Miss Webster, another part of her—a weak, foolish part, no doubt—wished she were a different kind of woman. A woman who could be content with his love…if she were capable of winning it.

Chapter Eleven

Following their boating excursion, the weather turned rainy for a few days. No one at Amberwood seemed to mind as they got busy preparing for their concert under the direction of Miss Webster with the capable assistance of Miss Fairfax.

Watching the two women in action amused Jasper. Though the governess appeared to defer to Miss Webster in every particular, he suspected she was the driving force behind the project. She assisted in the choice of pieces, helped arrange the order of the program and made certain everyone involved had sufficient practice.

In Jasper's experience, the qualities that made a strong leader often did not include compassion or a sense of fairness, but Evangeline Fairfax possessed both in abundance. The pupils at her charity school would be fortunate indeed to have her in charge of their care. He tried not to regret what *his* children would be losing.

As Margaret Webster immersed herself in preparations for the concert, Jasper was pleased to find that she no longer avoided his company. When they were together she seemed more at ease. He wished he could summon more enthusiasm for her company. She was an attractive, agreeable lady who suited him ideally. Yet he felt no great regret when he could not be with her. He kept hoping his early morning lessons with Miss Fairfax would suggest a cure for his strange apathy, but he was reluctant to raise the subject with her.

The day before the parish fair, the children grew anxious that continued rain might prevent them from going, but the sun came out at last, with every indication that it would return the next day.

When he rose early that morning, Jasper was pleased to see not a single cloud in the pearly dawn sky. Humming the melody of one of the concert pieces, he dressed, shaved and hurried to the nursery. Evangeline Fairfax was already up and waiting for him. Her expressive eyes sparkled with anticipation while her full lips bowed in an eager smile that was quite contagious.

Over coffee they talked about the upcoming fair.

Then, when Jasper expected her to begin his next lesson, Miss Fairfax asked a question he did *not* expect. "Are you certain you have not been hasty in dismissing Miss Brookes as a possible wife?"

Abigail? Jasper began to marshal his arguments against such a match.

But before he could get out a single word, Evangeline Fairfax launched into her rebuttal. "I know she may seem rather…boisterous at times. But that is only because she has been liberated from the scrutiny of her brother's parishioners. Like an overheated engine letting off a little steam, wouldn't you say?"

"Perhaps," Jasper agreed, "but see here…"

Miss Fairfax was not prepared to see anything until she'd had her say. "I believe Miss Brookes could love your children as sincerely as their own dear mother.

And I am certain she would run your household most capably."

Why was she suddenly pushing Abigail Brookes on him when he had decided days ago that Margaret Webster would be the more suitable choice? Did it have anything to do with their difference of opinion about the children coming to live in Manchester? He thought that had all been settled, as well.

Jasper raised his hand to signal his wish to speak. "What you say is true, but as I told you, my feelings toward Abigail are too brotherly for marriage. Besides, I fear she might be too strong-willed to be a harmonious match for me. I have enough trouble fighting tradition, greed and prejudice among the other mill owners. I do not need conflict at home, as well."

He expected Miss Fairfax to understand his reasoning, but instead it seemed to vex her. "I find it hard to fathom why a man who works so hard to make his workers *less* downtrodden is so anxious to subdue his wife."

Her charge offended his sense of fairness. "You are twisting my words, Miss Fairfax. It is *because* I would not wish to subdue her that I rejected the possibility of a match with Abigail. Miss Webster, on the other hand, would not need to be subdued since her opinions harmonize naturally with mine.

"Why are you suddenly so concerned with Abigail?" he continued before she could argue. "You did not object when I first dismissed the idea of courting her."

"That is because I was not fully aware of her situation," Miss Fairfax replied. "And how many people's future happiness depends on her finding a husband."

"What people?" he demanded. "And why does their happiness depend on Abigail getting married?"

"Her brother and Verity Dawson, of course." Miss

Fairfax sounded impatient with his lack of perception. "The vicar cannot afford to take a wife while he has to support his sister. It is plain that he and Mrs. Dawson are in love, but the poor woman has no fortune."

Jasper wondered how he had failed to notice what seemed so obvious to Miss Fairfax. "I will talk to Norton and ask what I can do to help…short of marrying his sister, that is."

When Miss Fairfax looked as if she meant to continue arguing, he cut her off. "It will not do, my dear. Much as I care for my friend, I cannot trade his happiness for my children's."

"I do not believe your children would be unhappy with Abigail Brookes for a mother." Her tone made the statement sound more like a fact than an opinion.

Jasper shook his head. "Children cannot be happy if their parents are always at odds, especially sensitive children like Emma and Owen. You may not understand that if your parents got on well together, but I assure you it is true."

The governess flinched, as if he had thrown the dregs of his cold coffee in her face. "Did your parents not get on well…before…?"

He gave a grunt of laughter as bitter as bile. Then he stared into the black pool at the bottom of his cup. "They fought like cats and dogs over everything and nothing. Being poor only made it worse."

He had not thought about that in years. The devastation of the fire seemed to have drawn a curtain between his early life and everything that came after. He was not certain what brought it back to him now, except that he did not want Evangeline Fairfax to think him unreasonable. He trusted that she, of all people, would understand what deep scars early experiences could leave upon a person's heart.

She did not reply right away. Perhaps she was trying to digest what he had told her.

At last, in a very quiet voice, she asked, "Is that part of the reason you try to ease the burden of poverty on your workers—to relieve the strain on their families?"

Jasper gave a slow nod. "I never thought of it that way, but I suppose so. It is ironic that trying to relieve that strain on my workers led to more in *my* marriage."

Miss Fairfax's bewildered look compelled him to say more than he'd meant to. "My father-in-law had made his fortune by the time Susan was born. He was determined to give her everything he'd never had, which made her accustomed to getting her own way."

He had loved his late wife and it pained him to speak ill of her, but he needed Evangeline Fairfax to understand why he was resolved to have a different kind of marriage this time. "You may not recall the tension between us in that last year. I tried as much as possible to keep our disagreements from the children. A person is better able to do that in a house of this size."

"Do what, Papa?" asked Matthew from the boys' bedroom door.

His son's question made Jasper's heart leap into his throat until he realized the boy could not have overheard much beyond that last sentence. He chided himself for speaking of such matters where the children might overhear, as they had more than once before.

He searched for a plausible, benign answer, but before he could think of one, Miss Fairfax came to his aid. "Why, hosting a party for so many guests, of course. Are you looking forward to the fair? I believe we will have a fine day for it."

Matthew nodded as he wiped the sleep from his eyes. "Granny said she would give us each sixpence to spend."

As his son chattered about the plans he and Alfie had made for disposing of their little windfall, Jasper and Miss Fairfax exchanged a long look. He tried to convey his gratitude for her assistance. He hoped she would realize that his disagreement with her was precisely the sort from which he was trying to shield his children.

Organizing five excited children to attend the parish fair kept Evangeline too busy to think a great deal about what their father had said to her that morning. But as the small parade of carriages set out from Amberwood to the village green, her thoughts returned to their early morning conversation.

Mr. Chase was right—she had not been aware of any tensions in his marriage when she first took up her position with his family. She had noticed Mrs. Chase became upset when her husband went away to Manchester. But whatever quarrels or pleading might have taken place before his departure, she'd never suspected.

Perhaps her employer was right to seek a wife who shared his opinions—one with whom he could have a placid marriage. Would being kept away from Manchester be any worse for his children than being raised in a household that seethed with conflict, as had? Possessing a comfortable income did not guarantee a harmonious family life, it only relieved some of the stresses and made differences easier to conceal.

In a strange way, it comforted Evangeline to know that Jasper Chase did not seek to dominate the woman he would marry. He only wanted to protect his children from the domestic strife he had suffered as a young child.

No one would ever guess that part of his past, today, if they watched him lift his children down from the carriage. Evangeline noted the protective way he held them and the tone of affection in his voice when he spoke to them.

When her turn came to alight, Mr. Chase offered her his hand. "Come, Miss Fairfax. You had better have a final word with the children before they scatter to the four corners of the fairground."

He spoke warmly and smiled at her as if they had never known a moment's disagreement. He grasped her hand with firm strength that promised to keep her from falling, yet did not clutch too tight. His touch kindled sparkling warmth that swept through her. When he let go, it felt as if something as vital as light or air had been taken away.

She must put a stop to this foolishness! With determined effort, Evangeline stood erect and imagined herself clad in an invisible suit of armor. Jasper Chase had told her plainly that he could not care for a strong-willed woman like her and he had told her why. Though she sympathized with his reasons, she could not change her nature for him or any man. Besides, she had important work to do.

"Children!" She clapped her hands to summon her pupils…and perhaps to quench the last embers of warmth their father's touch had ignited. "I do not want any of you going off by yourselves. Make certain you stay in the company of at least one of our guests at all times. Now, go have fun!"

The children scattered like autumn leaves before a

brisk wind. Joining their father's guests, they flitted from one bunting-decked stall to another.

Evangeline made a leisurely circuit of the fairground, keeping an eye on as many of them as possible. She took vicarious enjoyment in theirs even as she tried to ignore their father. Jasper Chase escorted Miss Webster around the various displays, accompanied by Emma and Miss Anstruther.

The latter seemed desperate to divert Mr. Chase's attention from his chosen companion by any means necessary. She made a great fuss over Emma, who appeared to find her pretense of interest uncomfortable. At last the child went off with Rosie and Miss Leveson to watch a puppet show. Miss Anstruther showed no interest in accompanying her but continued to trail after Mr. Chase and Miss Webster like a perfect gooseberry.

Evangeline vowed she would never make herself so ridiculous by pursuing a man who clearly had no interest in her. She should not pay the slightest attention to Jasper Chase now that Emma was no longer with him.

Instead, she turned her attention to Matthew and Alfie, who were investigating the wares of a pastry stall with Abigail Brookes. Evangeline wandered close enough to overhear the boys debating the merits of Blackburn cakes over gingerbread. Meanwhile, Owen and Mrs. Dawson were admiring Mr. Brookes's skill at the ring-tossing stall. Mrs. Thorpe, Mrs. Leveson and Mr. Webster sat in the shade sipping cider. Owen soon joined them, leaving the vicar and Mrs. Dawson to stroll off on their own.

A while later, Evangeline was watching Matthew and Alfie take turns tossing a large ball into a bucket, when Miss Anstruther stalked toward her with a stormy look on her face. "You there…governess, you seem to be watching everyone. Where has Verity gone?"

Though she was not well acquainted with Miss Anstruther's companion, Evangeline felt strangely protective of the meek little widow—just as she had of her school friends. Perhaps that was due to the harsh contempt with which she'd seen Verity Dawson treated. If circumstances would not allow the vicar to propose, Evangeline wanted them to enjoy this outing together at least.

She did her best to give a civil answer, but it was not easy after Miss Anstruther's sharp query. "The last I saw Mrs. Dawson, she and the vicar were admiring the needlework displays. Is there anything I can do to assist you?"

The lady turned up her nose at the very idea. "What on earth would I need with a governess? I want Verity to fetch me a cool drink. I mind this heat dreadfully."

Evangeline thought the temperature quite pleasant. But she could not deny the other woman's face had grown painfully red in spite of the parasol she held in one hand while fluttering her fan with the other.

Without a word of thanks, Miss Anstruther marched off in the direction Evangeline had indicated, like a battleship in full sail.

What could have put her in such a foul temper? Evangeline wondered. Had Mr. Chase finally made it clear he did not have the slightest interest in courting her? Whatever had vexed her, Miss Anstruther would likely take it out on poor Verity once she found her.

Evangeline glanced around to make certain all her pupils were in the company of an adult then she set off after the lady at a discreet distance. She was not certain what she meant to do, but she felt compelled to be on hand in case Verity needed her.

After a brief search, Miss Anstruther caught up with her companion and the vicar standing at the edge of the fairground in quiet conversation.

"I have been looking for you, Verity." Her fan flapped fast enough to raise a gale. "Why are you hiding away like this when you should be attending to my comfort?"

"I was not hiding." Verity Dawson offered a feeble protest. Her eyes were downcast and her cheeks flushed. "I didn't think you would want me following you and Mr. Chase."

Her mild contradiction seemed to inflame Miss Anstruther. "Of course you didn't think. You never do! I could have swooned from the heat for all you would notice. Instead, you are throwing yourself at the head of a man who feels nothing for you but pity."

Verity Dawson shrank from the woman as if her sharp tongue were a switch and every word bit deep into tender flesh.

"N-now see here," the vicar stammered. It was clear he wanted to defend Verity but was unaccustomed to confronting such a forceful opponent.

Penelope Anstruther dismissed him with a flick of her fan. "Do not try to be gallant, sir. It is obvious you cannot afford to marry a penniless nobody like Verity. If you had any sense you would pursue Miss Webster. At least she could improve your situation."

Even from some distance away, Evangeline could see Verity's lower lip begin to tremble. Outrage blazed through her in a way she had not felt since her school days. She could not bear to see the vicar and Verity bullied by this spiteful woman.

She flew to stand between them and their tormentor. "That is enough, Miss Anstruther! Request your companion's assistance if you must, but there is no need to insult her and the vicar in that way."

Miss Anstruther's nostrils flared. "How dare you speak to me that way? This is no business of yours. Even if it were, you are little better than a servant, while I am a guest in your master's house."

Evangeline refused to be intimidated. "I dare speak to you because it is the truth and it needs saying. You are a fine one to accuse Verity of throwing herself at a man's head. You have been doing it to Mr. Chase for days with far less encouragement than Mr. Brookes has given her. Everyone else in the party knows he would rather wed any of the other ladies than you."

Penelope Anstruther's color deepened from red to a shade nearly purple. "That is not... I never threw myself... You have no right..."

Her flustered stammer made it clear she was not accustomed to being confronted, especially by someone she considered her inferior.

By contrast, Evangeline strove to control her agitated emotions and speak with firm reason, as she would to one of her pupils if they misbehaved. "If you wish to attract a husband in future, I suggest you mind your temper and your tongue."

"Is there some difficulty?" The sound of Jasper Chase's resonant voice made Evangeline realize what she had just done and the embarrassment she might have caused him. "I heard raised voices."

She spun around to see him approaching. His bold features were tensed in a look of concern.

His appearance seemed to restore Miss Anstruther's power of speech.

"There most certainly is a difficulty, sir. I have never been so abominably insulted by this *governess* of yours." She infused the word with scathing contempt, as if Evangeline's profession was somehow disgraceful. "If any servant of mine dared to speak to a guest in my house with such insolence, I would dismiss them on the spot."

"Are you suggesting I do the same?" The fierce scowl on Mr. Chase's face made Evangeline fear he might.

She had no cause to fear for her future, like most women in her position, yet Evangeline regretted not having handled this situation with greater tact. Her vigorous defense of Verity might only make the poor woman's situation worse. Besides that, she was sorry to have embarrassed her employer.

The possibility that Jasper Chase might think ill of her dismayed Evangeline more than she could bear.

Dismiss Evangeline Fairfax? Jasper could not conceive of any action he would find more abhorrent. He had overheard enough of her exchange with Miss Anstruther to realize she had been defending Norton and Mrs. Dawson, the way the governess had once defended her school friends.

Admiration for Evangeline flared within him. He fought a bewildering urge to seize her and kiss her soundly. Was that because such a gesture might shock Miss Anstruther out of her wits…or could it be something more?

One thing he did know, with startling certainty, was that his children had been incredibly fortunate to have her example all these years. The way they'd reacted to hearing about conditions in the cotton industry showed they had learned well from it. Would his plan to keep them sheltered at Amberwood undermine the vital lessons they had absorbed from their governess?

Those thoughts rushed through his mind as Jasper came between the two women. He scarcely heard Penelope Anstruther's spiteful diatribe beyond her repeated demands to send Evangeline packing, which infuriated him. "I am sorry Miss Fairfax was forced to speak to you as she did. Since I might have said precisely the same things in her place, I cannot think of dismissing her. I would feel the same even if she were not essential to the happiness of my family."

"You defend this insolent creature?" Miss Anstruther blustered. "This insult is not to be borne! Come, Verity. We are leaving at once. I refuse to spend another night among such disobliging, ill-bred people."

With a poisonous glare at Jasper and Evangeline, she stalked away.

The beginning of a sob burst from Mrs. Dawson's lips but was swiftly stifled. Head bowed and shoulders slumped, she followed with obvious reluctance.

Had he and Evangeline made matters worse for the poor lady by trying to defend her? If so, Jasper regretted it, but what else could he have done? He had no intention of parting with his children's governess a moment before he must and certainly not at the bidding of Penelope Anstruther!

"Wait!" cried Norton. The poor man looked torn in several directions at once, as if his heart were being drawn and quartered. "Verity, please, I cannot bear to see you go away with that insufferable woman."

Penelope Anstruther turned back toward the vicar with a scornful sneer. "You should mind your tongue, sir. Of course Verity must come with me. She has nowhere else to go and there is nothing you can do about it."

For a moment Jasper feared his friend would falter in the face of such caustic contempt. But after a brief struggle, he straightened to his full, lofty stature and spoke in a ringing tone that would have sounded impressive from a pulpit. "Indeed there is something I can do and I intend to do it."

His long legs bore him swiftly to Mrs. Dawson then flexed to lower him before her on one knee. "My dear Verity, will you do me the honor of becoming my wife? I can offer you little by way of material comforts, but I promise that as long as I live, you will always be treasured and treated with the kindness you deserve."

Before her companion could reply, Miss Anstruther gave a derisive sniff. "Even Verity has more sense than to give up the advantages I can provide to make her home with a penniless clergyman and his hoyden of a sister."

The way Norton winced at her words made it clear they echoed his worst fear.

Jasper glanced toward Evangeline to find her staring at him intently. In her eyes he glimpsed an unspoken plea to intervene on behalf of the other couple. Much as he wanted to oblige her, he could not. Some intuition warned him that if their union was to succeed, they must both be willing to fight for it.

Unfortunately, life seemed to have beaten all the fight out of Verity Dawson long ago.

Or had it? Something in her bearing as she turned to answer Miss Anstruther made Jasper wonder if he'd been mistaken.

"Advantages?" She spoke the word in a mocking imitation of the other woman's scornful tone. "What do those advantages signify without respect or affection? I do not believe Miss Brookes is a hoyden and

even if she were, I would far rather live with a hoyden than a…a…shrew!"

Miss Anstruther's features went slack with shock. Then she gave a shriek of vexation and flounced off.

Verity turned her attention back to Norton, who looked suddenly hopeful. "Dear Mr. Brookes, I hope you have not proposed out of pity for my situation. I could not bear to be a burden to you."

Norton clasped her hand. "I beg you, let there be no talk of pity or burdens between us. I believe with all my heart that any burdens I bear in this life will only be lightened by your support…and love."

The lady inhaled a deep breath and braced her shoulders. "In that case, it will be my honor to marry you, Mr. Brookes."

Norton surged to his feet and raised both her hands to his lips. "You have made me the happiest man in the world!"

His long face glowed with joy. Yet Jasper detected a faint ripple of anxiety in his friend's eyes. Was he wondering how he would support a sister *and* a wife on his modest living, not to mention provide for children if they were so blessed?

"Congratulations, my friend!" Jasper swept toward the newly engaged pair. "I insist Mrs. Dawson stay at Amberwood as my guest until you are able to arrange the wedding."

"Thank you, sir." Verity Dawson looked astonished to be treated with such civility. "That is very kind of you indeed. I hope we have not spoiled your party by causing Miss Anstruther to leave."

Jasper shook his head. "I doubt her going will cast a pall over the festivities. Quite the opposite, I should think. Besides, it was I who provoked her to leave, not you."

Evangeline stepped forward to offer her congratulations. Then she said, "If you will excuse me, I must go check that the children have not sickened themselves on sweets."

"We should rejoin the party, as well," said Norton. "I want to share our happy news with Abigail. I am certain she will be delighted for us."

Seeing them so happy together made Jasper anxious to recapture similar joy…but not with Margaret Webster.

He offered Evangeline his arm. "Miss Fairfax, may I escort you back to the fair?"

"Thank you, sir." She slipped one slender hand through the crook of his elbow to rest lightly on his forearm. "It was good of you not to sack me after the way I spoke to Miss Anstruther. It was not my place to lecture one of your guests."

"I hope you did not believe there was any danger of that!" Jasper found it difficult to muster a coherent reply because so much of his awareness was concentrated on the touch of her hand. It filled him with a strange sweet lightness, like the froth on a mug of fresh cider. "As for your *place,* it is always the place of a true Christian to speak in defense of those who are being ill treated. I thought you were quite magnificent."

Her face lit up in a smile so radiant it made him long to…do something very foolish indeed. "You acquitted yourself well, too. If she had not behaved so badly, I might feel sorry for Miss Anstruther."

"Let us hope she will heed some of what was said to her and mend her ways. I fear Mrs. Thorpe may be vexed with me for making her goddaughter leave the party."

Evangeline chuckled. "If your mother-in-law scolds you, I promise I will come to your defense."

"Will you?" Imagining the scene made Jasper grin from ear to ear. "Then I reckon I have nothing to worry about."

They strolled back to rejoin the crowd still enjoying a fine summer day's entertainment. From the audience thronged around the puppet show, Margaret Webster waved to them.

Evangeline tensed and released Jasper's arm. "You should join Miss Webster and the girls. I must go find out what Matthew and Alfie are up to."

Before he could protest, she disappeared into the crowd, leaving his arm with a faint ache that he fancied only her touch could relieve.

Chapter Twelve

Jasper Chase had offered her his arm and told her she was *magnificent* for standing up to Miss Anstruther. The memory made Evangeline break into a furtive smile every time she recalled it that evening. Through the night, she relived that moment in her dreams.

Reason warned her that such a trivial incident should not mean so much to her. She tried to banish it from her thoughts with the familiar litany that Jasper did not want a wife like her and she did not want a husband of any kind.

But those convictions seemed to have lost their protective power. In their place came new ideas that intrigued and unsettled her. For instance, how pleasant it had felt to have someone she could rely on to come to *her* aid. Though Jasper claimed to want a submissive wife, she was not certain he truly did. There had been nothing submissive about the way she had confronted Miss Anstruther. Yet he had not rebuked her for it. If anything, he seemed to admire her more.

If she had required any further proof that he did not hold her actions against her, Jasper appeared in the nursery as usual the next morning, looking altogether too handsome.

"Drink your coffee quickly." He poured himself a cup and took a deep draft. "I have asked Jane to keep an eye on the children while we take a walk."

Evangeline strove to moderate her reaction to his words, but she could not keep her heart from bounding. "Do we have a sensitive subject to discuss?"

Jasper nodded. "About Norton and Mrs. Dawson. I thought you would want to know."

"Indeed I do." Evangeline was delighted with the match between Verity and Mr. Brookes, who reminded her of her soft-spoken, scholarly father. "I hope they can find a way to live in some comfort without having to marry off his sister, when she would prefer to earn her own living."

Jasper's head snapped up. "She would? How do you know that?"

"She told me so." Evangeline drained her cup and rose to her feet. "Miss Brookes would like to work as a governess, but her brother will not hear of it. Something to do with their mother."

Jane appeared just then. Though she tried to look as if it were a common occurrence for her employer and the governess to take early morning strolls together, Evangeline wondered if the nursery maid had commented about it below stairs.

"I will fetch my bonnet." Evangeline hurried off before Jane noticed the color in her cheeks and guessed more about her feelings than she could bear.

She returned as soon as she had tied on her bonnet… and her blush had faded. She knew it was not right for her to feel so elated about going off with Jasper on her own. She was trying to make a match between him and another woman, after all. Indeed, she had no business thinking of him by his Christian name. She was not certain when it had begun, only that she could not seem to stop herself now.

The countryside was swathed in mist when they emerged from the house, but the sky had a pearly glow that promised the haze would soon burn off.

Evangeline was grateful for the veil of mist that wrapped around her and Jasper, hiding them from curious eyes. It created an appealing illusion that they were in their own private world without obligations, plans or expectations.

"Did Miss Anstruther's departure make the atmosphere at dinner very awkward last night?" She hoped not. In spite of Jasper's insistence to the contrary, she felt responsible for provoking the unpleasant breach of his house party.

"My mother-in-law was rather dismayed." He did not sound troubled by Mrs. Thorpe's reaction. "But the rest of the party seemed happier for her absence. Norton and Mrs. Dawson announced their engagement, which put everyone in good spirits."

"Even his sister?"

"*Especially* his sister. She likes Mrs. Dawson and after what you have told me, she may assume her brother will be forced to let her earn her own living now. I wonder…" Jasper's voice trailed off.

"You wonder…?" Evangeline prompted him.

"Whether Abigail might consider filling your position at Amberwood," he continued in a bemused tone. "The children like her and Norton might be less resistant to her becoming a governess if it would help us out."

That did sound like a reasonable solution for everyone. Yet more than ever it troubled Evangeline to think of someone else taking her place at Amberwood—even someone as agreeable as Abigail Brookes. Could she command the respect a governess needed, after having been more of a playmate to the children?

Another idea occurred to her. "Perhaps Miss Brookes could come and teach at my school. Her brother might mind that less than having her become a private governess. It would benefit our pupils to have a teacher with her high spirits. My friends had wanted Leah Shaw to help me run the school, for precisely that reason. But then Leah married the duke."

"Leah?" Jasper repeated the name in a puzzled tone. "Wasn't she also one of your friends at the charity school who became a governess?"

"We all did," she replied. "Teaching is one of the few respectable means for a woman to earn her own living, however modest."

Her answer did nothing to dispel Jasper's puzzled look. "A charity pupil turned governess married to a duke?"

Evangeline nodded. "You may be amazed that Leah wed so well, but I am more surprised that she wed *at all*. I thought she valued her independence too much to be tied down that way. But she sounds happy in her letters. So do the others, though that surprises me less. Rebecca, Marian, Grace and Hannah were all well suited to marriage. I never expected they would make such advantageous matches, but I am delighted for them."

She pressed her lips closed to prevent a further rush of words. She had not meant to go on at such length.

But Jasper did not appear to mind. Indeed, he seemed to be listening most intently. When she paused, he did not seize the opportunity to turn the conversation back to Verity and Mr. Brookes. Instead, he asked, "Do you ever envy your friends the happiness they have found?"

"Never," she insisted. "My friends deserve all the security, comfort and happiness it is possible for women to be blessed with."

"Perhaps *envy* is the wrong word." Jasper's steps slowed as he searched for the right one. "What I meant to say was, do you never wish you could experience that sort of happiness for yourself? A home of your own, the love of a husband and children?"

Did she dare answer his question honestly? Evangeline feared not. More and more of late, she had begun to yearn for precisely those things—the love of a husband, especially. But not just any husband. Were such feelings a test to prove she was worthy to do the work for which the Lord intended her?

How could she think of letting down her friends who were depending on her, the orphan girls who needed her? Not to mention her late mother, who'd been so certain she was destined for some important task in life?

"I told you, my friends were well suited to marriage." She chose her words with care so she could speak the truth without betraying her feelings. "I am not and never have been envious of their marriages. I was meant for a different life."

"But not meant to be happy?" he asked in a tone of wistful pity that rasped against her pride. "I cannot believe the Lord intends you for that."

"Who says I will not be happy?" Evangeline bristled, though she feared it might be true. Now that her feelings for Jasper Chase had been roused, could she ever be truly happy if she were parted from him and the children? But his probing questions compelled her to deny it. "I expect to be very happy doing such valuable work and making a difference in the lives of so many children. I expect to be happy fulfilling the purpose for which I have been preparing all this time."

She cast a fleeting glance at Jasper as he walked by her side, not certain she was persuading either of them.

She made one final effort. "Do you think it would make me happier to give up all my hopes and plans to subject myself to the will of a husband? We would be at odds all the time. You told me yourself that can only lead to unhappiness."

As they walked, the hem of her skirts grew increasingly damp from the wet grass, until she fancied it weighing her down.

She expected Jasper to contradict her. That would prove she was right that they would be in constant conflict. Yet some traitorous part of her wanted him to persuade her that marriage could bring her happiness rather than regret.

But Jasper did not reply. Perhaps he realized she was right.

"Why are we wasting time talking about me?" she demanded. "You wanted to tell me something about Verity and Mr. Brookes. Was it only the announcement of their engagement?"

Jasper came to a halt and stared at her until she met his eye. "Talking about you is *never* a waste of time."

As they stood there in the mist, Evangeline felt the weight of unspoken words settling over them. She clamped her lips shut to keep from breaking their silence.

Just when she feared she would betray herself, Jasper turned and began walking back the way they had come. "There *was* something more I wanted to tell you about our friends. I invited Norton to help me with my work at New Hope Mills. He can preach to my workers and assist me in tending to their welfare. Perhaps he can take a few of the brighter boys to teach, the way Parson Ward did."

"Only the boys?" Evangeline muttered.

Jasper might not have heard her, or perhaps he did not want to start another argument between them. "I cannot pay Norton a large salary, but more than the living from his current parish. He seems eager to be involved."

Her happiness for Verity and Mr. Brookes soothed Evangeline's wrought-up emotions. "I am certain the vicar will be a great help to you."

"I expect so," Jasper replied. "What I did not expect was the renewed enthusiasm I feel for my work at the mill, knowing I will have his support. I only wish I had thought to ask him sooner."

Though she knew such a collaboration would benefit Mr. Brookes, Jasper and especially his employees at New Hope Mills, the thought of it gave Evangeline a wistful pang. She wished it had been possible for her and Leah Shaw to run the new charity school together, the way their friends had hoped. No doubt the two of them would have disagreed on occasion in a way Jasper clearly abhorred. But they would have supported one another all the same, as they had during their younger years. Even their disputes might have resulted in valuable compromise, to the benefit of their pupils.

"Why did you bring me out here to tell me that?" Evangeline nodded toward the house, the shape of which grew clearer with each step they took. "It is not a subject that should trouble the children if they happened to overhear. They like Mr. Brookes and Verity and their engagement is a happy event."

Jasper pondered his reply a good deal longer than he should have needed to. "I did not want them to hear me talking about the mill and start pestering me to take them to Manchester."

His explanation was perfectly reasonable, yet Evangeline sensed it might not be altogether true.

Of course, he had not wanted his children getting any more troublesome ideas about moving down to Manchester. So Jasper insisted to himself as he and Evangeline returned to the house. But that was not the chief reason he had invited her for an early morning stroll. Now that he had become aware of the true nature of his feelings for the lady, he wanted to spend time alone with her, without fear of being overheard or interrupted.

He had secretly hoped that telling her of his friend's engagement might provide an opportunity to speak of his feelings and inquire about hers. But when the subject of marriage came up, Evangeline's emphatic declaration was not at all what he'd hoped for. She had insisted she would never marry, least of all to an overbearing man like him.

She had not referred to him by name, of course. But when she spoke of having to subject herself to the will of a husband, he knew who she meant. Had she sensed his altered feelings toward her and tried to discourage him? If so, she did not know his character as well as she often seemed to. He had not risen to be master of his own mill by being easily discouraged from going after what he wanted.

And he wanted Evangeline Fairfax to be his wife—he grew more certain of the fact with every passing hour.

Watching her with his children as they ate breakfast

together, he could see the special way she interacted with each of them. He sensed how much they meant to her and how hard it would be for her to leave them. So why should she have to?

Her friends had all found happiness with families of their own. Why did they not encourage Evangeline to do likewise, after all she had done for them? No matter how valuable their contributions to the group might have been, she was the one who had brought them together. Had they appreciated her leadership, as she deserved, or had they secretly resented it? Might that be why they wanted her to operate the school endowed by their husbands—so she would be obliged to take orders from them?

Rosie jarred her father from his brooding by scrambling onto his lap and flinging her arms around his neck.

Much as her actions surprised Jasper, her words did even more. "Have we done something wrong, Papa? If we did, we're very sorry."

He wrapped his daughter in a reassuring embrace. "You've done nothing wrong at all. What put such a notion in your head?"

He cast a swift glance around the table at Rosie's brothers and sister to find them all staring at him with anxious expressions.

"You did look angry about something, Papa," Owen informed him in a solemn tone.

"Did I?" Jasper knew it must be true. When he recalled his thoughts about Evangeline's friends, his features began to tense. He struggled to raise a smile instead. "If I did, you may be certain none of you was responsible."

He sensed the children would only believe him if

he offered another explanation. "I was thinking about something unfair—a person who deserves much more from life than they are getting, a person whose friends may have imposed on them. It made me quite indignant on their behalf. I am sorry if I troubled you."

Jasper did not dare glance at Evangeline in case she guessed he was referring to her.

Emma had other ideas. "You mean, Mrs. Dawson, don't you, Papa? Miss Anstruther was supposed to be her friend but she did not treat her very well."

The other children nodded. Jasper had not realized they were aware of such subtleties in the behavior of his guests. Then again, Penelope Anstruther had not been particularly subtle.

Before he could decide how to answer, Matthew piped up. "You sent her away, didn't you, Papa, because she was so disagreeable to Mrs. Dawson?"

Jasper answered in a gentle but decisive tone. "I did not send Miss Anstruther away. The decision to leave was hers, though I cannot claim I am sorry to see her go. People who put upon others do not endear themselves to anyone. We would all do well to bear that in mind."

The children digested his advice with looks as solemn as Owen's. It made Jasper determined to raise their spirits. "I have some good news to share. Mr. Brookes and Mrs. Dawson have gotten engaged. That means they will be getting married quite soon."

He avoided any mention of the happy couple taking up residence in Manchester after the wedding. "I thought we could make the concert Miss Webster is organizing a celebration of their happy news."

His mention of the concert seemed to cheer his children more than news of Norton's engagement. Perhaps they did not understand how happy an event marriage could be. Certainly their governess would not have praised the benefits of matrimony.

How could he make her see that marriage and family life might be every bit as rewarding as running a charity school? Perhaps he should employ the lessons she had taught him. He must court her without appearing to court her. If she suspected his intentions before he succeeded in winning her heart, Jasper feared she would shut him out and he would never get another opportunity.

That evening, after he had heard his children's prayers and kissed them good-night, he turned toward Evangeline. "No doubt you are aware there is a small assembly hall in the village where they have dancing on Mondays and Thursdays."

"So I have been informed, sir." She replied without hesitation, though she seemed surprised by his remark. "Why do you ask?"

Jasper found he no longer liked her calling him *sir.* It emphasized the difference in their positions when he preferred to concentrate on the many things they had in common. "I plan to attend the assembly tomorrow evening with my guests and I would like you to accompany us."

"Me?" Her nose wrinkled in a way Jasper found rather endearing. "But why? It is not as though your party is short of ladies. Quite the contrary. Besides, there are some who might object to the inclusion of a mere governess at such an event."

In spite of her objections, Jasper glimpsed a golden sparkle in her brown eyes that made him suspect she secretly wanted to go. "I believe the only person who might have opposed the idea is no longer with us."

Evangeline strove to stifle a grin but did not quite succeed.

"Besides," he continued, sensing her receptiveness and wanting to take advantage of it, "apart from my mother-in-law and me, all the members of our party are strangers here. Your assistance in making introductions would be invaluable."

"I suppose…"

"There is another reason I would like you to come," he said. "You have borne a tremendous responsibility in my household during the past six years. I have no doubt you will bear even more as headmistress of your charity school. You deserve to enjoy yourself for one evening, surely?"

Did Evangeline realize that she deserved this and so much more? Or had her years in that miserable school made her believe otherwise?

"Please!" he concluded before she could raise any further objections. "Say you will come."

Her stalwart gaze faltered before his. Did she glimpse something in his eyes that she did not want to see?

"Very well," she replied. "If you wish me to accompany you."

"I do," said Jasper. "Very much."

At that moment, he wished for something else, too—a kiss from her full, generous lips. But he knew it was far too soon and this was not the right place. He would not risk spoiling his chances by acting prematurely. His years in business had taught him how to bide his time until the right opportunity presented itself then act decisively when it did. He must apply those hard-learned lessons to his pursuit of Evangeline.

"Until then." He made a courtly bow and withdrew before his romantic inclinations overcame his prudence.

Jasper headed down to join his guests in the dining room with a jaunty step and a mysterious smile upon his lips. Winning a wonderful but reluctant woman like Evangeline Fairfax would be a challenge, without a doubt.

But he had always relished a challenge.

Evangeline could scarcely recall the last time she had danced at an assembly. Certainly it was well before she'd come to Amberwood. Though she enjoyed dancing, she had resigned herself to avoiding such entertainments. She had not wanted another gentleman like Mr. Preston to get the mistaken idea that she wished to be courted.

But, as Jasper had reminded her, she would soon be safely ensconced at her school with no further need to be concerned about such matters. What would it hurt to enjoy this one evening before she took up her new responsibilities?

Her sense of caution warned that it might not be wise to mix socially with a man who appealed to her as much as Jasper Chase did. Particularly since the children would not be there to occupy her attention and act as a buffer between them.

She dismissed those qualms with a confident toss of her head. Their discussion about marriage had reinforced her priorities and made her view her situation in a clear, rational light. While it was true she felt more for Jasper Chase than she had ever expected or wanted to feel for any man, she knew there could be no possibility of a future together.

Even if she had been willing to give up the important task for which life had prepared her, she could never be the kind of wife he wanted. He had found that woman in Margaret Webster. Evangeline now recognized that her earlier reservations about the lady's suitability had sprung from unworthy jealousy, which she had no right to entertain. Having rededicated herself to founding a new charity school, she must renew her efforts to foster a match between Jasper and Miss Webster. An evening event, with no children to supervise, might provide the perfect opportunity to further her matchmaking efforts.

Having made up her mind about that, Evangeline seized a chance that presented itself when the children were in the great parlor, practicing for the concert.

"Is there some difficulty, Miss Webster?" she asked when she noticed the lady frowning over a neatly written list of the performers.

Margaret Webster sighed. "Say what you will about Miss Anstruther, she did have a fine voice. Her absence has left a few holes in our program."

"Surely you can sing in her place," Evangeline suggested. "Or, better yet, you and Mr. Chase could perform a duet. I happen to know he sings very well. I have heard him often in church."

It dismayed her to recall that she would soon lose the opportunity to stand near him in the family pew and drink in the rich resonance of his baritone voice. But she resolutely put that thought out of her mind.

"Will you, Mr. Chase?" Margaret Webster called over to Jasper, who was helping Alfie memorize his recitation.

"I suppose I could," he replied, "provided the song is not too difficult."

"I will play for you," Evangeline offered as another idea occurred to her. "I agree with Mr. Chase that the song must be one all three of us know."

She paused, pretending to consider the possibilities.

"I have it! You must both be familiar with 'Ellen the Fair.' It is an ideal choice for celebrating an engagement."

Unlike most popular love ballads, it was not too long and it had a happy ending. If anything could stir tender feelings between Jasper and Miss Webster, surely it was singing a love song together.

At first neither of them seemed as receptive to the idea as she'd hoped, but Evangeline managed to persuade them. "Here is the music. Why don't we have a quick practice now?"

Before either of them could object, she sat down at the pianoforte and began to play.

Though she congratulated herself on her well-executed plan, Evangeline was not prepared for the spasm that wrung her heart when she heard Jasper sing to another woman, *"And while I stood gazing, my heart, I declare, a captive was taken by Ellen the Fair."*

Her fingers fumbled over the keys, making a sour discord with Jasper's melodious voice. Rosie put her hands over her ears.

Alfie wagged his finger at his governess in an impudent imitation of the way she sometimes chided him. "You must concentrate on what you are doing, Miss Fairfax, and not let your mind wander."

Evangeline made a face at Alfie, but she took his advice and kept her thoughts firmly focused on the keys for the rest of the song.

When the piece concluded, a burst of hearty applause rang out and Mr. Webster cried, "Well done, indeed! I have always been partial to that old song. Your voices blend so well, I have no doubt it will be the high point of the concert!"

"It was Miss Fairfax's choice, Papa." Margaret Webster made it sound as if Evangeline deserved all the credit for their performance.

"She is a clever lady," the mill owner replied, "even if her playing is not quite up to your standard, my dear."

Though Evangeline could not deny Mr. Webster's comment, it still stung more than she cared to admit.

But his words scarcely had a chance to sink in before Jasper spoke. "That is hardly a fair comparison, sir. Miss Fairfax had no opportunity to rehearse the piece before she played it just now. With five children to educate, I cannot think when she ever finds time to practice."

It warmed Evangeline to hear him rise so quickly to her defense. Yet she feared Miss Webster might take offense that her suitor had challenged a compliment to her.

The lady proved more generous-spirited than Evangeline had expected…or deserved. "Mr. Chase is right, Papa. I have all the time in the world to devote to my music. Miss Fairfax has hardly any, yet she still manages to play and sing beautifully."

Her kind words made Evangeline ashamed of the selfish doubts she had expressed about Miss Webster's suitability to wed Jasper Chase. Clearly, the lady would make him a better wife than someone like her ever could. Yet that did not ease the ache in her heart when she looked to the future and pictured Margaret Webster at the heart of his home, while she took up her fulfilling but lonely post as the headmistress of her school.

Chapter Thirteen

That evening, as Jasper waited for his guests to assemble for their drive to the village, each of his internal organs seemed agitated in its own strange way.

His heart felt as if something had jarred it out of its reliable beat into a faster, more complex rhythm. His lungs performed their accustomed function, yet he found himself acutely conscious of every breath he drew, as if he could no longer take it for granted. His stomach tumbled about like a barrel rolling down a steep hill and he was not convinced his liver was behaving as it ought to.

His thoughts were every bit as unsettled, flitting from the past to the future and back again, scarcely aware of what was taking place in the present.

When his gaze fell on the pianoforte, he pictured Evangeline sitting at it, playing that love song. Though he had sung the words to Margaret Webster, who was as fair as the subject of the ballad, his heart had dwelled on the vivid russet loveliness of Evangeline.

Unlike the shallow nobleman in the song, Jasper was drawn to far more than her beauty. Indeed, he had scarcely noticed how attractive she was until he'd recently awoken to her many other admirable qualities. Evangeline Fairfax was clever and accomplished, brimming with leadership ability that *inspired* others to follow her rather than compelling them. Yet she had a warm, nurturing side, as well as an unexpected sense of fun.

More than any woman he'd ever met, she shared his compassion for anyone being kept down or mistreated. With her, compassion was not a passive, sentimental emotion, but an urgent call to right wrongs and improve people's lives. Was there a way he could make her see that *she* was a far better match for him than any of the others she'd tried to make?

While he was pondering that question, Evangeline slipped into the parlor with an air of discretion that did not apologize for her presence nor seek to call attention to it. Jasper was not certain she could avoid the latter. To him, she eclipsed every other lady in the room without the slightest effort. How could he have been so blind for so long to the treasure he'd harbored under his roof?

During her first year, it must have been his love for his wife that had prevented him from noticing any other woman. After Susan's death, grief and perhaps guilt had wrapped around him like a private fog, making it impossible to see a great many things. Lately, he had immersed himself so deeply in his work that he'd had no time to notice anything else except his children. Now he wished he'd noticed Evangeline before her friends had recruited her to run their charity school.

Jasper's practical nature silenced his regrets. There was no use wasting time on what might have been. He must act at once to discover whether she might feel more for him than she was willing to admit.

"Miss Fairfax." He approached her and bowed as

if she were an honored guest...which to him she was. "Thank you for agreeing to accompany us this evening. I know I can rely on you to make the necessary introductions for our guests and put them at ease."

She acknowledged his greeting with a confident smile. "I shall do my best, Mr. Chase. I expect the attendance of a number of new ladies will make quite an agreeable sensation at the assembly."

Her comment made Jasper realize that all his guests were assembled. "In that case, we must not keep the local gentlemen waiting."

He led the party to the waiting carriages and helped his mother-in-law into the first one with Mr. Webster, Mrs. Leveson and her daughter. Margaret Webster went in the next vehicle, followed by Norton Brookes, his sister and his fiancée.

When the second carriage pulled away, Jasper turned to Evangeline. "I hope you will not mind bringing up the rear with me in the gig, Miss Fairfax. I always prefer to drive myself when possible."

For an instant she seemed taken aback, but soon mustered her composure enough to rally him. "Given your independent nature, I suppose that should not surprise me. I have no objection to going by gig on such a fine evening. But I feel bound to point out that you should have detained Miss Webster so the two of you could have some time alone on the drive."

"Am I going to fail my courting lessons, then?" A deep chuckle rumbled through Jasper's chest. It settled his agitated organs but seemed to inflate them like air balloons. His chest puffed out and his step took on a buoyant lightness. "Do not fret. I am certain I will have all the time alone I want with Margaret Webster."

Before Evangeline had a chance to figure out what

he meant, he helped her into the gig. Then he climbed up beside her and they drove away into the twilit countryside. Off to the west, the sun was setting in bands of brilliant color over the lake-studded Cumbrian Mountains. To the east, a pearly moon and tiny diamond stars were becoming visible in the black velvet sky over the Pennines.

Jasper wished the drive to the village was longer, but since it was not, he refused to waste precious time admiring the sunset. "You know, Miss Fairfax, now that you will soon be leaving Amberwood, I regret how little I know of you. All these years you have lived under my roof and raised my children, yet so much about you remains a mystery to me."

She replied with a soft rustle of laughter. "I assure you, sir, there is nothing mysterious about me. My life has been quite ordinary. It has held its share of misfortune, but whose has not?"

"Misfortune? Is that what you would call being sent to that wretched charity school?" Jasper stole frequent glances at her as they drove, confident the horse could find its way to the village with little direction from him. "What about your life before that? How did you end up in such a place?"

Evangeline hesitated a moment, then inhaled a breath of calm evening air. "In the same way as most of my fellow pupils, I expect. My father was a clergyman of modest means, whose generosity exceeded his income. My mother died when I was eight years old and my father followed her within a year. They had no relatives able to offer me a home, so I was sent to the Pendergast School."

"Were you close to your mother and father?" Jasper asked. In spite of his parents' rows with each other, he knew they had loved him in their way and wanted the best for him. He was certain they would be proud of what he had done with his life. "What were they like?"

He was not certain Evangeline would reply. This was not the kind of lively conversation that usually preceded an evening of entertainment.

But perhaps she sensed his questions rose from something more than idle curiosity. "Father was a quiet man of deep faith and an inspiring preacher. My mother helped him a great deal with the practical work of the parish—visiting the sick and assisting the poor. From an early age, I accompanied her on her calls. She impressed upon me the importance of serving the Lord by helping others."

"She sounds like a remarkable woman," said Jasper. "What a blessing it must have been for your father to have such a willing partner in his work. How he must have valued her assistance."

Evangeline gave a brief nod. "He relied upon her far more than I knew at the time. I am not certain Father realized it himself, until she was…gone."

Speaking that simple, pain-drenched word, she sounded bereft, as well she might. The loss of someone so capable and compassionate must have left an aching void in the lives of those closest to her. If he and the children lost Evangeline, Jasper sensed it would be as if the heart of Amberwood ceased to beat.

"How did your mother die?" he asked gently, though he could guess.

"Influenza. There was an epidemic of it that winter. Mother insisted I remain at home while she paid her visits so I would not catch it. Father tried to persuade her to stay at home, too, but Mother insisted she could not neglect her duties when she was needed most. She came and went at all hours until the worst was over. Then she fell ill."

"I am sorry to hear it." Jasper wished he could do more than offer flat verbal condolences, twenty years too late. His arms ached to pull Evangeline close until her head rested against his shoulder. "Did your father take ill then, as well?"

"Not then." A soft sigh escaped her. "But he never truly recovered from Mother's death. It was as if he had relied on her so much that he could not figure how to get along without her. Some people claim it is impossible to die of a broken heart, but I have no doubt my father did."

A thought dawned on Jasper just then. He had never been given to analyzing other people's motives, or even his own. Perhaps that was why this unaccustomed insight had such an impact upon him that he could not keep it to himself.

"Was that when you decided you would never marry?" He turned to stare at her, hoping he had discovered the key to overcoming Evangeline's resistance. "Was that *why?* Because you were afraid to care for someone so much that losing him would threaten your very existence?"

It made a kind of sense. Evangeline was not a person to do anything by halves. Any task she set herself, she committed her whole heart and soul, whether it was raising his children, leading her school friends or finding him a wife. If she allowed herself to care for him, Jasper sensed she would hold nothing back. Such all-consuming commitment could be a powerful force... perhaps even dangerous.

It did not occur to him that he should have kept his thoughts to himself until Evangeline stiffened and inhaled a sharp little gasp. When she twisted about to face him, her roses-and-cream complexion was pale as snow, with small livid spots flaming high on each cheek.

Her large brown eyes flashed with sparks of amber lightning that Jasper could make out even in the gathering darkness. "Sir, this conversation is becoming far too personal. I will thank you not to speculate on my motives. They are no business of yours."

The magnitude of his mistake descended on Jasper like an avalanche. "Forgive me, Evangeline! I did not mean to offend you."

Sensing his apology required more than words, he reached for her hand, but she snatched it away. "Let us speak no more of such things! What is the point of becoming closer acquainted when I will soon be leaving your employ. You would do better to deepen your acquaintance with Miss Webster."

There could be no question she was vexed with him, but Jasper glimpsed something else behind her indignant glare. Sadness, perhaps, and…longing? Or did he only imagine a reflection of his own feelings that he wanted to believe she might share?

"It is not Miss Webster I wish to know better!" His vehement declaration violated all the lessons Evangeline had tried to teach him about proper courtship. But at that moment, with her so near and darkness falling around them, Jasper had no further patience for lessons and rules. "It is not Miss Webster I want with me now or to dance this evening away."

Before he could reach his obvious conclusion, Evangeline swept an alarmed glance around them and cried, "Here we are at the assembly! It seemed like a very short drive."

She scrambled out of the gig and dashed away to join

the rest of the party. As he watched her flee with the swift grace of a hind eluding a hunter, Jasper cursed himself under his breath.

But now that he had committed himself this far, he was determined to continue until Evangeline yielded to his suit or persuaded him beyond a doubt that she could never care for him.

She was running away from a man she cared for in a way she had never thought possible—a man who might have been about to declare his feelings for her if only she'd stayed to listen. Did that prove he was right and she was a coward when it came to matters of the heart?

As Evangeline approached the other two carriages, she slowed her steps and forced her racing breath to a less frantic pace. Then she fixed on a smile and tried to put Jasper's challenging questions from her mind.

Mr. Brookes was helping the ladies out of their carriage while Mr. Webster did the same for his fellow passengers. Evangeline found herself intensely aware of the tender glance that passed between the vicar and Verity when he escorted her into the hall. It filled her with a wistful ache that was not envy, only a longing to experience that deep, unspoken connection, which was surely one of humanity's greatest blessings.

This was no time to come over all dreamy and distracted! Evangeline chided herself as sternly as her teachers used to. She had promised to introduce Jasper's guests to his neighbors and put them at ease.

"Come along, ladies." She beckoned Miss Leveson, Miss Webster and Miss Brookes. "Let us not keep the gentlemen waiting."

Her prediction that their arrival would create a sensation soon proved correct. In no time at all, the ladies were surrounded by admirers and had promised the first several dances. Even Evangeline received an invitation and took to the floor with a mixture of relief and trepidation. Having avoided dancing for a good many years, she had to exercise all her powers of concentration to keep from making a fool of herself.

Before long, however, she got caught up in the movement and energy of the other dancers. Her false smile blossomed into a genuine one. By the time she had finished a reel and a country dance, she had pushed her unsettling conversation with Jasper Chase to the back of her mind, where she hoped it would stay.

But when he approached her with a cup of punch, the things he'd said came flooding back again and she could not dismiss them out of hand.

Jasper must have detected signs of alarm in her expression, for he asked, "Have I spoiled any chance that you will speak to me again, let alone do me the honor of a dance?"

"Not entirely." Evangeline reached for the cup of punch he held out to her. "This goes some way to redeem you."

She drank it down with grateful relish.

Jasper grinned, an expression that was as difficult to resist as the punch, for it contained an equally refreshing mixture of sweetness and tang. "If you ever give anyone else lessons in courting, you should add one on the value of providing a beverage at the proper time. I congratulate myself on coming up with it all on my own."

Evangeline tried to keep from smiling back at Jasper in case he took it as encouragement to continue in the vein he had begun earlier. She did not want that.

Or did she?

Duty and caution warned her that she should not. But could her caution be born of fear as Jasper had suggested? She had always prided herself on her stubborn refusal to be ruled by fear. Yet her employer's sudden attention caused her at least as much alarm as elation. It had made her turn tail and run as she never had before the harshest teacher or nastiest bullies at school.

"Thoughtful actions are always a good way to win the regard of others." Inwardly Evangeline winced at her prim, pedantic tone. Clearly she could use lessons in the subtle art of innocent flirtation.

Jasper chuckled as if he believed she meant to banter with him. He nodded toward the dance floor. "I am pleased to see Miss Webster's company is in such demand."

"No wonder." Evangeline watched the lady move with spirited grace through the steps of a longways country dance. "She is beautiful, an excellent dancer and very agreeable company. What more could a partner wish for?"

"I suppose that depends on the partner." Jasper lowered his voice. "She may be many men's idea of an ideal lady. I was inclined to think so, not long ago. But now I know what I truly want. I am pleased you made Miss Webster enough introductions that she will not miss my name from her dance card. That leaves me free to concentrate my attentions…elsewhere."

As his voice fell, he leaned closer to Evangeline, until his murmured words seemed to caress her ear.

The back of her neck prickled with gooseflesh. "That is not why I introduced Miss Webster around!"

"I know," Jasper assured her. "But if you had, I would not be displeased. Now, if, as you claim, I have not spoiled my chance of securing a dance with you,

I would like to request the honor. Will you prove your courage by obliging me?"

Prove her courage? Clearly Jasper knew the perfect means to persuade her to do what he wanted. It was no use pretending she wished to dance with him any less than he with her. But the manner of his request saved her pride a little.

"How can I resist such a challenge?" she asked with an intrepid tilt of her chin.

They left their empty punch cups on a nearby table. Then she took his hand and let him lead her to the dance floor, where a new set was beginning to form.

The warmth of his smile rewarded Evangeline for accepting his invitation, if she had needed any further reward than the pleasure of dancing with him. It kindled a sparkling glow that made her forget where her way-ward feelings could lead if she was not careful. All that mattered was this moment and her joy in his company.

They joined two long lines of men and women facing each other across the floor. Evangeline glimpsed several of Jasper's guests among the other dancers. A swift pang of shame gripped her when she encountered Mr. Webster's reproachful glare. But his daughter did not appear to notice that her suitor was paying considerable attention to another lady. Or was Miss Webster too proud to betray any sign of injured feelings?

The opening chords of the music banished those doubts from Evangeline's mind. Concentrating on the sequence of steps and following the more experienced dancers around her left no room for thoughts of Miss Webster. Her heart was too full of pleasure in Jasper's company to hold a single drop of guilt.

Some of the other dancers took the opportunity to converse at they bowed, crossed and turned, but Evangeline and Jasper did not. Perhaps he sensed that she could not tolerate any distraction or perhaps he also needed to concentrate on the steps he had not performed in a long while. But whenever their eyes met, he smiled at her and his gaze glowed with enjoyment. Whenever he clasped her hand, to bow over it or perform a turn, he gave her fingers a subtle squeeze that suggested a special connection between them. As the dance rollicked to its conclusion, Evangeline felt as if her feet scarcely touched the floor.

After it was over, Jasper applauded and gave a breathless chuckle. "I hope I did not disgrace myself or you too much with my performance."

She shook her head. "No more than I. Are you sorry now that you insisted on taking a turn with me?"

He answered with a look of mock derision tempered with fondness. "If you believe that, you are a good deal less clever than I reckoned."

"I must admit, you did not look sorry." His unexpected attentiveness made her feel light-headed, as if he had spun her around too quickly during the dance. "Indeed, you gave every indication of enjoying yourself."

"That's better." Jasper's eyes focused on her with such intensity, he hardly seemed aware of anyone else in the room. "Your powers of observation do not appear to have suffered, after all. Of course, if you wish to prove that you enjoyed our dance as much as I did, you will consent to join me for another."

"Must everything be a challenge with you?" she teased with a hint of asperity.

Jasper pulled a wry face. "Knowing my competitive nature, does that surprise you?"

Evangeline could not contain the laughter that bubbled out of her. It threatened to carry her away.

"I would say you and I are well matched in that regard. Come to think of it, we are well matched in a great many ways…" He looked as if he wanted to say more but managed to restrain himself. "Including on the dance floor. What do you say? Shall we try again and see if we can improve?"

The power of his personality and her own inclination urged Evangeline to agree at once. But her prudence and discretion were determined to mount some resistance. "I will dance with you again, if you wish, but not right away. It would be certain to cause comment and make Mr. Webster even more vexed with me. You really should not neglect his daughter so shamefully, regardless of what…strange compulsion has come over you this evening."

As the musicians tuned up for the next dance and new lines began to form, Jasper drew her away from the floor. "This *strange compulsion,* as you call it, is much more than that, Evangeline. And it did not come over me just this evening. It has been growing for some time without my being aware of it. I only wish I had recognized it sooner."

His words made her heart bound, for they described her feelings toward him with perfect accuracy. How could she doubt his sincerity when she had experienced the same emotions as he claimed to?

Though Jasper spoke softly and the people around them appeared too intent on their own business to take any notice, Evangeline pressed her finger to her lips. "This is not the place to speak of such things."

Jasper looked around as if becoming aware of the rest of the company for the first time. "You are right, of course. But I do mean to speak of them at my earli-

Deborah Hale 215

est opportunity. In the meantime, if you will not dance with me again so soon, at least let me fetch you another cup of punch?"

"I would be most obliged to you. I had forgotten what thirsty work dancing can be."

Perhaps a cool draft of punch would dampen the dangerous sparks of ardor his attentions ignited in her. If they blazed out of control they could threaten the life's work to which she had dedicated herself.

Jasper seemed to take her acceptance as further encouragement. "I shall return in a moment."

He had gone no distance when Squire Brunskill appeared before Evangeline and requested the honor of the next dance. The squire was a jovial little widower who often spoke kindly to her and the children after church. She accepted his invitation with a degree of eagerness that might have appeared rather forward.

While they waited to take their turn on the dance floor, Jasper returned bearing the promised punch.

The squire mistakenly accepted both cups for Evangeline and himself. "Why, thank you, Mr. Chase. It is very good to see Miss Fairfax enjoying a little local society. She is so devoted to your dear children, but surely the lady deserves a little life of her own."

The poor man seemed oblivious to the baleful glare he received from Jasper. For a moment Evangeline feared her employer might seize his neighbor by the collar and give him a sound shaking.

Before he had a chance, the squire bolted his punch and shoved the empty cup back into Jasper's extended hand. "Drink up, Miss Fairfax. The next set is about to form. If you will excuse us, Mr. Chase, I mean to take advantage of her unexpected presence this evening."

Evangeline did as the squire bid her, torn between alarm, relief and a wild urge to laugh. Finding herself suddenly the object of masculine rivalry was simply too ridiculous!

Did the squire have any idea how ridiculous he looked fawning over a lady nearly half his age?

Until that evening, Jasper had liked the plainspoken North Countryman who took a benevolent role in the activities of the village. Squire Brunskill had accepted him as a member of the community in spite of his being city bred and having bettered his fortunes by marriage. With no family of his own, the squire clearly doted on Jasper's children, losing no opportunity to praise their looks, cleverness and behavior.

But as Jasper watched his neighbor dance with Evangeline that evening and ply her with rustic gallantries, he found himself detesting the man. It was clear he had fancied the lady for some time but never found an opportunity to pursue her. The churchyard was hardly the proper place to conduct a courtship. Tonight, as the squire had proclaimed, he was eager to *take advantage* of her presence.

Worse than that, Evangeline seemed to be encouraging the squire in a deliberate effort to avoid Jasper! Could that be because she had no romantic interest in him and found his attentions distasteful? Or were her feelings quite the opposite and so strong that they alarmed her? After the silent communication that had passed between them during their dance, Jasper was inclined to believe the latter.

He must make Evangeline understand she had nothing to fear from him. But how could he persuade her of that if the squire insisted on monopolizing her company?

In a fever of anxiety, Jasper sought out Norton Brookes and drew him aside for a brief word. "Can I prevail upon you to claim the next dance with Miss Fairfax? A neighbor of mine is making a nuisance of himself."

His friend glanced toward the dance floor. "I shall always be happy to assist Miss Fairfax, though she does not strike me as a helpless damsel in need of rescue."

"Of course she's not helpless!" Jasper bridled at the thought. Even as a young girl, in that repressive school, Evangeline had found ways to stand up for herself and her friends. "But I fear he may take advantage of her good nature to impose upon her."

Still, his friend did not seem to appreciate the gravity of the situation. "If you are so concerned, why not have a word with the fellow? Or ask Miss Fairfax to dance yourself? That would be no hardship, surely?"

Of course it would not be a hardship! Jasper fought the urge to rage at Norton. His emotions felt raw, too easily inflamed. That was not a pleasant sensation, yet he felt more fully alive, somehow, than he had in a very long time. Perhaps this was part of what Evangeline feared about allowing herself to care too deeply for someone.

"If you will not oblige me, I suppose I shall have to ask her," he muttered darkly.

The worst she could do was refuse. Jasper told himself that would be a minor setback, though his heart regarded it otherwise. Perhaps a breath of fresh air would help him put the matter in proper perspective.

He turned away from his friend and stalked to the door, making a determined effort to avert his eyes from the dance floor. If he happened to see Evangeline enjoying the squire's company more than his, he feared he might do something he would regret.

A moment later, he emerged from the assembly hall into the cool air and relative quiet of the village square. A few coachmen had congregated within sight of the door, enjoying a little conversation and refreshment while they waited for their passengers. Jasper turned in the opposite direction and took several long slow breaths in an effort to clear his head.

Before he had managed that properly, Piers Webster appeared. Jasper doubted their meeting was a coincidence.

Mr. Webster wasted no time confirming his suspicion. "Have you and Margaret had a quarrel, then?"

"Nothing of the kind," Jasper insisted.

It was perfectly true. He liked Margaret Webster as well as ever. They'd never had the slightest disagreement, in contrast to his frequent clashes with Evangeline. He'd believed that was what he wanted from marriage—unbroken tranquility. Now he sensed it would only lull his heart back to sleep. While that might be a comfortable state, how much would he miss as a consequence?

Piers Webster gave a doubtful sniff. "Then why are you skulking out here while my daughter is inside dancing with every bumpkin beau in the parish?"

Jasper hesitated. He wanted to tell Margaret's father that there could be no match between them because his heart was committed elsewhere. But this was not the proper time. Perhaps he should go back inside, dance with Miss Webster and pretend his intentions toward her had not changed. But he did not want to lead the lady on any more than he had already. Neither did he wish to embarrass her with his obvious neglect. Evangeline had already chided him for that.

"It is not easy to get near her." Jasper offered the first excuse that came to mind, insisting to his conscience that it was true. "Your daughter is the belle of the ball and justly so. I do not wish to cheat her of her triumph by keeping her all to myself."

Piers Webster lowered his voice to a menacing rumble. "I did not make my fortune by being thick, you know. You've had no trouble getting near that chit of a governess. There looks to be more between you than is proper for master and servant."

"Miss Fairfax is not a servant!" Jasper could not bear to hear Evangeline referred to in that dismissive way. "There is nothing between us, nor has there ever been."

Not in the sordid way Mr. Webster meant, certainly. The last thing Jasper wanted was for ugly gossip about them to stain Evangeline's reputation.

"I am relieved to hear that." Piers Webster backed down in the face of Jasper's emphatic denial. "Can you promise me that your intentions toward my daughter are honorable? You haven't just been trifling with her, amusing yourself at her expense?"

"Of course not!" Jasper cried.

That sounded so deliberately callous. The truth was much more complicated. He'd sincerely believed he and Margaret Webster would make a harmonious match, even though he did not love her. "I have the greatest respect for your daughter. I would never wish to injure or embarrass her. I promise you that my intentions toward her have never been dishonorable."

The sincerity of his tone seemed to persuade the older man.

"That's what I wanted to hear!" Piers Webster

seized Jasper's right hand, pumping it up and down vigorously. "If that is how you feel, you had better quit shilly-shallying and propose to my daughter at your first opportunity."

"P-propose?" The thought rocked Jasper, making it impossible for him to do more than repeat the word like a simpleton who did not understand its meaning.

"Aye. What else?" Piers Webster chortled. "Consider this my blessing to ask her. I'll expect to see the pair of you engaged before we leave your charming house at the end of the week!"

Chapter Fourteen

"I beg your pardon, sir!" Evangeline cried as she tread on the poor squire's toes for the second time in as many minutes. "You must be sorry you ever invited such a clumsy partner to dance."

When she'd danced with Jasper, the need to concentrate on the steps had helped her push troublesome thoughts to the back of her mind. But now they crowded forward to distract her when she most needed to pay attention to what she was doing. Every word he'd spoken that suggested tender feelings for her ran through her thoughts over and over. She was powerless to banish them. Could that be because she did not want to?

One particular idea that he had expressed struck an answering chord in her. More than once he'd mentioned that his feelings had been growing for much longer than he'd realized. Perhaps that was true for her as well. These past years, as she'd witnessed his devotion to the children she loved, had the seeds of trust and tenderness been sown? Had they lain fallow in her heart just waiting for a change of season to blossom?

The squire winced but quickly covered it with a forced smile. "Not to worry, my dear. You are out of practice, that is all. I hope we shall be able to remedy that in the future."

Evangeline did not contradict him, though she knew it was most unlikely. She would soon be leaving Amberwood to set up her school.

Leaving Jasper and the children? Her heart protested painfully. How could she think of going now that she knew he cared for her the way she did for him?

The very thought brought her heart and soul into such anguished conflict that she turned left when she should have turned right and bumped into Gemma Leveson.

"Forgive me!" She scrambled to correct herself. "I seem to have two left feet this evening."

Her cheeks blazed. Everyone in the assembly hall must be staring at her, whispering to one another behind raised hands and fans. What had possessed her to come here tonight when she could not execute a simple step without injuring one of the other dancers?

Jasper Chase, her conscience accused her, he was the reason she had come. She'd wanted him to see her in her modest finery, wanted him to converse and dance with her. Had she secretly hoped he would fall in love with her like the young lord in that love ballad?

That had only been an idle fancy, surely. If Jasper truly cared for her and declared such feelings, it would complicate her life and future unbearably. She had only allowed her foolish infatuation for him to grow because she'd been so certain he would never return her feelings. Now that it appeared he might, she could be forced to make some very painful choices.

Evangeline breathed a sigh of relief when the dance finally came to an end without any further disasters. The squire escorted her from the floor, making all manner of kind excuses for her awkwardness. His words washed over Evangeline, scarcely registering in her mind as her gaze darted here and there in search of Jasper.

Would he tease her over her dreadful performance, challenging her to do better when she took the floor with him again? The prospect almost made her forget her embarrassment.

But Jasper was nowhere to be seen.

Was he vexed with her for accepting the squire's invitation? Had her skittish reaction to his attentions made him think she did not care for him? That might make her situation easier—lifting the burden of decision from her shoulders. Yet her feelings demanded some sort of expression and acknowledgment, even if nothing could come of them.

Squire Brunskill must have sensed her inattention, for he seized her hands and raised his voice to attract her notice. "I should be honored to put my carriage at your disposal any evening you wish to grace us with your presence, Miss Fairfax."

There could be no mistaking his interest in her. Evangeline wondered why she had not noticed it before. A qualm of shame gripped her for having made light of it earlier. There was nothing amusing about such feelings, especially when they could not be returned. The squire was a good, kind man and she did not want to hurt him. But if there was a man she dared encourage, it was not he.

"That is a very generous offer, sir." She chose her words with care. "I will bear it in mind if I wish to attend another assembly."

The squire beamed and gave her hands a squeeze before he released them. Evangeline struggled to hide her distaste. Fortunately Mr. Brookes appeared just then, providing a welcome diversion.

He bowed to her and the squire. "I beg your pardon, Miss Fairfax, but I wonder if you might do me the honor of a dance?"

Squire Brunskill looked as vexed with the vicar as Jasper had with him. "The lady might prefer a little rest and refreshment before she takes the floor again."

His presumption in answering on her behalf made Evangeline fret less about sparing his feelings. It made her wonder if even the kindest of men were apt to overbear the women they claimed to care about.

"I am not tired in the least." She took Mr. Brookes's arm. "Dancing requires less energy than keeping up with five children. If you are brave enough to risk my clumsy dancing, I shall be happy to oblige you."

As they made their way toward the floor, she murmured, "You are my hero, sir. In gratitude for rescuing me, I shall do my best to avoid treading on your toes."

The vicar chuckled. "I would appreciate that, but any gratitude you owe is to Mr. Chase. It was he who asked my help to extract you from an awkward situation. He seemed quite concerned on your behalf. I fear I was not as obliging as I might have been. I suggested he should do the honors himself if it mattered so much to him. I thought he intended to, but then he went off somewhere."

Why had Jasper asked his friend to intervene rather than doing it himself? Evangeline wondered as she and Mr. Brookes took their places.

During their dance, she managed to keep her promise not to lame her partner, but it required considerable effort. Afterward she received a few more invitations and was able to avoid Squire Brunskill.

But even as she danced with those other partners, Evangeline was intensely aware when Jasper rejoined the company. Would he ask her to dance again, or had he taken her earlier rebuff to heart?

She made herself available for an invitation from him, but none was forthcoming. Her heartbeat picked up tempo whenever Jasper took a step in her direction. It slowed again when he approached one of the other ladies in the party instead. Clearly he considered it his duty to take a turn with each of them, even Mrs. Leveson and his mother-in-law. Had he only danced with *her* out of a sense of duty? Had all the thrilling things she thought he'd said been no more than products of her futile yearning?

At last Jasper managed to catch Margaret Webster between partners and invited her to take the floor with him. Evangeline turned down an invitation to dance that set, for she knew it would be impossible to keep her mind on the steps. Instead, she sipped punch and pretended to converse with Abigail Brookes, who was content to do most of the talking.

She could not deny that Jasper and Miss Webster made a handsome couple, his dark coloring an attractive contrast to her fair, golden beauty. They danced well together, too. Miss Webster was so sure and graceful in her movements, Jasper seemed more relaxed and confident than when he had danced with Evangeline.

Reason reminded her that she had practically ordered Jasper to pay more attention to Miss Webster. But reason could do nothing to ease the jagged pain that ripped through her heart when she watched them clasp hands or exchange a smile.

"P-pardon me." She interrupted Abigail in midword. "I must excuse myself. I am not accustomed to such late hours and so much excitement. I should get home…that is…back to Amberwood."

She tried to slip away, but Abigail followed her. "Are you unwell? Can I help?"

"I am not ill." Evangeline tried to wave her away. "Only tired and my head aches. It is not far to walk back, and fresh air may be all the remedy I need."

"Nonsense." Abigail refused to be dismissed. "You cannot walk that distance alone after dark. I will drive you home in Mr. Chase's gig."

"Please do not trouble yourself," Evangeline begged. "This part of the country is perfectly safe. I do not want to spoil your evening."

"You will do nothing of the kind," Abigail insisted as Evangeline collected her bonnet and shawl. "If I take another sip of punch, I will turn into a lemon and I cannot dance another step in these slippers for they pinch something vicious. Wait here while I tell the others we are going."

Much as she appreciated Abigail's concern, Evangeline could not do what she asked. It was vital she get away on her own into the cool, calm night, where she could compose herself. If that failed, at least the darkness would hide any tears she was foolish enough to let fall.

The instant Abigail disappeared from view, Evangeline slipped outside and hurried away. Even the waiting coachmen took no notice of her early departure. She made her way though the darkened village, careful not to draw any attention to herself. Once out in the moon-dappled countryside on the road to Amberwood, she heaved a great sigh that was part relief and part anguish.

The night seemed to want to comfort her. The breeze rustling through the leaves and the distant gurgle of the river were two of the most soothing sounds she could imagine. The summer air was scented with the wholesome sweetness of new-mown hay and clover. From the heavens, the lady in the moon looked down on her with a pitying gaze.

But before she had a proper chance to reflect on the events of the evening, Evangeline heard a vehicle approaching from behind and glimpsed the bobbing glow of a lantern. A moment later, the gig overtook her.

"Really, Miss Brookes," she called in a sharper voice than she intended, "it was not necessary for you to come after me like this."

"I am not Miss Brookes," Jasper replied. "And I believe it was entirely necessary that I find you."

Hearing Evangeline's voice, as intrepid as ever, set Jasper's heart beating properly again for the first time since he'd set off after her. He was torn between the urge to rage at her for frightening him by running off and an equally powerful one to gather her in his arms and deluge her face with kisses.

He doubted she would react well to either of those.

So instead he said, "Climb in. I will fetch you the rest of the way home."

It was not a very gallant offer, but she had managed to get herself out of the gig very capably only a few hours ago. Besides, he did not trust himself to help her up without giving way to his longing to embrace her.

To his relief, Evangeline did as he asked with no argument. When she was seated safely beside him, Jasper jogged the reins, and the horse continued on its way at a more sedate pace than it had come from the village.

After considering and discarding several possible

openings, he said, "You should not have gone off on your own. You know that, don't you?"

"Indeed I do not," she replied stoutly, though her voice sounded as if it had been stretched thin. "What I do know is that I should never have come in the first place."

"Please don't say that," he begged her.

"Why not?" she demanded. "It is true. I made a fool of myself stumbling around the dance floor all evening."

Jasper sensed there was more to it than that. Had his forward behavior made her regret attending the assembly? "I doubt anyone else noticed. Folks around here know you have more important things to do than practice dancing."

"So have I." Evangeline shifted a little on the seat beside him. Was she trying to inch as far from him as possible? "I am a working woman with responsibilities and plans, not a fine lady with no aim in life but to secure a husband. I had no business traipsing about an assembly at all hours, drinking punch and chattering away about a lot of nonsense."

Jasper flinched. Had he deluded himself that she might be receptive to his approaches? Perhaps he should have asked his courting teacher for a lesson on how to tell when he was winning a lady's regard and when she was trying to politely discourage him. "I suppose you think I was chattering nonsense this evening when I tried to tell you how I feel?"

"Perhaps you were. You might have been practicing your courting technique on me to prepare yourself to propose to Miss Webster. The two of you made a very well-matched pair on the dance floor."

There could be no mistaking the plaintive note in

her voice. It wrung Jasper's heart even as it gave him a sweet taste of hope.

"Did we? Is that why you left early, because seeing Miss Webster and me together made you feel the way I did watching the squire make up to you?"

"Why should you care about the squire?" she demanded. "He means nothing to me!"

"Perhaps not, but *you* mean a great deal to me, Evangeline." There, he'd said it as plain and bold as could be—the thing he'd been trying to tell her all evening in spite of her efforts to discourage him. Was it too soon to declare his feelings or years too late?

Evangeline did not reply, which made him fear he should have held his tongue. The last thing he wanted was for her to lump him in with Squire Brunskill—a man of long acquaintance who had destroyed her respect for him with his sudden clumsy overtures.

Since it was impossible to take back his declaration, Jasper forged ahead, even if it meant digging himself in deeper. "Life is not a dance floor, you know. It does not matter how well matched a couple may *appear*. The important thing is how well in step they are in essentials and how much they care for one another."

How he wished it were light out so he could see Evangeline's expression and look into her eyes. They would tell him whether or not he dared hope, even if she refused to speak…or could not bring herself to.

Desperate to provoke some response from her, he demanded, "Do you want me to marry Miss Webster, even if it is you I care for?"

"Yes!" she cried as if he had tormented the confession out of her. That one outburst seemed to uncork a jug of potently fermented emotion. It spewed forth in a torrent of frenzied weeping, amid which Jasper thought he heard her sob, "No!"

He had been paying almost no heed to his driving, trusting the horse to find its way home at whatever speed suited it. Now he abandoned any pretense of attention. Dropping the reins, he reached for Evangeline, as he had longed to do all evening. He had never thought he would hear her in tears. Not long ago, he would have believed her incapable of weeping. Now he knew it must require terrible provocation. Delighted as he was to glimpse her feelings at last, he reproached himself for distressing her.

"Shh!" He wrapped his arms around her the way he would one of his children if they were hurt or upset. His feelings for her were every bit as strong as for them. He wanted to provide for Evangeline and protect her, comfort her and care for her. After a lifetime spent caring for others, she deserved all that and more. "There now, dear heart, it will be all right. I will not do anything you don't want. You do care for me a little, after all, don't you?"

She was still weeping too hard to speak, but he could feel her head move up and down against his shoulder in a welcome nod of agreement.

"That is the best news I have heard in years!" A powerful wave of happiness swept over Jasper, leaving behind a film of briny moisture in his eyes.

"We were meant for one another, you and me." He savored the sensation of her in his arms, where she so obviously belonged. "I wish I'd seen it sooner, but I am thankful I found out before it was too late."

Evangeline's weeping eased to a series of sniffles. No doubt she realized she had nothing to cry about now that they understood one another. A happy, fulfilling life stretched ahead of them—one he was eager to begin.

He fished out a handkerchief and swiped it over her face in the darkness, his touch awkward but tender. "Dry your eyes now, my sweet, and I will do everything in my power to give you no cause for tears again."

Evangeline reached up and took the handkerchief from him. She wiped her eyes properly then blew her nose. Her bonnet had slipped back off her hair, allowing Jasper to press his cheek against the silken strands.

That did not provide enough of an outlet for the tenderness he felt toward her. When Evangeline had finished drying her tears, Jasper cupped her chin and raised her face to his so he might kiss her properly on the lips.

He began with a soft, almost tentative approach. Part of him still could not quite believe he had been blessed to find love a second time, especially with such a fine woman, who was every inch his match. He marveled that he could still remember how to kiss a woman after years of bereavement, during which he had driven himself in an effort to forget what he was missing.

But at the first brush of her soft, full lips, it all came back to him. Evangeline's response, hesitant yet sweetly eager, told him that she had not been kissed by another man. Jasper considered that a precious gift and a treasured responsibility. He sought to make it an experience that would stir her senses and her heart, leaving her without a doubt of the depth of his feelings for her.

Earlier, Jasper had wished it were day so he could divine Evangeline's feelings by looking at her. Now he realized sight was far too limited a sense to fully communicate all the subtle complexities their hearts held. He blessed the warm, fragrant summer night that cast a veil of privacy over them, giving the delightful illusion that nothing and no one existed outside the circle of their embrace.

Then suddenly the gig lurched and sped up as the horse neared home. It dragged Jasper and Evangeline into the well-lit courtyard of Amberwood. A stable boy, who must have been watching for the party's return, ran toward the gig calling out to them.

Jarred from the quiet shadows of intimacy, Jasper pulled away from Evangeline and seized the reins. She drew back just as abruptly as he, adjusting her bonnet to cover the chestnut tresses he had kissed only moments ago. It felt like much longer. And it seemed like a whole other lifetime ago they had set out for the village assembly.

So much had changed since then and a bright new future stretched before them. Jasper could scarcely wait to share their happiness with the children, for he knew they would be almost as delighted as he to have Evangeline as part of their family.

For twelve blissful hours, Evangeline lived in a hazy dream of perfect happiness.

Jasper's kiss tingled on her lips. His heartfelt declaration of his feelings and the tender endearments he had addressed to her echoed in her thoughts, drowning out any reluctance. Emotions she had long stifled welled up in her heart, leaving no room for fear or doubt. She knew only that the man she cared for returned her feelings without reservation.

Her heart seemed to dance on air, encased in a delicate soap bubble of shimmering rainbows. She fell asleep with Jasper's handkerchief clutched in her hand and woke from the sweetest dream to find it still there, proof that the events of the previous night were more than some moonlit fancy.

The children were already awake and eating their breakfast with Jane when Evangeline emerged, drowsy but smiling, to join them.

"Did you enjoy the dancing last night?" asked Matthew, his head cocked to one side in a quizzical way that reminded Evangeline of a bright-eyed bird.

"Very much," she said, ruffling his dark hair. How like his dear father's it was.

"Did you dance with Papa?" inquired Emma in her shy manner that seemed to ask something more. Had the perceptive child sensed the feelings her father and governess had managed to conceal, even from themselves, until last night?

"Of course." Brushing Emma's cheek with the back of her fingers, she recalled the way Jasper had clasped her hand, as if she were a priceless treasure he was proud to touch with care. "Your father was kind enough to dance with all the ladies."

She was the one he had wanted to dance with, though. Evangeline knew he would have claimed her company exclusively if propriety had not decreed otherwise.

"I wonder if that is why Papa did not come to breakfast with us this morning," Alfie pondered between spoonfuls of porridge. "Perhaps dancing with all those ladies tired him out and he needs to rest."

"Perhaps so." Evangeline beamed at Alfie as if he'd made the cleverest remark she had ever heard.

In truth, she thought it more likely that Jasper did not want the children to see them together and guess their feelings before they had reached an understanding. They had been prevented from discussing their future last night by the arrival of the other carriages so soon after them. Not wanting to risk embarrassing Jasper or Miss Webster, Evangeline had slipped away to the nursery before any of the guests noticed her tear-stained face and the radiant smile she could not hide.

"You look different this morning." Owen regarded her with a grave countenance.

Evangeline tried to quench the hot tingle in her cheeks, without success. "It is probably the effect of my late night—pallor, dark circles under my eyes. That's one of the reasons it is important to get a good sleep."

Owen's nose wrinkled up in a way that made her want to kiss it. "That makes no sense. You look better... prettier."

"He's right," Rosie agreed before Evangeline could pretend to dismiss the compliment she secretly cherished. "You look like one of the princesses in my book of fairy tales."

Evangeline brushed a kiss on Rosie's plump cheek, something she did not do nearly as often with her pupils as she would have liked. "I think you and your brother need to rub the sleep out of your eyes. Now, let's finish eating so we can go for a walk. It is a glorious morning."

As they finished their breakfast, Evangeline caught Matthew and Emma exchanging puzzled looks.

"Are we going to practice more for the concert with Miss Webster?" asked Rosie as they headed off for their walk a while later.

"Perhaps." Evangeline smiled down at the child, trying not to betray her uncertainty.

Would the concert go ahead as planned, with Jasper and Miss Webster singing a love ballad after he had declared his feelings for someone else?

Evangeline wondered how the lady would react when

she found out. Had Margaret Webster come to care for Jasper, the way she had? Of course, she must. What woman with a functioning heart could keep from losing it to such a man, especially if he made the slightest effort to win her? Jasper had gone to great lengths to secure Miss Webster's affections—even seeking courting lessons to aid his efforts.

A wave of bilious shame rolled through Evangeline's stomach. Never in her life had she stolen anything that belonged to someone else, but suddenly she knew how a thief with a conscience must feel. It seemed as if her soul was shriveling into something small and hard.

While the children plucked wild raspberries from a patch of brambles they had discovered, Evangeline told herself she had not *stolen* Jasper's heart from Margaret Webster. She had never intended to care for him nor tried to make him care for her—quite the opposite, in fact. It was not her fault he had developed feelings for her.

But try as she might to assuage her conscience, the fact remained that her happiness would surely cause heartache, perhaps even heartbreak, to an innocent woman who had never been anything but kind to her.

The shimmer was rapidly coming off Evangeline's fragile soap bubble by the time she and the children returned from their walk.

"Go wash your hands now so you don't stain your clothes," she bid her pupils in a no-nonsense tone they were more accustomed to hearing from her. "And you must change your stockings, Alfie. Those brambles snagged them terribly."

Jane appeared then to help tidy the children up. But first she handed Evangeline a letter. "This came in the post for you, miss."

Evangeline thanked her and sank onto the nearest chair to read a few lines while her young charges were occupied. They returned shortly to find her still reading and gnawing at her lower lip.

"Is it bad news?" asked Emma in an anxious tone.

"There's nothing the matter with Kit, is there?" added Matthew, referring to the stepson of Evangeline's friend Leah, with whom he and Alfie corresponded.

"I'm certain Kit is quite well." Evangeline did her best to mask her distress for the children's sake. "My letter is not from Leah...I mean, Lady Northam."

"Who sent it, then?" Rosie peered at the letter.

"Mar...er...Mrs. Radcliffe." Even though Marian had been wed for four years, Evangeline still found it hard to think of her and the others by their married names. "Remember, I told you about her. She has two adopted daughters close to Emma's age and a little son. They live near Newark in Nottinghamshire."

Even as she spoke, she tried to think of a way to secure a few moments' privacy so she could finish reading Marian's letter and digest its contents. "Jane, will you please take the children out to the garden? I shall be along shortly."

"Yes, miss." The nursery maid beckoned the young Chases. "Come along, everyone."

A very subdued group followed her. Poor dears! They must wonder what mysterious events were rocking their secure little world this morning.

Evangeline read a few more words of Marian's letter then realized she was not alone. She glanced up to find Owen watching her from the door.

Before she had a chance to bid him go join his brothers and sisters, the child spoke in an uncanny imitation of the words and tone she sometimes used with him. "Is there something you want to tell me?"

In spite of the tempest within her, Evangeline could not help smiling. She shook her head. "Later, perhaps, but thank you for asking."

He seemed to accept her answer.

"Go on, then," she repeated in a gentle way that was almost an endearment.

Owen nodded, but instead of heading off, he darted toward her and threw his arms around her neck. The next instant he scurried away, leaving Evangeline on the verge of tears for only the second time in as long as she could remember. Reading the rest of Marian's letter did nothing to restore her shaken composure.

When she heard footsteps approaching through the door Owen had left ajar, she thought it must be Jane returning with the children. Had she been sitting there that long?

The calm, ordinary world her body inhabited seemed miles away from the stormy inner realm of her thoughts and emotions. She willed herself to rise from the chair even as she grappled with a horde of regrets, questions and longings doing battle for her heart and soul.

The door flew open the rest of the way and Jasper strode through it looking so handsome and happy it was like an exquisite jeweled dagger plunged into Evangeline's chest. She almost cried out in bittersweet torment.

"Dearest Evangeline!" He swept toward her and seized her hand, raising it to his lips. "Jane told me I would find you here. Forgive me for not coming sooner. I was on my way when I saw you go off with the children. You haven't told them yet, have you…about us?"

She shook her head slowly as if it belonged to a puppet she had trouble operating. "What is there to tell?"

"A great deal, I would say." Jasper chuckled as if she were teasing him and pressed her hand to his cheek. Only the parts of her in contact with him felt fully alive. "I suppose you do not want to announce anything until the formalities are settled. I cannot believe I let you get away last night without asking…without making certain. It is all understood, of course, but I do not want to deprive you of this special moment."

Still grasping her hand, he sank to the floor on one knee. Evangeline knew what he was going to say next, but she could not utter a word to prevent him. That was because part of her wanted so much to hear it.

"Evangeline Fairfax," he began, smiling up at her. "May I request the singular honor and happiness of your hand in marriage?"

Her tongue seemed paralyzed by the conflict of two very different answers, both of which she felt powerfully compelled to give him.

The radiance of his smile faltered and his black brows drew together over eyes grown suddenly wary. "Don't keep me waiting, dear heart. Say you will marry me."

If only he knew how much she ached to do exactly that!

His clasp of her right hand tugged her one way, but the letter she held in her left pulled her even harder in the other direction. "Forgive me, Mr. Chase. I cannot marry you."

Chapter Fifteen

"What did you say?" Jasper demanded, gazing up at Evangeline.

If this was her idea of a jest, it was a poor one. But no twitch of her lips or twinkle in her deep brown eyes betrayed even a hint of levity.

Perhaps his ears were playing tricks on him. Or perhaps this was all a bad dream.

"Must you make me repeat it?" Evangeline wrenched her fingers from his grasp. Only then did he realize how cold they were. "It was hard enough to say the first time. I cannot marry you. I wish I could, but it is not possible!"

She had the gall to sound vexed with him? Jasper had never felt like such a fool as he did now, kneeling before the woman who had spurned his proposal after he'd given her his heart.

That organ, so tender and vulnerable, felt as if she had kicked him in the chest with a copper-toed boot. He wondered how it managed to keep on beating, but somehow it did.

He staggered to his feet. "How can you refuse me? Last night you told me you care for me. You let me kiss you. A lady has no business letting a man kiss her that way unless she is willing to marry him."

Evangeline drew herself up, spine stiff, chin tilted at a defiant angle. "Are you questioning my virtue? I assure you I have never permitted any other man to kiss me as you did last night. Nor do I mean to ever again. That was a grave lapse in judgment, which I very much regret."

Her voice broke on that last word, as if it might not be true. Jasper hoped it was not, for the thought of her repenting that wondrous moment between them was more than he could bear.

Much as his injured pride urged him to lash out at her, he took a deep breath and moderated his tone. "Was all that a lie last night? Do you care nothing for me? Then why did you make me believe you do?"

Her vibrant features twisted into an expression of wretched misery that tore at his injured heart. "It was not a lie. I do care for you, though I wish I did not. It only makes what I must do more difficult."

Her words tormented Jasper with a sliver of hope. "What must you do?"

"Have you forgotten?" Her wounded gaze reproached him as she held up a sheet of paper he had not noticed in her hand. "My school. This letter is from my friend Marian Radcliffe. She says they cannot wait any longer. If I cannot undertake the project immediately, they will be forced to find someone else."

Was that all? Relief almost took Jasper's knees out from under him. "Then let them find someone else, by all means! It is a worthy project and I will gladly contribute toward it, but there is no need for *you* to sacrifice your happiness and mine for the sake of a little charity school."

Her full, generous lips compressed into a thin, stubborn line. "Would you not be willing to sacrifice our happiness for the sake of your sooty old cotton mill? These past years, you have not hesitated to sacrifice your family life for it."

"That is not a fair comparison and you know it!" Jasper stabbed the air with his forefinger to emphasize his words. "New Hope is more than just another cotton mill. It is the means to a better life and some kind of dignity for every person I employ and their families."

Evangeline crossed her arms in front of her like a shield against him. "That is exactly what my school would provide for the orphans I would teach and care for. Working men have a great many more opportunities to better their lives than those poor girls do."

Much as he wanted to deny it, Jasper could not. The thought of his own dear daughters, friendless and penniless, shook him to the depths of his soul. But so did the prospect of his family's future without Evangeline. "New Hope Mills is a kind of beacon I pray others may follow until this country's industry is run on Christian principles."

Evangeline refused to back down, which Jasper supposed should not surprise him. It was one of the things he admired most about her, much as it tried his patience at times. "Do you not think that having a charity school operated on true Christian principles might inspire others to do likewise?"

"Perhaps," he conceded. "I admit it is important work. But must you give up your own happiness and mine and the children's? Surely there is someone else who could do it just as well—a woman who has no opportunity or no wish to marry and raise a family."

He could tell that arrow had found its mark. Evangeline's stance of stiff defiance softened. Her squared shoulders slumped a little and her countenance betrayed some uncertainty. Yet she still refused to surrender.

"Knowing what you do of my character and my past, do you honestly believe there is any woman better suited than I for this task?"

Something about the way she asked the question made Jasper wonder if she hoped he could suggest someone else who might fill that role. He wished with all his heart that he was able to, but he could not lie about something so important, least of all to her.

So he stubbornly refused to say anything.

Evangeline unfolded the letter from her friend. Her gaze ranged back and forth over the lines of small precise writing. "According to Marian, there was an epidemic of typhus at the Pendergast School last winter. Several girls died. There has been an investigation of some sort and the place may be closed."

"Good riddance to it," Jasper growled. After the way Evangeline and her friends had been treated at that miserable excuse for a school, he would have liked to tear it down stone by stone with his bare hands. "Surely it is good news that the place could be closed."

"Don't you see?" She shook the letter at him. "It is more vital than ever to prepare a place for those children who will have nowhere to go."

A vast sigh gusted out of Evangeline, which seemed to deflate her entirely. She sank back onto the chair where she had often read bedtime stories to his children and cuddled them when they were ill. "If I had not thought so much about your convenience and your children's feelings and my own selfish reluctance to leave Amberwood, the new school might have been built by now. And those girls would not have died cold and hungry and neglected, as I know they must have been."

"Are you trying to say those deaths were your fault?" Jasper demanded. "Or mine? And that we must be punished for it?"

"I can only speak for myself," Evangeline replied softly. Why did her sorrowful tone burden him with more guilt than any amount of sharp recrimination? "I do feel I must share responsibility with the staff and trustees of the Pendergast School. I do not blame you. I should have insisted on leaving here long ago."

"You are not to blame!" Jasper fell to his knees beside her chair. "You were trying to do your best for my children. You did everything in your power to make me stop dragging my feet so you could go—even organizing this daft house party to find me a wife. But it did not turn out the way you expected, did it?"

"Not by half." Evangeline made a brave attempt at a smile, which affected him more than tears would have done. "I promise you, I am not trying to punish anyone, Jasper, least of all your children. But I cannot bear to have any more deaths or misery on my conscience. You and your children have each other. It may not be easy at first, but I know you can manage without me. I cannot say the same about the girls who need the care a new school could provide."

Much as the philanthropist of New Hope Mills sympathized with her mission, the father of her five young pupils and the man who had come to care for her could not let Evangeline go without a fight. "It may not be easy? A fine piece of understatement that is! Do you remember what it was like for the children and me after Susan died?"

She nodded. "Better than you do, perhaps. I remember

answering Matthew's endless questions about Heaven and why his mother could not have taken him along if it was such a lovely place. I remember how Emma cried at night after the others had gone to sleep and would not let me comfort her. I remember Alfie acting the f-fool trying to make the rest of us smile."

Evangeline was right. He did not remember the aftermath of Susan's death in the acute, aching detail she did. He had run away to Manchester to drown the pain of his loss in his work, leaving her to comfort his children and knit his fractured family back together. How could they bear to lose her?

"My leaving will not be like that," Evangeline continued. The distracted manner in which she folded and unfolded her friend's letter suggested she was less certain than she tried to sound. "I will write to the children and visit when I am able if you will permit me."

"Of course," he muttered gruffly. "I will not forbid it, just to make you stay."

Agreeing to letters and visits troubled him, though, for it suggested he was giving up on trying to change her mind.

Evangeline seemed to take it that way. "I am certain it will be for the best. A marriage between us would never have worked out."

Jasper shook his head vigorously. "I refuse to believe that. We are better matched than Susan and I, much as I loved her. You understand the importance of my work. You would support me in it and not try to distract me from it."

Wasn't that what he was trying to do to her? his conscience demanded.

She gave a bitter laugh. "If you think I would have sat patiently at Amberwood, being mother and father to your children so you could devote even more time to New Hope Mills, you are mistaken indeed. As your wife, I would have insisted you take the family with you to Manchester and let us share in your work."

Was she only saying that to soften the blow of losing her? Jasper wanted to believe it, but he sensed Evangeline was perfectly sincere. "You know why that would not be possible. We have been all over it before."

"So we have and quite heatedly if you will recall. That is also why we would do better not to wed. You want a wife who would agree with you all the time and I could not."

"Why? Am I so unreasonable?"

"In most respects, no. But my feelings for you cannot blind me to the fact that you are not always right. We would either be bound to argue, which you could not abide, or I would have to suppress my true nature, which I could not bear."

He hated the thought of them always rowing like his parents, and yet the notion of a spiritless Evangeline who accepted his every edict without question disturbed him even more. "Is there nothing I can do that will persuade you to stay and marry me?"

"Would you promise to take the children and me to Manchester once we were married?" she asked. "If you could, then perhaps…"

All the reasons he could not consider such a thing flooded Jasper's mind, challenging his past decisions, questioning his love for his children and stirring his indignation.

He sprang to his feet. "You don't mean that! You are only demanding the impossible to shift the responsibility for your going onto me."

"Am I?" She seemed to weigh his charge impartially, only to reject it. "I do not believe so. What I am trying to do is make you understand how difficult this is for me and how I wish I could find some other way. But I must do as I believe the Lord is guiding me and so must you."

Against her arguments he might conceivably prevail. But how could he stand against Evangeline and the Almighty?

When Jasper turned and stalked away, it seemed to Evangeline that he was taking all the light, color, music and flavor out of her life with him. Her heart pounded against her ribs as if it wanted to batter its way out of her chest and follow him.

While they had argued about whether she could give up her plans and destiny to marry him, she had been able to resist. But the moment he stopped opposing her, she began to have second thoughts. Had she meant what she said about reconsidering her answer if Jasper promised to relocate the family to Manchester? Or had she only been trying to avoid responsibility for a decision that would hurt the people she cared for most in the world? She now realized that would be no easier to escape than her responsibility for those lonely little graves in the churchyard near the Pendergast School.

Was she truly turning her back on Jasper and the children for the noble, selfless reasons she had given him or because she was afraid, as he had accused her of being? Did she fear committing her heart to them for fear of losing them as she had her parents? Yet, knowing the pain of such loss, how could she walk out of their lives?

Duty sternly reminded her that she could not sit there all day and mull over a problem that might well be insoluble. Drawing a shaky breath and contriving a smile, she rose and headed off to the garden, stuffing Marian's letter in her pocket as she went. Considering how it weighed on her, that flimsy sheet of paper might have been a sack of bricks.

In her earlier foolish euphoria, her young pupils had felt especially dear to her. Now, as she faced the immediate prospect of leaving them, they all seemed dearer still. Even their little faults, which had sometimes annoyed her, took on a strange appeal.

Hard as she tried, she could not fool them. They sensed something was wrong. Matthew was clearly making an effort not to pester Evangeline with too many questions. Emma offered her a nosegay of flowers picked from the garden, while Alfie turned an impressive series of cartwheels. The younger children just stayed close and smiled up at Evangeline whenever they managed to catch her eye.

Their efforts to cheer her up had quite the opposite effect. How could she leave them and their dear father for a group of young strangers? Some of the orphan girls in need of care might be like her and her friends at that age, while others might be worse off, without a circle of love and loyalty to sustain them. But some might be like the bullying "great girls" she recalled with such distaste from her school days. They would require a kind but very firm hand to keep them in line and show them the error of their ways. Were they worth abandoning her chance to be a mother to these five precious young ones and wife to a fine man?

Hope and fear, resolution and doubts swirled and tumbled in Evangeline's mind as she fetched the children in from the garden and gave them something to eat.

They were just finishing when Abigail Brookes appeared at the nursery door. "Miss Webster asks if the children might come down to practice their concert pieces."

"Yes, of course," Evangeline replied. "I shall bring them as soon as we finish here."

"We are all done." Matthew indicated the children's empty plates and hers, which she had barely touched. "You are the one who still needs to eat."

"I haven't much appetite today." Evangeline rose from her place. "Let's not keep Miss Webster waiting."

"You should not leave food on your plate," Owen said in a respectful yet strangely authoritative tone that was difficult to disregard. "There are plenty of people who would be glad to have a full belly. That's what you always tell us."

What could she say to that?

Miss Brookes came to her rescue. "Why don't the children come down with me while you clean your plate?"

Evangeline nodded. "That is an excellent idea, thank you. Go along, children. I know I can rely on you to behave well for Miss Brookes and Miss Webster."

Her pupils trooped away with a subdued air. When they had gone, Evangeline forced forkful after forkful of food between her lips until her skittish stomach rebelled. Duty urged her to join her pupils as soon as possible, but the prospect of playing accompaniment to Jasper and Miss Webster's love ballad duet held her back.

At last, she knew she could delay no longer without raising awkward questions. Inhaling several slow breaths to gather her composure, she practiced her facial expression in the looking glass. Clearly her miserable attempt at a smile was not fooling anyone. Perhaps a placid, sober countenance would raise less suspicion. She fixed one in place like a mask and headed off to the great parlor.

As she descended the stairs, she met Mr. Webster on his way up.

"How fortunate we should meet, Miss Fairfax," the big mill owner declared, though Evangeline suspected he had been watching for her. "I would be grateful for a word with you, if I may."

"Of course, sir." Drawing on the harsh lessons of her girlhood, Evangeline refused to let him intimidate her. "First, I must join the children at their concert practice. But as soon as they finish—"

Mr. Webster cut her off without ceremony. "The children are in excellent hands with my daughter. She is very fond of them all and they get on well with her, wouldn't you say?"

"I would indeed, sir," she answered truthfully.

If she heeded reason rather than her rebellious, selfish heart, she knew Margaret Webster would make a far better wife and mother to the Chases than she ever could.

Mr. Webster softened his tone. "I will not take much of your time, Miss Fairfax. There is just a thing or two I would like to say."

"Very well, then." She continued down the stairs. "The small sitting room should be empty. I will be able to hear the children from there if they need me."

A moment later, she turned to face Mr. Webster, who had shut the sitting room door behind them. "What is it you wish to discuss, sir?"

He planted his feet wide and clasped his hands behind his back. "I won't beat about the bush. It's you and

Mr. Chase I want to talk about. What does he mean to you and you to him?"

"I am his children's governess." Her guilty blush surely contradicted her prim reply. "I have worked for him these past six years."

"And you feel nothing more for him than any loyal worker feels for a good, fair employer?" Mr. Webster shook his head. "Do you think I am blind or daft, young lady? I saw the way you lit up when he danced with you last night. I've spotted the two of you out walking more than one early morning. Last night you stole away from the assembly to make him go after you. It will not do, you know. Jasper Chase is going to marry my daughter and I will not have you spoil it."

As he spoke, Evangeline's blazing blush cooled until her face felt as if it had been carved out of hard-packed snow. "I have no intention of spoiling anything, Mr. Webster, and I most certainly did not want Mr. Chase to follow me back from the assembly. If he wishes to marry your daughter, I will do nothing to stand in their way—quite the contrary, in fact."

"Do you mean that?" Mr. Webster looked doubtful.

"This house party was my idea," Evangeline replied. "Ask Mrs. Thorpe if you do not believe me. When you saw me walking with Mr. Chase, I was giving him advice about how to court your daughter."

She savored the look of confusion on Mr. Webster's beefy face. "What made you do all that?"

As briefly as possible, Evangeline explained her plan to find Jasper a wife so she would be free to start her charity school. When she finished, Mr. Webster looked as remorseful as Alfie after he had gotten into some serious mischief. "Well, I got the wrong end of that stick and no mistake. I beg your pardon, lass, for suspecting you of any impropriety. I just want to see Margaret married to a good, steady man like Jasper Chase who won't tolerate any foolishness. Becoming a mother of his brood will settle her down soon enough."

Though she wasn't entirely certain what he meant, Evangeline nodded.

"So he was telling me the truth last night," Mr. Webster continued, more to himself than to her.

"The truth about what?" The words burst from Evangeline before she could remind herself it was no business of hers.

"About wanting to marry Margaret. He asked my blessing to propose to her."

Mr. Webster's words seemed to freeze Evangeline's whole body to match her face. Why had Jasper kissed her last night if he intended to propose to another woman? Why had he asked her to marry him only hours ago? Had he meant to hold Margaret Webster in reserve in case she refused him?

If that was the case, how dare he plead with her and urge her to abandon her life's work, tearing her heart in two, while he had other marriage plans waiting in the wings?

Her outrage denounced Jasper in her thoughts so loud that she almost missed Mr. Webster's next words. "How soon will you need to leave Amberwood to start this school of yours?"

She explained how long Jasper had delayed her and told Mr. Webster of the recent need for haste.

"Bless me," he replied. "It sounds as if there is not a moment to lose."

It was good to hear someone else acknowledge that. Evangeline nodded.

"Then you should go at once."

"What, now?" she cried. "Today?"

"When better? There are plenty of others to look after the children until their father can make arrangements for a new governess. With the concert and all, they'll hardly notice you've gone." Mr. Webster meant to reassure her, Evangeline knew, but instead his words dealt her a cruel blow.

Could he be right? Much as she loved the children, was she not as indispensable to them as she liked to believe?

"I will do all I can to help you, my dear," he offered with an air of fatherly solicitude she found hard to resist. "I owe you that and more after the way I misjudged you. Whenever you need to go, I shall put my coachman and carriage at your disposal."

Where would she go to begin her mission and her new life? "Even as far as Nottinghamshire? I could not impose upon you so much."

"Do not think of it." Mr. Webster waved away her objections. He rummaged in his pockets and began unfolding banknotes. "My coachman can deliver you to Nottinghamshire and be back before I need my carriage again. Here, you will need a bit of brass for inns and meals and such. What you do not spend, consider a donation to your school. Write to me when you get settled and I will arrange a more substantial contribution."

Evangeline blinked at the value of the banknotes he pressed into her hand. "That is vastly generous of you, sir."

"There are things worth a great deal more than money, Miss Fairfax. I shall sleep sounder at night knowing those poor orphaned girls are being properly cared for. Now, you will want to make a start while you still have a good bit of daylight to get on your way.

You go pack while I tell the coachman to harness the horses."

"But the children..." Evangeline knew she should not turn down this blessed opportunity. Yet the thought of leaving Emma, Matthew, Alfie, Owen and Rosie so abruptly was almost more than she could bear. "What will I tell them? Then there is the concert..."

"We will all manage, my dear." Mr. Webster patted her arm. "It will likely be easier on the young ones if you go quick and don't draw out your leave-taking."

He was right, of course. Hadn't she seen that with Jasper's departures for Manchester? The children recovered sooner when his goodbye was swift and clean. The more he prolonged it, the more it upset them.

That was the last thing she wanted.

"What is all this?" Jasper surveyed his children, lined up outside the nursery in their best clothes with their faces scrubbed and their hair neatly brushed. "You look as if you're going to a funeral not a concert. Where is Miss Fairfax? Perhaps she can tell me what ails you."

No sooner had he spoken than Rosie's lower lip began to quiver ominously and her eyes filled with tears. Emma rushed to comfort her little sister. Though she did not weep, her delicate face looked positively stricken. The boys' eyes were all downcast and their lips pressed tightly together as if clinging to their composure by a thread. What had come over them all? And why were Abigail Brookes and Verity Dawson hovering nearby with guilty looks on the faces?

As Jasper knelt to put his arms around his daughters, Owen announced, "She's gone, Papa."

Matthew found his voice, too. "She said it might not be for long, but she took all her things away with her. She wouldn't do that if she meant to come back, would she?"

Jasper did not have to ask which *she* they meant. Part of him had known before the children even spoke.

Alfie lost his battle to keep up a brave front.

"I don't want to have the concert without M-Miss Fairfax!" he wailed.

"Neither do I." Owen shook his head. "I couldn't sing or recite because I have a big lump in my throat."

"I have one, too," said Matthew. "I wonder what it is and why it comes when I feel saddest?"

Jasper did not know what to tell his son. That same lump of misery had been lodged in his throat ever since he'd marched out of the nursery that morning. He wasn't sure it would ever go away.

He gathered all the children close to him and tried to comfort them as best he could. Soon they were all weeping, even Owen, in a way that rent his heart. He cast a questioning, reproachful glance at Abigail Brookes.

"I'm sorry!" she cried. "Miss Fairfax made us promise not to tell you. She left a few hours ago. She didn't say where she was going."

"She went in Mr. Webster's carriage," Verity volunteered with a hesitant air, as if she feared she would get in trouble for speaking.

Piers Webster's carriage? Urgent questions seared away Jasper's shock and sorrow. "I agree we should postpone our concert under the circumstances. Now, I need your help, my dears. Will you do something for me?"

They looked at him with tear-streaked faces that made his heart ache. But every one of them nodded bravely.

"Dry your eyes and go along with Miss Brookes

and Mrs. Dawson. Have your tea early then get ready for bed."

"But why, Papa?" asked Matthew.

"I'll explain later." Jasper kissed each of them on the forehead. "For now just trust me and do as I ask. I will be back later to hear your prayers and tuck you in."

Alfie swiped at his brimming eyes with the back of his hand and announced fiercely, "I know what I'm going to pray for."

"So do I." Jasper ruffled his son's hair. "So will we all."

He watched them go off with the ladies then he stalked down to the great parlor where he found the Websters, the Levesons, his mother-in-law and Norton Brookes.

Jasper marched up to Piers Webster and demanded, "Who gave you the right to meddle in my life?"

"I beg your pardon?" Webster had the gall to look bewildered by his question.

"What has Father done, Mr. Chase?" As Margaret Webster approached them, the others discreetly withdrew from the room.

"I have done nothing that concerns him or you," Mr. Webster protested to his daughter.

"Are you saying Evangeline Fairfax *stole* your carriage to leave Amberwood?" Jasper thundered.

"Nothing of the kind." The older man scowled as if gravely offended. "The lady asked for my assistance and I was happy to oblige her. If you call yourself a Christian, you would have done the same two years ago."

Jasper flinched. Was it so wrong to want to keep Evangeline here with him and his children when other children might need her even more? Ever since their encounter that morning, he had not been able to stop thinking about what she'd said and the impossible challenge she had set him. He had begun to glimpse a possible compromise, but now the chance to work things out was gone with her.

"Perhaps I should have." He acknowledged his wrong and lifted a silent plea for forgiveness. "But something tells me it was more than Christian charity that made you pack Miss Fairfax off to who-knows-where without my knowledge."

Guilt blazed on Piers Webster's broad features. "What does it matter that she's gone? You and Margaret can hire a new governess for the children. If you have any sense, you will get one who's older and not so pretty."

"Father," Margaret Webster spoke in a quiet yet ominous tone. "What have you done? And why should I have anything to do with hiring a governess for Mr. Chase's children?"

"You know…when the two of you are…married. He would have proposed by now if he hadn't been distracted by that Miss Fairfax. Not that she wanted it, mind you. The lady did her best to bring about a match between the two of you." Mr. Webster turned toward Jasper. "Now that she is gone, the least you can do is honor her wishes by proposing to my daughter."

Jasper cast Margaret Webster an apologetic look. Poor lady, caught in the middle of all this. He had given far too little thought to her feelings. Perhaps, for the sake of peace, he ought to give in and do what everyone else seemed to expect of him.

Should he try to forget Evangeline Fairfax and ask Margaret Webster to marry him instead?

Chapter Sixteen

Seated in the library of Knightley Park, Evangeline leaned forward and gave Marian Radcliffe's hand an affectionate squeeze. "I do hope you and your husband can forgive me for appearing on your doorstep without a word of warning. It was kind of you to make me so welcome, under the circumstances."

"Tosh." Marian chuckled as she drew back and began to pour them tea. "It was a lovely surprise. I wish our other friends would drop in on me like this, but it's not so easy now that we all have families to consider. That is one selfish reason I will be so pleased to get our school up and running, so we can all get together for regular meetings of the trustees."

"Ah, yes—the school." Evangeline pulled a wry face. Seeing Marian again after so many years brought their school days much closer and made her feel guiltier than ever about how she had neglected her duty. "I cannot tell you how sorry I am for taking so long to get started. When I think if those poor children at Pendergast, sick and dying, I wonder if I can ever forgive myself."

"That was not your fault," said Marian in that reassuring way Evangeline remembered so well. "I hope my letter did not make it sound as if I blamed you."

She passed Evangeline a steaming cup of tea. "I did not mean to drag you away from the Chases. I only wondered—well, we all did—whether you might have changed your mind about wanting to run the school. We worried you might think you'd be letting us down, but of course, you wouldn't. We wanted to give you an excuse to change your mind if you were so inclined."

She fixed Evangeline with her perceptive gaze, which had a way of always getting at the truth. "*Are* you so inclined? Believe me, none of us will think any less of you for it."

"I want to do this." Evangeline strove to persuade her friend of her certainty…and perhaps herself, as well.

On the long journey from Amberwood, reading Marian's last letter over and over, she had clung to Mr. Webster's assurance that establishing the school was a matter of great urgency and importance. The sights she'd glimpsed while traveling through England's industrial Midlands had opened her eyes to the hardship so prevalent outside the peaceful Vale of Eden. All those things had reinforced her commitment to the work she knew she was meant to do.

But even in the short time she'd been a guest at Knightley Park, doubts had begun to gnaw at her resolve. Seeing how happy Marian and Captain Radcliffe were in their marriage and their family made her long to experience that sweet domestic fulfillment for herself. When she spent time with Marian's adopted daughters and little son, she felt the loss of Emma, Matthew, Alfie, Owen and Rosie as if the five fingers of her right hand had been amputated.

"I don't doubt that you *want* to." Marian's tone of

loyal sympathy made it sound as if she understood far more of Evangeline's situation than her friend had told her. "But is that *all* you want?"

It was no use trying to conceal anything from someone who seemed to know so much already. Evangeline shook her head. "I cannot deny I want more than just that. But I cannot have everything I want and since I must choose…"

"The other things you want," Marian prompted her. "Do they include the love of a husband and children? None of your friends would want you to give that up and I do not believe the Lord would, either."

Evangeline wished she could share her friend's staunch certainty. "There is more to it than that. I feel if I give up one for the other, I would lose a part of myself."

"Why is that?" Marian's brow creased with a look of fond concern.

Her entreaty was too powerful for Evangeline to resist. Laying the whole complicated situation before her friend might not yield a solution, but at least it might confirm in her own mind that she had done the right thing in coming here. "Do you remember when we were at school how the teachers used to say I would never get a husband if I did not subdue my strong will and independent streak?"

Marian gave a rich chuckle that seemed to ring with a gloating note. "According to them, none of us had a chance of ever being married. Rebecca and Hannah and I weren't pretty enough. You and Leah were too willful. Poor Grace was too vain. We all knew it was nonsense when it came to the others. But for ourselves, I reckon we took those predictions more to heart. Trust me, Evangeline. They were no truer for you than for any of us."

"Weren't they?" She cradled her teacup in her cold hands. "I wish I could be sure."

She told Marian about Jasper Chase, what a strong, compassionate man he was. How he wanted a wife who would support him and agree with him in everything he did.

"And Mr. Chase cares for you?" asked Marian when Evangeline fell silent. "We thought he must, the way he kept delaying your departure. What fine work he is doing with his mill! I have heard of a philanthropist in Scotland who is doing something similar. If only there were more men of business like them. I must say, you and he sound well matched in your strength, your determination and your practical concern for those who need your help."

"That is half the problem." Evangeline sighed. "We were *too* much alike—both leaders, not followers. A marriage between us could never work out."

"Not easily, perhaps." Marian seemed to agree while doing exactly the opposite. "Here in the country, I have often seen how a strong team of horses or oxen can work better when harnessed side by side than when one is behind the other."

Evangeline could not suppress a bittersweet grin at the image of her and Jasper yoked together to pull a load. "That only works when the creatures have a skilled teamster to lead them."

"Exactly." Marian lifted her gaze upward. "Could Our Lord not be as good a teamster as a shepherd? After all, horses are clever animals, but sheep, poor things, are so very dim-witted."

Her friend's words made Evangeline laugh, but they

also shed a ray of sunlight into her soul. For a sweet, breathtaking instant, nothing seemed impossible.

Then she remembered how she had left Jasper's children in tears and deserted him without even a word of farewell.

"No doubt He can." She set down her cup with trembling hands and a heavy heart. "But it is too late for Jasper and me."

"Are you certain?" asked Marian.

As Evangeline pondered her friend's gentle challenge, a knock sounded on the library door.

"Yes?" Marian called.

The grandfatherly butler of Knightley Park entered. "A caller to see you, miss."

"Can they wait or come back later?" asked Marian. "I am occupied at the moment."

The butler shook his head. "It is not *you* they want, my lady. It is Miss Fairfax and they have come rather a long way."

"Mr. Chase, is it?" Marian rose, her eyes alight.

When Mr. Culpepper nodded, she cried, "By all means, fetch the gentleman in at once!"

Had he made a great mistake acting on impulse and coming so far to show up uninvited at the Radcliffes' door? As Jasper waited for their butler to summon Evangeline, doubts began to assail him. Would she view his pursuit of her as a sign that he did not respect her choice? Would she think he meant to coerce her into following his wishes? Would she be vexed with him for imposing on her friends?

He silenced those thoughts by reminding himself that he would get to see her. Even if she rejected him again, at least he would be able to say a proper goodbye.

A tall, fair-haired gentleman descended the stairs just then with two pretty young girls holding his hands. One of the girls looked a bit older than Emma, but with the same quiet, responsible air. The other child Jasper guessed to be two or three years younger. Her bouncy step and bright smile put him in mind of Alfie.

"Welcome to Knightley Park." The man let go of the younger girl and extended his hand to Jasper. "I am Captain Gideon Radcliffe. Can I help you?"

Jasper shook the captain's hand warmly. "My name is Jasper Chase. I've come from up north to see Miss Fairfax. I believe she is a guest here. Your butler has gone to fetch her for me."

"I see." Captain Radcliffe nodded as if he understood far more about Jasper's errand than he had been told. "I wish you the very best, Mr. Chase. If you find yourself staying in this part of the country, I hope you will be our guest at Knightley Park. Cissy and Dolly love company, don't you, girls?"

The girls nodded, one more vigorously than the other but both with winsome smiles that assured Jasper of a warm welcome.

"That is very kind of you, but I fear it might be more inconvenient than you realize," Jasper said, briefly explaining why.

"That is no excuse not to stay!" The younger girl headed for the door. "In fact, it is a better reason that you should."

"Dolly!" The captain chuckled at her forwardness, which did not offend Jasper in the least. "There will be no getting away for you now, I fear, Mr. Chase."

Jasper wanted to believe that was true. But how could he stay if Evangeline turned him down?

The butler reappeared just then, followed by a pretty little woman with an indomitable air.

"Mr. Chase!" She greeted him as if they were old friends. "I am Miss Fairfax's friend, Marian Radcliffe. I see you have met my husband and our girls. Do come in and see Evangeline. We were just taking tea in the library. You will not be disturbed there. Take as long as you need."

Without letting him get a word in, she led him toward the library and practically pushed him through the door, which she shut behind him with some force.

At the sight of Evangeline rising from a narrow settee, Jasper seemed to lose his powers of speech and movement. This was his last chance and so much depended on his success or failure.

"You must excuse my friend," she said. "I do not recall her being so bossy when we were at school. That was my role. I believe marriage has had an unfortunate effect on Marian in that regard."

Thanking Providence for such a promising opening, Jasper forced himself toward Evangeline. "You reckon marriage has made Mrs. Radcliff more strong-minded? How can that be? I met her husband just now and he seemed to have a determined character, as well."

Evangeline nodded. "I believe it is a requirement for a captain in the Royal Navy."

"Do they get on well together, in spite of it?"

"Very well indeed." Evangeline sounded surprised as she sank back onto the settee. "Marian is not under the captain's thumb, nor he under hers. From everything I have seen since I arrived, they seem very happy together."

Jasper looked around the Radcliffes' library and saw

no chairs near enough to allow for comfortable conversation.

Casting Evangeline an apologetic glance, he took a seat beside her on the settee. "Forgive me for following you here. I could not leave matters between us as they were after our last conversation."

"How did you know where to find me?" She regarded him warily, making Jasper wonder whether she was flattered or vexed by his pursuit.

"I made Piers Webster tell me where you'd gone. He had no business to spirit you away like that, with so much unresolved between us."

"I thought it *was* resolved when you walked out of the nursery," Evangeline replied. "Besides, Mr. Webster did not spirit me anywhere. He was kind enough to offer me his assistance and I accepted."

"Piers Webster was not being kind!" Jasper rolled his eyes. For such a self-reliant woman, Evangeline could be too trusting. But could he persuade her to trust him? "He wanted you gone from Amberwood, so that I might forget you and propose to his daughter."

"Why did you not oblige him?" Evangeline's temper flared. "I thought that was your plan—to hold Miss Webster in reserve, poor lady, in case I refused you."

"Where did you get a daft idea like that?" Jasper demanded, though he could guess who had planted it.

"Mr. Webster." She sounded as if she considered the man an unimpeachable source. "He told me you requested his permission to propose to his daughter the evening before you proposed to me."

"He *gave* me permission," Jasper insisted. "I did not *ask* for it!"

Evangeline folded her arms in front of her. "And I

suppose you gave him no reason to believe you might want to marry Miss Webster?"

Jasper squirmed a little on the Radcliffes' small settee. It was a tight fit for the two of them. Besides, his conscience was not entirely easy. He might not be guilty of what Evangeline had accused him, but he was not altogether innocent. "I might have, though I did not intend to deceive him. The night of the assembly, Mr. Webster asked me if my intentions toward his daughter were honorable or if I was only toying with her affections. I denied that, of course, not thinking what he might suppose I meant."

"So you never thought of asking poor Miss Webster to marry you?" Evangeline looked doubtful of his explanation.

Jasper was not certain what she wanted to hear. One answer would slight his feelings for her. But the other might make him seem callous toward Margaret Webster. The truth lay somewhere in between, and cast him in a bad light with both women. "I cannot deny I did consider it after you left so suddenly. For the sake of the children and my work, I was tempted to secure a wife who would manage everything at home and leave me free to concentrate on the mill."

"That must have been powerful temptation." Evangeline did not sound as vexed by his admission as Jasper had expected. "Yet you did not succumb to it. You came all the way to Nottingham instead. Poor Miss Webster."

"You keep calling her that." Jasper shook his head. "The lady is not so much to be pitied as you imagine. Nor is she as meek and obliging as we both believed."

Evangeline raised her dark, well-shaped brows. "What makes you say that?"

His lips twitched, remembering the scene in his parlor. "I witnessed a most enlightening exchange between Miss Webster and her father after I had words with him for sending you away. She told him she would not marry me if I asked her and he must put the idea out of his head once and for all."

"She would not marry you?" Evangeline sounded disbelieving and rather offended on his behalf. "Why?"

He made a wry face. "Hard to imagine her turning down such a fine catch, isn't it?"

"You are a fine catch! If I had been in her position, I would have accepted you at once."

"Thank you for saving my pride." A hopeful smile tugged at the corner of Jasper's mouth, though he feared it might not be justified. "After hearing two women say they would not marry me in the course of a few hours, it took rather a beating. I could not be too injured by Miss Webster's rejection, since I never did propose to her. It turns out she is in love with someone else—a music master from Bath, whom her father is convinced must be a fortune hunter. She only came to Amberwood to oblige Mr. Webster so he might look more favorably on her young man. She was not pleased to discover how hard he had been trying to marry her off to me and she told him so in no uncertain terms."

"Oh, dear!" A trill of surprised laughter burst from Evangeline. "That explains a great deal. Bravo to Miss Webster for standing up to her father."

Jasper found himself grateful to the Websters for providing a topic to break the ice between him and Evangeline. Now he must take advantage of the thaw. "I thought that bit of news might interest you, but I did not travel all this way only to share it."

The laughter faded from Evangeline's face. "I suspected there might be something more."

Was this his chance, he wondered, to offer Evangeline a different kind of proposal—a compromise that might be better than what either of them had originally wanted? Or had he come all this way for nothing?

Jasper Chase was a man of his word. Evangeline believed that with all her heart. If he said he had never intended to propose to Margaret Webster, it must be true.

But did that change anything between them? Her mistaken belief that he had planned to ask for the other woman's hand might have provoked her sudden flight from Amberwood but it had no bearing on her original refusal of Jasper's proposal.

Had he come all this way to tell her something that would make a difference between them? Or did he hope the resolution of that misunderstanding, and her longing for his children, would make her forget everything else that stood between them?

She recalled Marian's comment about draft animals working better in tandem. It had struck a chord with her, but could a dynamic man like Jasper Chase ever be willing to share the lead? Did the fact that he had come so far in pursuit of her only prove the lengths to which he would go to get his own way? If she gave in to her feelings for him and his children, her duties as wife and mother and her contribution to his important work might keep her content for a while. But sooner or later, Evangeline was certain she would begin to chafe at her subordinate role and resent what she had been obliged to give up.

She did not want that for either of them, and especially not for the children.

"I want you to know," said Jasper, "that I gave a great

deal of thought to what you said when you…rejected my proposal."

Evangeline could tell those words were hard for him to speak. Clearly his reference to his injured pride had not been altogether in jest.

"Even before you…left," he continued, "I debated with myself whether I could do what you asked."

"Settle your family in Manchester, you mean?" After their recent misunderstandings, Evangeline wanted them to be quite clear.

Jasper nodded. "I cannot deny that at first I did not believe I could do it."

At first? Evangeline tried to keep her rising hopes in check.

"It was not only because I am pigheaded and must have everything my own way." He seemed determined to explain. Was that to persuade her he was right…or some other reason? "To me, Manchester is a place of danger and hardship—a place of sights I would do anything to forget. I did not want that for my children. Amberwood seemed like a haven where they could grow up as far away as possible from my past."

Part of her wanted to argue with his reasoning, but another part sympathized all too deeply. One thing Evangeline realized without any doubt was that she had asked Jasper to do one of the hardest possible tasks for him. She had made it a condition of his marriage offer, without any assurance that it would induce her to accept. Her sense of fairness reproached her.

"Oh, Jasper…" She reached out and laid a hand on his, which were clasped tightly over his knees.

"Please let me finish," he begged her. "Once you've heard everything then say what you will."

She replied with a silent nod, but she did not move her hand. Jasper gave no sign that he wanted her to.

"The more I thought about it," he continued, "the more I realized I was letting myself be ruled by fear—just as I accused you of doing."

"You were right!" Hard as she tried, Evangeline could not hold the words back. "I *have* been afraid of what would happen if I let myself love anyone too much. Afraid that if I did, I would lose myself!"

He did not chide her for her outburst but nodded as if he understood the depth of her fears as well as she did his. "That is when I decided I must overcome my fear. Not only to prove how much you mean to me, but for my own sake and my family's."

Until that moment, her attention had been so focused on Jasper Evangeline had not been aware of anything else. But suddenly she caught the sound of children's voices drifting in from the Radcliffes' garden.

It was not only Cissy and Dolly or even little Harry with them. It could be no less than half a dozen youngsters. The cadences of their voices were some of the most familiar and beloved to their devoted governess.

"Alfie?" She leaped up and dashed to the window that overlooked the garden. "Rosie? Are they all here?"

Indeed they were, for she could now see them as well as hear them, running about with the Radcliffe girls. Only when she glimpsed them again did it hit home how dreadfully she had missed them in a few short days.

She turned toward Jasper, who had risen and followed her to the window. "You dragged them all the way here? The poor dears! How tired they must be! And what have you been feeding them—inn fare?"

Jasper gave an infuriating chuckle at her outburst, perhaps because he recognized the protective love behind it—love for his children, which was one of their strongest common bonds. "Look at them. Do they seem any the worst for our journey? I had to bring them. When I told them where I was going they would not give me a moment's peace until I promised they could come. Besides, I hoped it would convince you of my sincere willingness to do what you asked."

She felt a light touch on the small of her back as they stood there at the library window staring out at the garden full of children. Jasper was a strong, forceful man, but he had a gentle side too, just as she did. Perhaps...

"We stopped one night in Manchester on the way here," he went on. "While we were there, I did what you suggested. I showed them the mill and the workers' flats. I told them more about my hopes and plans for the place. You were right. They want to be involved. They want to help now and when they grow up."

Evangeline nodded, brooding over her darlings as she watched them play. "They will be an invaluable asset to you with all their different talents. They may turn out to be your most valuable legacy to the people of Manchester and beyond."

"Indeed." Paternal pride and love warmed Jasper's voice. "But that is only part of what happened."

"There is more?" Evangeline's gaze turned from the children to rest upon their father.

Jasper stared back with undisguised love and a mysterious glow of wonder. "After I had shown the children around, they informed me that my workers' children need a school. Not only a Sabbath school for some of the boys, but a place for girls to learn, as well. I realized that education is the missing piece of my plan."

"Of course," Evangeline murmured, her imagination

fired by the possibilities. "With an education, those children will truly have new hope, just as you did."

"There is only one difficulty," said Jasper.

To her questioning look, he replied, "I have no experience in education. I would need someone to organize a school for me."

Now it was his look that asked the question.

"Me?" The prospect of assisting him in such vital work appealed to her. "But what about *my* school? Am I supposed to simply forget about it?"

"No, indeed!" Jasper reached for her hands and clasped them in his. "Such a place is badly needed and there is no one better qualified than you to bring it about. But could we not combine your school and mine? I have a vacant building we could fix up nicely for the purpose. It is on the outskirts of town where the air is healthier."

Combine the work that was so important to each of them and help one another achieve their dreams? It sounded too good to be true.

Jasper seemed to mistake her speechless amazement for resistance. "I know I once told you I wanted a wife who would always see eye to eye with me and never argue. But you have shown me that intelligent opposition can yield a compromise that is better than either original idea. I believe this is such a compromise. Are you willing to give a little to gain so much for us both and for those we care about?"

Evangeline found her voice again. "It is a truly inspired idea. I am willing to recommend it to my friends. I believe they will be in favor of it since a building would be one of our greatest expenses. But is that all you are asking—for me to establish this combined school?"

"I must admit there is more to it." Jasper's eyes sparkled with eagerness even as the set of his full, dark brows conveyed apprehension of laying his heart open to rejection once again. "The truth is, I love you, Evangeline. Not as a convenient mother for my children, but as the delightful, determined woman who is more than a match for me in so many ways!"

His words made her throat tighten, but the final barrier around her heart began to crumble.

Before she could answer, he continued. "I know you are afraid that you will lose yourself if you become part of a family again. But I do not believe that will happen any more than it did when you brought together your circle of friends. Look how well that turned out. I hope that if I can prove myself capable of being the kind of husband you need and deserve, you will change your mind about marrying me."

Evangeline glanced out at the garden, where Marian was supervising their children at play. *Their children.* Suddenly her heart acknowledged its long-denied secret wish for Emma, Matthew, Alfie, Owen and Rosie to belong to her.

Overwhelmed with happiness and gratitude for this second chance, Evangeline raised Jasper's hands and pressed her lips to them. "I am no longer so afraid of what I might lose by giving you my heart. It belongs to you now along with all the love it can hold. Whenever you choose to propose to me again, I shall be honored and delighted to accept."

His dark, rugged features glowed with joy as bright and tender as that which overflowed from her heart.

Jasper released her hands only so he could open his arms and gather her close. She raised her face to his and kissed a man she loved with her whole heart, keeping nothing back.

A brief lifetime later, when Jasper held her, his cheek pressed against her hair, he murmured, "Is it too soon to propose yet?"

Evangeline burrowed deeper into his embrace. "Not a moment too soon."

Epilogue

Manchester, England
October 1817

An enthusiastic crowd had gathered to watch Hannah, Countess of Hawkehurst, untie a large ceremonial ribbon stretched across the main entrance of a large, handsome stone building.

After a brief speech about how she and her fellow trustees had met and grown close during their years at school, she announced, "Today it is my honor and pleasure to declare the Faith and Friendship School now officially open!"

The spectators applauded, none louder than Jasper Chase, while Evangeline stood by his side beaming.

Her friend the countess stepped out of the way to let the crowd stream inside for a tour of the school and refreshments. Soon the only ones left outside were the original circle of friends and their husbands. Grace, Lady Steadwell, had christened them "glass slipper brides" after the heroine of her stepdaughter's favorite fairy tale.

Rebecca, Lady Benedict, shook her head with an air

of amazement and admiration. "Well done, Evangeline! You more than made up for any earlier delays by getting this place running so quickly."

Marian, Hannah, Grace and Leah nodded.

Jasper spoke up in Evangeline's defense, even though he knew she was more than capable of standing up for herself. "The responsibility for any delays rests entirely with me, ladies, and I beg your pardon with all my heart. Though I may not have recognized my feelings for your friend in the beginning, I was wise enough to know that I did not want to lose her."

The gentlemen all smiled at him as if they understood perfectly. Though most of them where noblemen, Jasper had found them all fine fellows and looked forward to getting to know them better.

"Enough, my dear." Evangeline gave his arm a playful tap then grasped it warmly. "You will make me blush."

To the others, she added, "I did want to make up for lost time once we had come to an understanding. But I cannot take all the credit. Mr. and Mrs. Brookes and his sister provided invaluable assistance. In fact, once the school is running smoothly, I may turn over the day-to-day operation to Miss Brookes."

The ladies murmured in agreement. They had met Abigail earlier and clearly believed she would make a fine headmistress.

Glancing toward Jasper, Evangeline continued. "I must not forget to acknowledge the help of a certain gentleman. We could never have accomplished what we did without his energy, enthusiasm and practical advice."

The Duchess of Northam gave a dignified nod, lightened by a mischievous grin. "It sounds as though you have more than atoned for any delays you may have caused, Mr. Chase. It is clear that you and your bride-to-be make an excellent team."

When Jasper, Evangeline and Marian Radcliffe all laughed, the duchess protested, "What is so amusing? For once I did not mean to make fun."

"I will explain later," Mrs. Radcliffe murmured to her friend.

"Hadn't we better get inside?" Lady Steadwell suggested. "Before the children devour all the food."

"An excellent idea, my dear," said her husband as he offered her his arm.

"Speaking of the children…" The Duke of Northam addressed Jasper as he and his wife followed the Steadwells. "My son Kit was delighted when we received your invitation. He has enjoyed exchanging letters with your children and could hardly wait to meet them in person. I hope someday your family will pay us a visit at Renforth Abbey."

"Thank you, your grace." Jasper marveled at the thought of a former bobbin boy rubbing shoulders with a duke. "That is very kind of you."

"Please call me Hayden," the duke replied, "or Northam if you prefer. After all, we will soon be like family."

"Very soon indeed." His wife winked at Evangeline with unladylike glee. "To think we shall all be married—entirely confounding the predictions of our teachers."

"Now, Leah," Jasper's bride-to-be responded. "I do not believe our teachers are the only ones who would be surprised to see the two of us married."

The other ladies nodded and chuckled.

"I am as amazed as anyone." Evangeline squeezed

Jasper's hand and smiled up at him. "I never expected to wed and have a family...especially such a large one, but I could not be happier that I soon shall."

Jasper's heart echoed her words. The past three months had been the happiest and most fulfilling of his life, working side by side with Evangeline, to realize their hopes and dreams, being a full-time father to his children and making them part of his world.

As he had foreseen, once Evangeline overcame her fears and committed herself to loving him and his children, she had plunged in, holding nothing back. The only thing left to crown their joy was for them to stand before the Lord and pledge themselves to one another.

"Wasn't yesterday a wonderful celebration?" said Hannah as she and her friends helped prepare their intrepid leader for her wedding. "It was the achievement of a dream and our final triumph over our past."

"So it was." Marian caught her friend in a warm embrace. "And today will be another."

Leah draped a gauzy lace veil over Evangeline's bonnet. "I have not seen such a beautiful bride since I looked in the mirror on my own wedding morn!"

Evangeline laughed with the others. "It is thanks to all of you that I look remotely presentable for my nuptials. I was so busy preparing for the school opening that I scarcely thought about getting ready for my wedding."

"My dress fits you perfectly," said Rebecca. "It means a great deal to me having you wear it today."

"The same goes for my veil," said Hannah.

They had all contributed something to her wedding attire—Grace a sapphire pendant, Marian a pair of dainty kid slippers and Leah a lavish bouquet of roses from the greenhouse of Renforth Abbey.

Once Evangeline was ready, they all kissed her and wished her the joy in marriage that they had found.

"I am certain I shall have it in abundance," she replied confidently, "if these past months have been a foretaste."

The friends walked together to the nearby chapel where Jasper and their wedding guests were waiting. In the vestibule, Emma and Rosie greeted the bride.

"You look lovely," said Emma with a happy sigh.

"So do you, my dearest." Evangeline caressed her cheek.

"After the wedding, may we call you Mama?" asked Rosie.

Evangeline nodded with a sidelong glance at Emma. "If you wish, but only if you really want to. Now I think we had better head in before Matthew and Alfie get too restless."

The girls walked ahead of her up the aisle, Rosie strewing fragrant petals of her namesake flower.

At the foot of the altar stood Jasper and his sons, all looking very handsome. The radiant smile on Jasper's face and the warm glow of love in his eyes made Evangeline feel she was the happiest and most fortunate woman in the world.

Reverend Mr. Brookes opened his prayer book and cleared his throat. "Dearly beloved, we are gathered together here in the sight of God, and in the face of this congregation, to join together this man and this woman in holy matrimony."

When he asked, "Who gives this woman to be married to this man?" Evangeline answered in a firm, clear voice, "I do."

Behind her, she heard whispers and muted chuckles from their guests, but Jasper gave a decisive nod to signal his approval of her unorthodox declaration. She was giving herself in marriage to him just as he was giving himself to her, to share the rest of their lives.

As they repeated their vows, she and Jasper stared deep into each other's eyes, making private, unspoken promises about respecting, supporting and challenging one another in the years ahead.

The children cheered when Mr. Brookes pronounced them husband and wife.

"To think," said Verity when the ceremony had concluded, "two matches came out of your house party at Amberwood. There may be another, for I hear Mr. Webster is courting Mrs. Leveson!"

"I do not wonder that *my wife's* matchmaking efforts were such a success." Jasper seemed to savor those words. "Even if the result did not turn out exactly as she planned!"

* * * * *

Dear Reader,

With this story, I come to the end of the GLASS SLIP-
PER BRIDES series, which makes me a little sad. I have
enjoyed getting to know Rebecca, Marian, Grace, Hannah, Leah and Evangeline, discovering how each was
marked by her experiences in a harsh charity school
and seeing how they have overcome their pasts to find
love and a happy future.

Evangeline Fairfax is the most resistant to marriage
of all her friends. She believes the responsibility of a
family will interfere with the Lord's work she feels
called to do. She also fears marriage will curb her strong
will. Widowed mill owner Jasper Chase does not want
his children to lose their capable, caring governess.
But if Miss Fairfax is determined to leave, perhaps he
should find a wife to manage his home so he can devote
himself to improving the lives of his workers.

When Evangeline organizes a house party to find
her employer a suitable bride, Jasper begins to realize
he need seek no further than…her. But can he persuade
the wedlock-shy governess that her special calling may
include a loving family?

Deborah Hale

Questions for Discussion

1. Even though Evangeline has worked for Jasper for several years, they only begin to truly know one another as she is about to leave. Is there anyone in your life you wish you knew better? What is holding you back and how might you overcome those obstacles?

2. Evangeline believes it is the Lord's will for her to set up a new charity school. Have you ever felt a Divine call to do something? Were you eager to follow the call or ambivalent? How did it turn out?

3. The character of Jasper Chase is modeled after pioneering social reformer Robert Owen. Do you think it is possible for businesses to remain competitive in today's economy while applying Christian principles to their operations? What are some ways they might accomplish that?

4. Though she lives during the Regency era, Evangeline Fairfax faces the modern woman's dilemma of trying to "have it all," including marriage, children and a meaningful career. How do you strike a balance in your life between family and work? Does your faith play a role in achieving a balance that works for you?

5. Jasper wants to shield his children from the harsh realities of life in industrial England. Why do you think that is? Do you agree with him? Why or why not?

6. Evangeline reflects on how her teachers criticized her and her friends, and how easy it was to dismiss the criticism of the others but not of herself. Have you ever experienced that? Was there anything that helped you overcome it?

7. What advice about courting would you give Jasper Chase?

8. When Jasper and Evangeline confide in one another about their pasts, they realize they have more in common than they ever expected. Has that ever happened to you? How did it change your relationship with that other person?

9. Through most of the story, Jasper believes that differences between a husband and wife can lead to conflict and unhappiness in the home. Why does he feel that way? Do you agree? Why or why not?

10. Evangeline's friend Marian tells her that the Lord may be a teamster as well as a shepherd. What metaphors for God are most meaningful to you? Why do you think that is?